Let Love In

MELISSA COLLINS

This is a work of fiction. Names, characters, businesses, places, events, and incidents are either the products of the author's imagination or used in a fictitious manner. Any resemblance to actual persons, living or dead, or actual events is purely coincidental.

LET LOVE IN
Copyright © 2013 by Melissa Collins
All rights reserved

ISBN 978-1484085905

*For those who have been hurt, yet still found
the strength to let love in*

Let Love In

Chapter 1

MY PARENTS ARE DEAD. Don't get me wrong—I am affected by it. I'm trying to get over it, but in all honesty, there's no way I'll ever be completely healed. They died when I was ten years old—eight years ago. I'll never forget the day I lost them, because when I lost them, I lost everything. It was a car accident that killed them—jackknifed tractor-trailer, to be more specific. Since I was only ten, I didn't need many more details than that. They were gone, and that was that. I have no siblings, and my grandparents on both sides were long gone. I had never known them—they died before I was born. It seemed like my life was plagued by death, and I was only in fourth grade.

But life has a funny way of going on. You don't have a choice, really. You wake up, force yourself into some clothes, drag your ass to school, smile and nod as if on cue, do enough work to keep your head above water so as not to raise concern—in short, you deal. You deal with the fact that at ten you are uprooted from the only life you've ever known, the only sources of love and warmth horrifyingly ripped away from you in the middle of the night. They were only supposed to be going on a date—dinner and a movie. A funeral and burial weren't supposed to be part of the package deal.

But this was my package deal—dead parents and relocation. I was taken away from my quaint little suburban home on Long Island and transplanted to the middle of nowhere. That's what I like to call it, but it's really just a few hours outside Manhattan. There isn't much in upstate New York; I learned that my first winter here. There's snow and cows—and plenty of both. My dad's aunt—his mother's sister, my Aunt Maggie—adopted me. She is sweet and caring, but let's face it, a sixty-six-year-old spinster taking care of a ten-year-old is not ideal for either party.

But, like I said, I was—maybe still am—in survival mode. I don't remember much from the first few years with her. I was in a fog. There was no proverbial light at the end of the tunnel, and I was certain that I was doomed to live a gray life. The snow and the cows just helped to support that color scheme.

My first glimpse of color came in the form of a bubbly redhead. She sat next to me in seventh grade homeroom—we were arranged alphabetically, and

Melanie Crane came right after me, Madeleine Becker. Her face was covered in freckles and split impossibly wide with a huge smile pretty much all the time. It was difficult not to notice her—not to be nice to her, not to open up to her. I still remember our first conversation.

"What's your favorite color? Mine's purple. Not the real dark kind, but lavender or lilac. It's just so pretty. Lilacs are my favorite flower, too—they smell *so* pretty. My whole room is covered in purple. It's so me!"

Okay, so it wasn't so much of a conversation as a monologue, but when she spoke to me, something inside cracked open just a tiny bit. The part inside that remembered I was just a little girl and that forever was a long time to wade through the sea of gray loneliness engulfing me, weighing me down.

My lips curled up into the tiniest of smiles, and that was all she needed to know that I was in there somewhere. Maybe she had some kind of ESP to know I was sad. I wasn't really sure at the time; however, when I look back on it, she definitely did. Melanie is the kindest, most caring and gentle person I have ever met. She is the quintessential "not a mean bone in her body" kind of girl, and because of that, because of my need for kindness and love and warmth, we've been best friends ever since. After her praises of the color purple, she invited me to her house the next day. When I told Aunt Maggie about my "playdate," she was excited, saying that "it would be good for me" to finally make some friends.

Walking into Melanie's house the next afternoon was like walking into my past. The house was the definition of warm and cozy—a sofa and love seat anchored the living room with their rich chocolate color, but the rest of the room was airy and light, in varying shades of pale blues and sea greens. It was home, someone else's home, but a home nonetheless. The bookshelves were jam-packed with kids' books and overflowing with family pictures—a stark contrast from the doily-covered coffee table overloaded with old lady tchotchkes that characterized Aunt Maggie's living room.

I know it's cliché, but what really made it home was the smell. It was a mixture of some kind of spring meadow air freshener and fresh-baked cookies. No one has ever made me cookies except my mom. I missed her instantly, but I couldn't dwell on those feelings for long because Melanie grabbed my hand and led me toward the kitchen, where her mom was piling the chocolate chip cookies on a plate for us.

"Hey, sweetie, how was your day?" Mrs. Crane's voice reverberated through me, but all I heard was my mom's voice—crooning sweet comforts in my ear when I was sick, rousing me from sleep when I was drowsy, singing me lullabies when I had a nightmare. "This must be Madeleine. I've heard so much about you from Melanie. She just can't keep shut now, can she?"

I managed to squeak out a whispered "hi," but that would never do with Momma Crane. She insisted I call her that. And since everything about her was motherly—slightly graying hair, bright blue eyes set in a warm round face that, just like Melanie's, was never without a smile—agreeing to call her Momma Crane didn't even get a second thought in my head.

I later learned that Momma's husband, James, was the one true love in her life. He was an architect, and there was some kind of freak accident at work. In an instant, he was pulled from her life. They had been married less than a year, and she was six months pregnant with Melanie when he died. When I found all of this out, I knew that I wanted to be just like Momma. Not that I wanted to lose the love of my life or anything like that, but I wanted to learn how to deal with such life-altering loss in a graceful and strong way. I wanted to survive, just like she had.

Melanie and I spent the rest of that afternoon—and pretty much every free minute of our teenage existence—in her room singing songs from our favorite boy bands, watching chick flicks, experimenting with our hair and makeup, and occasionally doing some homework. But in between all of those insignificant moments of singing and dancing and daydreaming, something miraculous happened. I came to life. I was happy. Being a part of Melanie's family made me whole again, and when Aunt Maggie passed away from a sudden heart attack at age seventy-four in the spring of our senior year in high school, it was only natural that I would move in with Melanie and Momma. I practically lived there anyway, so aside from the sadness of having to say goodbye to the only family I had left, the move had been easy.

It is now late August, and Melanie and I are getting ready to move into our dorm at Ithaca College in a few days. We spent hours flipping through old pictures—the whole walk down memory lane thing, but in all honesty I am not interested in reviewing the past. Even though my time here with the Cranes has been nothing but loving, I miss my own family. Having to move out of the Cranes' house makes me realize that I am truly alone.

I find a picture from middle school, and I am shocked by the sadness that pervades my features. My whole body sags under the weight of my life. The tears spilling down my cheeks as I look at who I used to be just can't be stopped. I want a do-over. I want to be happy for once. I want so badly to love myself and to love my life—to know that someone really and truly loves me. I want my family back, and seeing this picture just makes me want all of that even more.

"Do you think I should bring these Uggs? I don't want to ruin them in the snow, but they are just so comfortable. I'm not sure I can leave them behind. Mad? Maddy? Hello, earth to Ms. Madeleine? You in there somewhere?"

Seriously, take a breath every now and then, Mels.

When I turn to her, my tear-streaked face is pretty much a dead giveaway to my emotional state. She sinks next to me on her ruffled lilac bed and wraps her arms around me.

"What's the matter, Maddy? Why the tears? This is a happy time. We're out of here and on our own in just a few days."

"That's just it, Melanie. I'm going to miss this place. It's the only real home I've ever had. I have nowhere else, no one else." Somehow all of that manages to come out past the lump in my throat.

"What do you mean 'miss this place'?" Her face is etched with genuine confusion.

"I just mean—I—well, what I..." Stammering through my words, I just can't find the right ones to express my fears. "Melanie, the last few months being here, living with you and your mom, have been the best."

She opens her mouth to agree, but I stop her mid-breath so I can finish.

"They have been the absolute happiest days of my life, and you know exactly how sad my life has been and how it's not so easy for me to say that I've been truly happy. But we're moving out—well, I'm moving out, I mean. Your mom was kind enough to take me in for a few months, but I'll be on my own in a few weeks, and as exciting as it is that I'll be rooming with you, I'm just sad that I don't have a real home anymore."

The tears come on in earnest at this point, and my frustration mounts. I throw my hands up in the air and try to play off my emotional outburst in a flippant sarcastic burst.

"Who am I kidding, Melanie? I haven't had a home in the last eight years!" I flop back on the bed and huff in frustration.

"That is absolutely the most ridiculous thing I have ever heard, Madeleine Renee Becker." Momma Crane's voice rings through from the doorway. She moves swiftly, sitting on the other side of me, sandwiching me between her and Melanie. "This has been your home since Melanie first brought you here. Now you just get your mail here, too!"

That gets a snicker out of me. "Momma C, it's okay. You don't have to keep taking care of me anymore. I've been enough of a burden these last few months, and I couldn't imagine you having to…"

"Now, shut that pretty mouth of yours with all this 'have' to. You live here because we want you to. We love you, not because you're like my own daughter, but because you are. It's just that, plain and simple. You may have lived with your Aunt Maggie, but I was the one who had the privilege of watching you grow up—of seeing you transform into the beautiful woman you are today."

Damn tears. They just will. Not. Stop. When I finally get some air back into my lungs, I tell her that I love her, too, but I just can't shake the uncertainty that, once I leave here, I won't have a home of my own.

"Are you sure, Momma C? I don't want to be a bother. I'm sure when Melanie is home for vacations and holidays, it'll be stressful enough without having to worry about me."

"Maddy, don't you get it? It'll be more stressful if you aren't here. I'll be up day and night wondering where you are and who is taking care of you. This is your home. Got it?" The finality in her tone makes me smile and sigh in relief. "Now, clean up that pretty face and get downstairs for dinner in twenty minutes."

"Your mom's the best, Mel. I'm pretty sure that I'd be living out of Aunt Maggie's old beat-up car if it wasn't for her."

"Yeah, when I grow up I want to be just like her. Maybe less gray hair, though." Mel's teasing gets a laugh out of me, and just like that my little outburst is over. We get the last few things packed away and cleaned up before dinner. The sadness is still there beneath the surface, but for once life is starting to feel good—really good.

Chapter 2

AFTER DINNER, MELANIE AND I start getting ready for
a little going-away party. It isn't a party dedicated just
to us; we're all headed down to the lake with a group of
friends for a last "hurrah," if you will, before we all start
leaving next week. Everyone is heading their own way,
and even though we've vowed up and down to stay in
touch, there is a part of me that just knows it won't happen. Call me cynical, but it's more that I know I can't
count on anyone in my life other than Melanie and
Momma C. It's just how it is.

Jay will be there, too. We've been together for the
last six months, and while it's been going pretty well, I
don't think that I'm in love with him. Actually, I know
I'm not in love with him, and the sad thing is that I
want it that way. I know it's foolish and cliché, but if

I don't love him, then he can't hurt me. If I don't get close, then there won't be an aching void in my life when he's gone from it. Self-preservation is a double-edged blade—it keeps you safe, but at a fairly large cost. I'm not sure that I'll really ever let anyone in, and yet, on the other hand, letting someone in and sharing who I am and my entire existence with them is really all I've ever wanted. I'm the first to agree that I'm a bit young to have these feelings, but hell, losing both of your parents when you're ten sure as fuck will make you grow up quickly.

Jay is your typical all-American "good boy." Stellar good looks—light blond hair and deep, rich brown eyes. He is pretty much six feet of muscle, but not in that "I'm at the gym ten hours a day" kind of build. He's lean and just so damn gorgeous. Yup, gorgeous—that's the best way to describe him.

He wants more out of our relationship than I do; he's told me that much. If it were up to him, we'd been "doin it like bunnies"—his words, not mine, and we'd only come up for air and food. I'm not there yet—not sure that I'll ever be. I mean, we've done pretty much everything, but—well, you know. He's sweet and kind and funny as hell, but I just can't bring myself to love him. And if I don't love him, I know for certain that I can't give myself to him. I'm not super conservative or anything like that—I certainly don't oppose premarital sex. That's not why I won't sleep with him. I just don't love him, and I think if you're going to give someone your body, you need to be in love with them. If that makes me too conservative, then oh, well.

After Melanie is done styling her hair, she comes into the bedroom and lets out a long, loud wolf whistle.

"Damn, girl! You look hot!" Her words prompt a heated blush to my cheeks. "Quit your blushing, Maddy. One day you will realize just how beautiful you are. I don't mean to sound shallow, but do you think you could land a guy like Jay if you were anything less than beautiful?"

"Yeah, I guess so, Mel. I just don't see it, but find me any teenage girl who sees her own beauty. I'll get there one day, maybe." Even I can hear the lack of conviction in my own words. I know I'm not completely unfortunate-looking, but I just don't feel beautiful. I never had that mother-daughter bonding time; she never had the chance to teach me how to put on makeup and dress to my advantage. So I had to figure it all out on my own. I'm still figuring it out.

As Melanie steps out of the room to let Momma C know our plans for the evening, I steal a glimpse in the mirror to try to see what Melanie sees.

Legs? Check. I am five foot seven, after all. They're slender but not too skinny. I run every morning, so my legs have always been slightly muscled, but in a feminine way—at least I hope they look feminine; bulky is not a word I'd want someone to use. I think the not too short, but short enough to still be very stylish, pleated and thickly cuffed navy blue shorts show my legs off nicely. My cork and white wedges with a cute little bow at each ankle are the perfect finishing touch. A simple dove-gray ribbed tank completes the outfit and hugs my curves. Maybe there is something to Mel's theory after all.

My golden-blonde hair is sun-kissed in the summer, and its soft waves cascade to the middle of my back. I usually have it up, but tonight Melanie insisted that I leave it down and wavy. I let her play Barbie, and I can't say I hate it. The real show-stopper, though, is my eyes. They're a bright, vibrant green. They look almost fake, but as I lean into the mirror to get a closer look, I catch small little flecks of gold around the outside that I know no contact lens could replicate. I have always loved my eyes. I have my mother's eyes. I've seen them in the few pictures I have from my childhood. Even if my eyes were the murkiest, dingiest, dullest brown, I still would have loved them, as long as they were my mother's. It's really the only thing I have left of her.

I gave in on the hair and let Melanie have a field day, but I insisted on keeping my makeup simple—a soft pale pink blush, clear lip gloss, and a light dusting of gold eye shadow is all I need. A quick swipe of some mascara, and the look is complete.

Okay, so Melanie's theory definitely has some merit. I do look hot. Maybe it was the emotionally cathartic cry before with Momma C and Mel that has me feeling a bit lighter, but I really feel great tonight. I know not everything is perfect in my life—God, do I know that better than anyone—but I feel a change coming on.

We park Aunt Maggie's old beat-up Honda Civic and make our way down to the lake. The guys have already got the bonfire going, and the flames are licking toward the night sky. Everyone is lounging around the fire—they haven't gotten their drink on yet. I'm not a big drinker, never have been. Don't get me wrong, I've thought about it—numb the pain and all, but I just don't see the point in it. The alcohol-induced haze will wear off eventually; unfortunately, the pain is forever.

There's some loud rock music pumping bass out of someone's car. I vaguely recognize the lyrics to Fun's "We Are Young" as I walk toward the group. The girls, Katie, Julia, and Lyndsay, are already up and dancing. Mel joins them, and I make my way over to Jay.

"Hey, babe! Wow, you look....um...wow...yeah, you look good tonight." He manages to get that out before planting a sweet, soft kiss on my cheek. He knows I'm not one for PDAs.

"Thanks, Jay. You always say the sweetest things."

He seems a bit out of it—distracted, but I'm not sure by what. "Wanna take a walk? It's a bit quieter down by the water."

Yeah, definitely distracted. His normal cool confidence is completely absent as he grabs my hand and brings me down by the water's edge.

"What's up, Jay? You seem a bit off tonight. Is something wrong?"

"If you consider that my girl is leaving here in two days and she won't give me an answer as to where we'll stand when she does, then yeah, I'm off a bit." Cool and confident just completely walked out the door, and in walked angry and hurt.

"Jay, we talked about this. I just don't think long distance will work. Why can't we stay friends and just see how it goes? We've only been together a few months. It's not even anything serious."

Exit angry and hurt, and enter pissed off. "It's not serious?! Really, Maddy, is that how you feel about us? I've been trying to tell you how I feel about you for a while now, but every time I bring it up, you change the subject, push me away. Okay, fine—it's only been a few months, but in my heart it feels like more than that."

His tone has changed again, and I can tell he's trying to shut down the "pissed off." He's being sweet and romantic. I have a giant soft spot for him when he's like this. I may not be in love with him, but he definitely has a piece of my heart.

He nestles my hand inside his and pulls us down to the sand. We sit looking out at the shimmering water for what seems like an eternity. Neither of us wants to break the silence, yet ironically we both start talking at the same time.

"You go first," I tell him.

"No, Maddy, you first. Please talk to me."

His sweet words are too much to hear. I know I'm going to break his heart, but I can't do this any longer.

"I'm sorry, Jay. Really, I am. I didn't mean to push you away or change the subject. We do need to talk about us. I guess I'm just afraid. It's scary thinking about moving away from here and starting over again in a few days."

"But, Maddy, that's why I'm here. I…ah, shit there's no easy way to say this, because I'm just so afraid of scaring you away, but I love you. I've known for a while now, but I know you wanted to take things slowly and I've been trying to, really I have. But you're just so sweet and funny and, goddamn, you are the most beautiful girl I've ever laid eyes on."

My chest constricts, and I just can't get oxygen into my lungs. Jay notices the shocked look in my eyes. He cups my face with his palms and gently rubs my cheeks with his thumbs.

"Maddy, I love you. I want to be with you. Tonight, and when you leave. I don't want us to break up." His plea is so painful to hear because just a few minutes ago I was ready to take this conversation down a completely different path.

He takes my silence as a cue to move forward. He leans his face toward mine, and I'm too shocked by his revelations to move even an inch. His mouth slants over mine in a sweet and innocent way. His tongue dances along my lips, begging permission to deepen the kiss. I grant it, not because I want to go further, but because I know this will be our last kiss.

He moves one of his hands around to cup the back of my head and pulls me closer. His tongue dances around my mouth, and mine meets his stroke for stroke. It's intense, maybe the most passionate kiss we've ever shared. But we're both getting lost in it for two entirely different reasons, and that's enough to make me pull back. When I do, he gazes into my eyes. His are hooded and lust filled. I feel terrible, but I have to say this.

I place my hands on his chest, not to caress, but to put some more distance between us. "Jay, I can't be with you. I'm not in love with you. Honestly, I can't even say that I want to be in love. You're kind and sweet and a great guy, but I just can't. I'm sorry, Jay, but we can't be together anymore."

My words paralyze him. He mutters out something that sounds remotely like "fuck," but his jaw is clenched so tightly that it's difficult to make out. Exit sweet and romantic; make room for REALLY PISSED!

Slamming his fists into the sand, he makes me jump back a little. The force behind his words makes me shudder even more. "What the fuck, Madeleine! Why the fuck not? What the fuck is your problem? I should have seen this coming. You never want to talk to me. You've never opened up. Fuck, we barely even see each other anymore. Here I am opening my heart to you, telling you I want you, that I want us, and you're just being a bitch about the whole thing. You know what?

Fine, have it your fucking way. We're done. Go off into your own little world and leave me here." He stalks off and begins pacing along the shoreline.

When I catch up to him, he's staring off into space, thinking about God-knows-what. I try to grab for his hand, to offer him what little comfort I can, but he pulls away the second he feels my fingers brush up against his.

He takes a step back, and the blistering look in his eyes knocks me off-kilter a little. "You know what, Maddy? I take back what I said earlier. I don't love you. I could never love someone as cold-hearted and as shut-down as you are." He doesn't scream this. That would have been easier to understand. His words are barely a whisper—a venomous, hurtful whisper. I visibly cringe at them, and the tears that I so desperately did not want to shed are definitely going to make an appearance.

The tears are quickly followed by sobs—gut-wrenching, chest-heaving sobs. I sink down to the sand and cover my face. I'm crying because I've hurt Jay, but more so because I hurt. Just when I thought that maybe, just maybe, I could start to feel better about my life, it all comes crashing down around me. I know I don't love Jay, but not loving him makes me feel like I'm never going to love anyone. If I can't love someone like him, then I am broken beyond repair.

Jay stands in front of me, deathly still. It takes him a few minutes to find his voice, but when I look up at him, I see him trying to catch his breath through his tears. He sinks down beside me and turns my face to his.

"You broke my heart, Maddy. I hope one day I'll get over it, but I love you, and it's because I love you that I'll say this. You deserve love. You are not broken and empty like you think you are." He places his finger over my lips as I try to interrupt him and wipes the tears from my eyes, intent on finishing his "Maddy is worth loving" speech.

"You are. Now let me finish. I know losing your parents was difficult and that, in a lot of ways, you're still reeling from it, but it will never get better until you let it get better. You have to let them go and move on with your life. I know that you deserve to be loved. And for fuck's sake, I was so hopeful that I would be the one deserving enough of the honor to do so, but I'm not. I just hope that one day you realize you deserve it—that one day you'll be able to let love in."

He stands up and grabs my hand to pull me up with him. The sobs have stopped, and I wipe the tears away. I want to say something, but I don't have the right words—what would the right words even be at this point?

"Jay, I'm sorry. Really, I am." Yup, that's all I can come up with. He's all sweet and heartfelt, and I'm all lame and feeble.

"Shhh. It's okay. I'm a big boy—I'll deal. Let's head back to the group and enjoy the rest of the night."

" Okay. That sounds like a plan." Lame and feeble—that's me.

The rest of the night passes by in a blur, mostly because everyone else is more than slightly intoxicated. Mel and I were able to steal away for a few minutes so I could fill her in on what happened with Jay. She wasn't surprised. She knew my issues. She knew them better than anyone. She told me that she understood how I felt, but she also agreed with Jay—all that crap that I was deserving of love and that I've got to stop shutting down.

Mel's theory was proven right earlier in the night. Maybe I should follow her advice on this front as well.

Chapter 3

I WANTED A DO-OVER, and a do-over is what I'm getting. Okay, granted, I am never going to get my parents back, but a fresh start is definitely on the horizon. After Jay and I broke up and Mel and I had an even deeper heart-to-heart later that night, I made a few promises to myself. They're very simple promises, but ones that I hope will wipe the slate clean.

Choose happy.

Appreciate beauty.

Let love in.

Like I said, simple, refreshingly simple.

Melanie and I moved into our college dorm suite yesterday, and even though it was beyond difficult to say goodbye to Momma C, it was so thrilling and exciting to be on our own. Our suite mates also moved in yesterday. They are awesome. Beyond awesome, actually. Lia and Camryn are cousins. They're also sophomores, so we didn't just get kickass roommates, we got built-in tour guides, too. Our suite is kickass as well. Actually, I wouldn't even call it a suite; it's an apartment. Melanie and I share a room, and Lia and Cammie share the other. They're not small rooms, either—there's more than enough room for a bed, desk, dresser, and full closet for each of us. We share a common living area that the college furnished so it's kind of boring, but after we all added our own personal touches, it really felt like home. There's a modest kitchen area—an apartment-sized stove and fridge. The sink is nestled in a small length of pale blue Formica countertop that forms an L-shaped breakfast bar opposite the appliances. It's not high-tech or anything like that, but it's functional, and for the first time ever, it's mine—really and truly mine. This is the first time in my life that I've actively chosen to live somewhere—that I've actually felt comfortable enough to put my personal stamp on it.

Lia, Cammie, Mel, and I are headed out to lunch at the local pizza place, and I am beside myself with how much has changed in the days since I left home. I feel lighter, freer. I feel good, really good, and I just can't stop smiling about it.

"So what are you guys up to tonight?" Cammie interrupts my daydreaming. "There's a house party at Jack's tonight. He said you guys should come. He'd love to meet you." Jack and Cammie were high school sweethearts, and unlike Jay and me, they loved each other enough to make things work. They've been together for the last three and a half years, while Jack was starting here and Cammie was finishing up high school, and from what Cammie has shared so far, they're both in it for the long haul.

"Oh, my God! You guys should definitely come. Jack's parties are always awesome. Please, please, please—you don't want to be without your new roomies for the whole night, now, do you?" This is from Lia. She's a little bubbly, to say the least. I wish I had a quarter of her energy and spirit, though considering my new promises to myself, spending more time with Lia might be in my near future.

Mel and I share a glance over our slices and simultaneously say "hell, yeah." We spend the rest of lunch chatting about how we grew up, where we're from, how we're feeling about college—well, they share; I just smile and nod.

"Why so quiet, Maddy?" Cammie chimes in, and I immediately freeze.

It's not like I'm embarrassed or ashamed that my parents are dead, but I just wanted to move beyond it, and here it is staring me down. I take a deep breath and choose happy—just like my new rules said I should.

"No reason, really. Just not much to share. My parents died when I was a little girl. My aunt adopted me. She died this past spring. Then Mel and her momma kinda sorta adopted me. I've lived with them for the last few months, and now I'm here on my own." Wow, so that's what my life looks like in a nutshell.

Stunned into silence, neither Lia nor Cammie can formulate a response more eloquent than "oh."

It didn't take more than a beat for Lia to regain her effervescence. "You are not on your own. You've got us, and we've got you. I don't know what it's like to lose parents, and I won't ever pretend that I do, but if you ever need anyone to talk to about it, I'm here." She smiles at me reassuringly. "Now, let's finish this pizza and get ready for Jack's later."

Cammie and Mel raise their sodas in a mock "cheers" to Lia's proclamation of friendship.

"Same from me, Maddy," Cammie says. "I'm here for you. Let's focus on happier things and have a blast tonight. It'll be good to cut loose before classes start on Monday, and I know Jack is dying to meet you girls. His housemates are pretty excited, too. For your information, they're real easy on the eye—his housemates, I mean. Now, don't get me wrong, I love Jack more than anything, but oh, my, he has got himself some gorgeous friends."

Cammie's little tidbit stirs a sea of laughter from the three of us. I'm definitely excited for tonight now.

Jack's house is practically vibrating from the bass of the music. It's so loud that I can't even figure out what song is playing. Cammie opens the front door and drags us all in behind her. She maneuvers her way through the crowd and up the stairs. She stops in front of one of three doors in the hallway and digs through her purse for a key.

"This is Jack's room. Our stuff will be safe in here. I'm the only one other than him who has a key." Cammie tucks the key into her back pocket, and we all put our bags in his closet. Before we go back downstairs, Cammie fills us in on Jack's housemates.

He shares the place with two other guys—Logan O'Rourke and Reid Connely. They are all seniors and have shared the house since the beginning of junior year. Jack is studying physical therapy and is hoping to set up his own practice after finishing grad school. Logan is the football star. Cammie jokes that he was born with a football in his hand. Reid, apparently, is the loose cannon of the group. He's changed his major so many times that Cammie isn't even one-hundred-percent sure what it is anymore. She knows nothing of his home life; no one does. Maybe the guys know something about him, but anytime Cammie asks Jack about it, he tells her, "Guys don't talk about that shit," and she just leaves it alone. The only thing she does know is that Reid is hot. Like, really fucking hot—her words, not mine. After the brief background bio on the boys, we are off to party.

The crowd seems to have multiplied in the ten minutes that we were upstairs. Cammie brings us into the kitchen and grabs some red Solo cups for the keg out on the back patio. The entire house screams "bachelor pad." Well, bachelor pad/college frat house combo. It works, though. It isn't so dirty that you fear contracting an STD if you sit on the couch, but it is pretty far from clean.

When we get outside, Cammie's face softens, and her eyes light up. She has locked eyes with who I assume is Jack, who is manning the keg.

"Hey, ladies." His voice oozes smoothness. "Thanks for coming. Did you put everything up in my room? These parties can get a little crazy."

"Yeah, we're good, Jack. Pour me one?" Lia holds her cup out for Jack to fill.

"Jack, this is Melanie and Madeleine." Cammie introduces us as he moves on to filling her cup and then ours.

I take a sip, and he notices the look on my face. "Thanks, Jack, but I'm just not much of a drinker."

"No problem, Madeleine. There's water in the fridge. Help yourself to whatever you want," Jack instructs.

"Thanks. A college kid who doesn't drink—I guess I belong in the Smithsonian or something, huh? Oh, and by the way, you can call me Maddy. I'm going to head inside and take you up on that water. I'll be back out in a minute." I hear their "okay" as I head back into the kitchen.

There is a group playing quarters on the island and another group lining up shots on the breakfast bar—so not my scene. I just shrug, open the door, and pull out a bottle of water, and, when I turn around to walk back outside, I face-plant into a wall of solid muscle.

"Hand me one?" His voice is smooth and gruff at the same time.

Red-faced, I turn back around and get him his water, glad for the cool respite that the opened refrigerator door offers.

"Here you go." I can't peel my eyes away from his mouth as he moves the bottle to his lips. They are perfect - beautiful and full in a completely masculine way. I watch, completely fascinated, as his throat moves, downing the water in three or four large gulps. He wipes his mouth with his forearm, and I can't help but let my eyes travel up the rest of his arm to his biceps and shoulders. Those are the same as his lips—perfect. Amazingly, gorgeously, utterly, divinely perfect. Muscled and tanned, his arms are mouthwatering.

My knees wobble. My heart thuds. Thousands of butterflies spread their wings in my belly.

I've never felt like this before, even with Jay. I'm caught completely off guard.

"Thanks…" He stares blankly at my face for a minute, and I can't help but wonder if he likes what he's seeing. He clears his throat and rouses me from my little daydream where the gorgeous boy is mesmerized by the maybe-a-little-above-average-looking girl. That's when I realize he is asking for my name.

"Maddy. Sorry, my name's Maddy." I nearly choke on my tongue over my freaking name.

Dork.

When I regain the ability to speak like a normal human being, I continue, "My suite mate Cammie is dating one of the guys who live here." My mouth goes dry and it takes a monumental effort to even get those simple words out.

He just nods in return and pushes past me to grab another bottle of water. He is covered in sweat, and when he brushes my arm, he gets some on me. I am not grossed out; in fact, suddenly I wish he would get me all sweaty in an entirely different way. He's obviously just finished working out. He is wearing a lightweight gray T-shirt and black mesh shorts, and even though he is drenched in sweat, he smells delicious. He is that divine combination of sweat and cologne and man that I'm pretty sure every woman swoons over.

The silence is killing me, so as he's chugging down his second bottle of water, I wiggle my bottle in front of me and say, "I'm not that much of a drinker, so I hope you don't mind if I steal one of these from you?"

"Help yourself. It's just water. I'm going to go grab a shower. Maybe I'll see you later, Maddy."

And with that he is gone. Don't get me wrong, I don't mind watching him leave—his back is just as glorious as his front—absolutely yummy, but I wouldn't have minded talking, or, um, staring, just a little longer. Knowing his name would have been nice, but seeing as he said he was going to grab a shower, he must live here. So his name was either Logan or Reid.

I go back outside as the girls are mid-laugh about something Jack is telling them. Melanie immediately notices the blush on my face. "Are you okay, Maddy? You look a little flushed."

"I'm good. It's just a little hot and crowded in there."

Like six feet, two inches of solid, gorgeous, beautiful man hot and crowded.

I keep that to myself, though.

"Come on, girls, let's go dance!" Lia, bubbly as ever, is in full-on party mode. She drags us back into the living room, changes the music to some techno dance beat, and starts moving. It's hard not to follow her lead. She is just so much fun.

We really get into it, too. The party is in full swing, and Cammie, Lia, Mel, and I are having so much fun in our small dance group that I don't really care that I'm not drunk like the rest of the people there. I promised myself that I would choose to be happy, and that is exactly what I am doing. I dance and dance and dance. My arms swing over my head in a languorous, smooth movement as my hips move to the beat. As I turn around, I look over at the stairs, where mystery man from earlier is walking down.

I lean into Cammie's ear and try to keep my voice low so no one can hear me, though I'm sure the music does a good job of drowning out my question.

"Who is that, Cam? I talked to him earlier, but I didn't catch his name. I figured it was either Logan or

Reid since he said he was grabbing a shower, but he never told me."

Cammie's lips curve up into a knowing smile as she starts to respond to my question. "That, my dear, is Reid. I told you Jack's housemates are easy on the eyes! He's delish, right? Logan won't be here tonight. He's got a mandatory study session and then films for football."

"Delish" does not even begin to cover it. I thought Jay was good-looking, but Reid puts him to shame. Reid is the epitome of tall, dark, and fucking amazingly handsome. And even that description doesn't seem to cut it.

Based on his attire from earlier, it is clear that he works out, but his body seems even more defined in the fitted black tee and loose, but not-too-loose, faded jeans he is currently wearing. His all-over-the-place, messily styled medium brown hair is still a little wet from his shower, and I can see a few droplets of water on his neck. Lucky water droplets. I want to lick them up.

He catches me staring and shoots me a quick look of recognition and a brief nod—so calm and cool, when I am over here stifling the urge to jump up and down, flailing my arms to get him to come over to me. I maintain my cool, though, and just keep dancing, my inner voice telling me that it would be so very lame to be "that girl" at my first party.

An hour or so and who knows how many dances later, and my feet are killing me. I am ready to call it quits when I feel hands grab at my waist from behind. I can't see who it is initially, but I can tell just from the smell; it isn't as sweaty as it was earlier, but it is the same combination of cologne and man, with the new addition of body wash, that makes me give my thighs a tight squeeze.

"I think you owe me a dance." His warm breath on my neck makes my legs turn to Jell-O and my heart thud in my chest.

"Owe you? For what?" My voice sounds breathy even to me.

He spins me around so that we are face to face. "For the water, of course," he says.

"Oh. I'm sorry, I didn't realize …." My voice trails off, and his lips quirk up into a little smile. A gorgeous little smile. Call me crazy, but the look in his eyes is one of flirtation. Reid is flirting with me. Well, color me confused!

"It's okay, Maddy. I'm kidding. C'mon, let's dance a little." His voice relaxes me a little, but my heart refuses to beat anything other than a furious tattoo against my ribs.

The bastard is laughing at me. Well, you want to dish it out, I'll dish it right back. I lower my lids to a sexy, sultry look, wrap my hand around his neck, and bring his ear to my lips. Without a centimeter of space between us, I murmur, "I could pay you back with more than a dance, Reid."

I place my hands on his chest and push back just slightly. I see his pupils dilate and hear the hitch in his breath. Score one for Maddy!

"So you did a little digging, huh?"

I'm pretty sure my face conveys my confusion, as my brows are furrowed. Digging? Huh?

"My name—you just had to find out who I am, didn't you?" He is amused and playing along.

"Of course I dug. I needed to know who was responsible for getting me all hot and sweaty before." I realize my error as soon as the words are out of my mouth.

"So I got you all hot and bothered, hmm? Let's see if I can do it again." With that, he grabs my hand and pulls me to the dance floor.

The music has slowed a little. It is no longer a techno club beat. It is smooth and rhythmic—what I would imagine sex would sound like if it were music. Not that I would know anything about that.

He wraps his arms around my waist and brings me in close to him. I don't know where to put my arms at first, afraid that I'll go up in flames if I actually touch him, so I bring them up in the air above my head.

Wrong move. He raises his arms, too, and caresses them down over mine, lightly grazing my skin with his callused fingertips, causing goosebumps to pimple my flesh. My nipples harden instantly and almost painfully. I try to squeeze my legs together to keep myself from convulsing on the spot.

When his hands reach mine, he laces our fingers together and brings my arms around his back so that I can go exploring over the hard planes and ridges of his muscled and sculpted back. Damn T-shirt for getting in the way. I want to touch his skin, but somehow ripping off his shirt in the middle of his living room just doesn't seem appropriate. Hell, nothing that I want to do seems appropriate.

He must see the look in my eyes because he chuckles lightly; the rumbles from his equally ridged and sculpted chest move through my body in waves and pulses. Our bodies move together as one—swaying and grinding to the music. His large hands roam all over my back but always return to the small expanse of skin that is exposed between my tank top and my denim skirt. At one point, I'm pretty sure he leans down to inhale the scent of my hair. I could be imagining that though; I am just so lost in the feel of his body next to mine that I can't be sure. He cups my face at one point, and we hold each other's gaze for long moments.

As our eyes lock, wow—just wow. Endless seas of the deepest blue I have ever seen meet my green eyes, and I am transfixed. He is beautiful; that is certain. But there is something in those eyes that makes him so familiar to me. It takes me a minute to put my finger on it, and I think he catches my quizzical stare.

He spins me around a few times ballerina-style and then dips me as the song ends. By the time he rights me and releases my waist, I figure it out. It is pain. It is the pain I see in my own eyes all too frequently.

Sensing that I'm seeing something he doesn't want me to see, he abruptly lets me go and says thanks for the dance. There is an edge to his voice that was not there before. The change in his demeanor is instantaneous. I feel cold and bereft in his absence, and I can't ignore the pang of jealousy that I feel as I watch him stalk off to some leggy blonde dancing on the other side of the room.

By the end of the night, Reid and leggy blonde are lip-locked on the couch. I haven't said more than a handful of words to him, and he's already done with me.

I guess I can choose happy as much as I want, but it doesn't mean much if I'm not chosen back.

Chapter 4

I TRY NOT TO THINK OF REID for the rest of the week-end. I am not successful. He is in my dreams. I can feel his hands on my body. I can see the pain in his eyes, and to say my curiosity, and my lust, for that matter, are piqued is an understatement. I want to get to know him more because in our short time on the dance floor, I felt something. I felt a lot, actually. I relaxed into him, and there was a definite connection—one he apparently doesn't want to acknowledge, but one that is there nonetheless. I try not to think of him, but sadly spend most of the weekend doing just that.

When my alarm buzzes at 6 a.m., I am already awake. I always run in the morning, and a good run before my first day of classes is exactly what I need to clear my mind. I don't have class until 10:30, and since

I don't really know how safe the local trails are, I figure I will make my way to the gym and hop on a treadmill.

It is quiet at the gym. There are a couple of guys in the weights section, and every single treadmill is free. The treadmills all face a wall of one-way mirrors—I can see out, but I know from when I walked up to the gym, no one can see in. The glass wall provides a picturesque view of the lake out in the distance. The sun is still low in the sky, and the pink and orange hues reflecting off the water are amazingly beautiful. I will definitely have to find a trail outside soon.

I stretch out, put my earbuds in, jack up the volume, set my pace, and run. As Florence and the Machine's "The Dog Days Are Over" blasts in my ears, I feel for the first time in my life that I am running toward something rather than away from it.

Forty-five minutes and five miles later, I step off the treadmill and wipe the sweat from my face. I feel good, damn good. I've worked out all of my confusion over the weekend. I know that I'm bound to cross paths with Reid again, so I decide to just pretend as if the moments we shared, or that I thought we shared, never happened. I promised myself that I would choose happy, and Reid leaving me longing on the dance floor while he goes to make out with some other chick is *so* not happy.

On my way back to the showers, I sneak a peek into the weight room. Just when I decide to forget him, there he is. Reid is with a group of his friends, laughing. They look like they are really enjoying each other's company as they work out. What the freak? He was so moody and cold Friday night, and now he looks like a completely different person. He is smiling and laughing, and there is a light in his beautiful blue eyes that is just breathtaking.

The second he catches me staring, he stiffens. It's like he's steeling himself against a harsh blow. I've done nothing but look at him, and he's shooting me daggers. What the fuck is his problem? What the fuck have I done to piss him off so much? Why am I saying "fuck" so much? He must bring out my inner swearer. My runner's high evaporates instantly, and I stalk off to the locker room.

About twenty minutes later, Reid arrives at the exit at the same time I do. I smile at him, trying to be nice, while his face remains as hard as stone—lightly stubbled, roughly delicious stone. I have a choice here: I can be pissy and moody, or I can be cool and calm. I bury my anger; I remember my promises, and I choose the latter.

"Hi. It's Reid, right? I think we met this weekend at Jack's party." I try for innocent, hoping that the knowing looks he shot me before can be erased by my faux confusion.

He smirks at me, knowing that I'm full of shit. Through his stifled laughter, he says "Yeah, it's Reid. Ashley, right?" Now it's his turn to be full of shit.

I roll my eyes and try to bite my sarcastic tongue,

but I fail miserably. I lean into him a little seductively and say, "If you hadn't left me after one dance for Miss Leggy Blonde, then you would definitely remember my name. There's no way you would have forgotten it after screaming it all night." Okay, I'm a virgin, but definitely not a prude, and it seems like Reid brings out not only swearing Maddy, but sexy Maddy as well.

He stands at the door, mouth agape. I stride past him and head off to class. I'm walking across the quad when I feel him catching up to me.

"It's Maddy. Even if I hadn't had the privilege of calling it out all night, I wouldn't have forgotten your name. So why are you following me?" His question leaves me more than a little confused, because he's the one who is following me out to the quad.

"What do you mean?"

"To the gym—are you stalking me or something?" He's trying to make the question seem light, but there's a serious undertone to his voice. He really thinks I'm following him. Doesn't he realize that I am not some clueless desperate freshman?

I huff an exasperated sigh and lay into him a bit. "No, Reid. I am definitely not following you. I was going for a run before class this morning. I didn't even know you were at the gym. I didn't see you until I was finished running and you shot me the nastiest look. I wouldn't have even said hello to you if you hadn't met me at the door. Happy? You can go on your merry way now knowing that I had no intention of even seeing you today."

I pick up the pace toward the library to get a little bit of reading done before class starts, but his long legs eat up the distance I am trying to put between us in no time.

"I'm sorry, Maddy. I didn't mean to piss you off. Really, I didn't. I guess I was just surprised to see you there. Definitely surprised to see you run like that. I'm not one bit surprised to see how much of a firecracker you are, though." His words are a stark contrast to the icy stare he shot at me before. They're sweet and sincerely apologetic.

"Oh, Reid, you have no idea," I snip back at him. For some reason, his rather mercurial reaction to me gets me very fired up, very annoyed. "Now, if you'll excuse me, I need to get some work done." And with that, I walk into the library, find a cubicle, and open my book. Unable to focus, I stare blankly at the words on the page, my mind lost in the enigma that is Reid Connely.

The next two weeks continue in much of the same pattern. I get up early, head to the gym, get in my five miles, and go to class. I'd be lying if I said my only motivation for going to the gym every morning is my run. Reid also goes to the gym every morning. I know he looks for me. I've caught his glance a few times, so he knows I'm looking for him, too. We seem to be stuck in this push and pull, yet neither of us is willing to do much of anything about it.

It's Friday and I'm done with classes early, so I head back to the suite to catch a nap. Cammie has the afternoon off as well, and when I walk into the living room she lifts her nose out of her textbook.

"Hey, Maddy! How was your day?"

"Not too thrilling. This psychology class is going to kill me, though. Synapses and neurotransmitters and blah blah blah." I flop down beside her on the couch and debate whether or not to talk to her about Reid. She's already said that she doesn't know much, but I figure what the hell. It's worth a shot, right?

"I know I've already asked about him, but what can you tell me about Reid? He's at the gym every morning when I get there, and we swap stares all morning. We spoke once last week, and it was rough and edgy, like I'd pissed him off by being in his precious gym, and then he was all apologetic and sweet for nearly biting my head off. I'm usually pretty calm and collected, but he brings out this sarcastic snippy side to me. I just don't know how to deal with him, and I have no clue what I did to bother him."

Yeah, that pretty much sums it up.

"Um…" She pauses while she tries to gather her thoughts. "I'm not really sure. Reid really keeps to himself while I'm at Jack's. I've never gotten more than a tight smile and a quick 'hello' when he sees me there."

Oh, not what I expected. He seems pretty loose and friendly with his boys at the gym.

"Look, Maddy," she continues, "you might not want to hear this, but the few things I do know about Reid don't exactly paint him in the best light. He's a player. In the three years that he's been here, he's never been with a girl for more than one night—maybe a weekend if she was really good. He sleeps with pretty much anything that moves, and he doesn't seem to be ashamed of it at all. The fact that you say he was sweet and apologetic is actually really shocking to me."

Her words hit me in the gut. It is completely ridiculous of me to think that Reid can't have any girl he wanted; I just didn't want to think he took them up on the offer as frequently as he did.

Thoroughly confused about how I should feel about all of this, I harrumph and slouch down further on the couch. "I just don't know what to make of it. We danced at that first party at Jack's, and I swear we had some kind of connection, and in a heartbeat he went from completely into me to ice-cold and distant. Then he thought I was stalking him at the gym. He played it off like he was pissed that I was there, but then there was a hint of hopefulness in his words that I might actually be there to see him. I've seen him every morning since then, but he hasn't said two words to me, and I won't make the first move at this point."

I see a light bulb go off over her head as a mischievous grin curls her lips into a tight smile. "Well, there's another party tonight. Why don't you come with me and see if we can push a few of his buttons —get him to make the first move."

There's a sneaky look in her eyes, and I'm not sure if I'm down with her plan.

"I don't know, Cam. I'm not the type for a player." Even as I say the words, I have this gut feeling that he wouldn't play me. I don't know why. Maybe it's that I know I wouldn't let him play me. I kept my walls up around Jay, and I genuinely liked him. Reid doesn't have a shot in hell at breaking them down at this point.

"Come on, it'll be fun. We'll get you all smoking hot and make him realize what a jerk he's being. We'll give him a taste of his own medicine and then head home. And if that doesn't work, we'll just dance and have fun and find you some other hottie."

Cue the big puppy-dog eyes, and I'm a goner.

" Okay, I'll go, but I'll pick my outfit. And I am NOT going there to be one of his tramps."

Though getting to touch him again wouldn't be horrible by any means. After all, I have seen him at the gym with his shirt off. That was a good morning, indeed.

Cammie's excited voice breaks into my steamy musings about Reid. "Yay! It'll just be me and you, though. Lia has a study session, and Mel is at work tonight."

I forgot about that. Melanie got a job at the computer lab. Since she's new, she got stuck with the Friday night shifts, which cut into her social time, but it's like she's getting paid to get her homework done, so she doesn't complain much. For the first time in our lives,

Melanie and I are actually going to have to carve some time out for each other.

"Okay, you and me it is, then! It'll be fun. I could definitely use some time to cut loose." I'm slowly warming up to her little plan.

The fact that Reid will be there has nothing to do with it.

No, it's not about Reid and his bright blue eyes, and his gorgeous body, and his sexy smile. No, not at all.

When we get there, the party is in full swing. The music is pumping, and everyone is up dancing. I don't see Reid anywhere, not that I'm looking for him.

Nope, definitely not looking for him.

I follow Cammie out into the kitchen while she grabs us a drink. It's not beer this time; it's some girly pink punch concoction. It doesn't taste horrible, so for the first time in my life, I decide that I'll actually drink. Just one or two—not enough to get smashed like everyone else already is. Jeez, it's only 10 p.m. How is it even possible to be *that* drunk *this* early?

It takes us about fifteen minutes before we find Jack, who is laughing with Logan.

"Hey, babe!" Jack smiles lovingly at Cammie, and her face glows. They really are adorable together.

"Hey, Maddy! I don't think you got to meet Logan last time you were here." He introduces us, and Logan reaches out to shake my hand, but turns it over and brushes a soft kiss all courtly-like on the back of my hand.

My face heats, and he smirks at me. He's very good-looking in that typical all-American football star way. He's got short brown hair and warm brown eyes. Where Reid is all hard and masculine, Logan is pretty. Without sounding too snarky about it, he is a pretty boy. Very easy on the eyes, but so very different from Reid.

Not that I compare every guy I see to Reid. No, I don't do that at all!

"It's very nice to meet you, Maddy. Can I get you another drink?"

As I look down into my cup, I realize I hadn't even noticed that I finished the first one. Logan grabs my hand and walks me back toward the kitchen to the girly punch.

As he fills my cup, he asks, "So how do you like it here? How are your classes getting on?"

"It's great. I really love it. Cammie and Lia are fantastic. Classes? Ehhh—they're okay. Not so hot at psychology, but I'm in love with my poetry class," I reply.

I take a big sip and start to feel the effects of the alcohol. I definitely need to slow down. I do not want to be a sloppy mess. Logan and I continue our conversation, and he's really nice. Cammie is right; he pretty much eats, breathes, and lives football. It turns out that he's an athletic training major. He says if he can't spend his life on the field playing, the next best place to be is on the sideline helping others play better.

The night carries on, and we make our way out into the living room. Logan spins me around and we start dancing—jumping up and down to some crazy frantic hip-hop beat. I feel the stress of my schoolwork and all of the crap with Reid melt away, and I give into the dance.

Eventually the pace changes, and it's a slow R&B rhythm flowing through the room. Logan pulls me closer and aligns our bodies. He starts moving and swaying, and I willingly go with him. The alcohol has made me looser, and I place my hands on his chest. He wraps his arms around my waist and leans his head down to my face.

Just as he moves to brush his lips against mine, someone bumps into me. Hard. So hard, in fact, that I almost lose my footing. I have to grab onto Logan's shoulders in order to regain my balance. When I turn around to see who the freak that was, all I catch is Reid's back as he stalks up the stairs. He turns around at the top and glares at me. If I thought he was cold and harsh last week at the gym, then this look can only be described as arctic.

"I'll be right back," Logan yells above the music, and takes the stairs two at a time to catch up to Reid. They scuffle at the top of the stairs, and I catch bits of the conversation.

"What the fuck, dude? That was not cool," Logan grumbles at Reid.

Reid just offers a shrug of his shoulders and says, "What did I do? I didn't do anything."

He's trying to play it off like nothing, but I see the edge in his eyes. He's looking at me in his peripheral vision, and he's seething anger.

Logan scoffs out a "whatever" and comes back down to me.

"I'm going to get another drink. Do you want one?" Logan asks.

I know I said I would take it easy, but after Reid almost knocking me over I'm pissed, and a third drink seems like an excellent idea. By the time Logan and I re-enter the living room, Reid has made his way back downstairs, too, and is grinding away on the dance floor with a girl I can only describe as supermodel beautiful. They are practically having sex out there. His hands are roaming all over her body, just barely skimming past parts that should not be touched in public—unless you're into that sort of thing, of course.

I gulp back the rest of my drink and lose my balance. Logan is right there to grab me, and he pulls me farther into the living room to go sit on the couch. I follow him and sink down next to him. He puts his arm behind me and around my shoulder as his fingertips make lazy circles on my upper arm. It feels nice, and goosebumps start to break out across my arms. I close my eyes and try to enjoy his touch—even though it's Reid I want touching me. What I'm really trying to do is move all thoughts of Reid and the chick he's dry-humping out of my mind.

Logan leans down to kiss me, and I don't fight it. He's been sweet all night, and I've resolved myself to the fact that I'm not who Reid wants, even if I do look fan-fucking-tastic in my black mini skirt and hot pink top. As Logan moves his lips across mine, I feel the atmosphere in the room shift.

Reid is in front of us in seconds. He grabs Logan by the collar and lifts him off the couch. Before Logan can even get a word out, Reid cocks his arm and lands a nasty right hook across Logan's jaw. I scuffle off the couch and move to the edge of the room, where everyone else has retreated to give them space.

It takes Jack and few other guys a minute or two to break Reid and Logan up, and when they do, I can see that Logan's cheek right under his eye is split and his jaw is already swollen from Reid's first punch. Reid mutters out a "fuck you" to Logan before he storms out the front door.

I grab some ice for Logan's face and sit back down on the couch with him. At this point, most of the partygoers start to leave. The crowd has definitely thinned out, and within half an hour of the fight, it's just me, Logan, Cammie, and Jack sitting in the living room.

"I'm beat," Jack says and then starts laughing. "But I guess not as beat as you, huh, Logan?" He's beside himself with laughter now.

"Oh, you're just so fucking hilarious, Jack!" Logan's words are dripping sarcasm as he reaches up and touches his bruised cheek.

"Aww, baby, leave him alone. Come on, let's go up to bed."

Cammie leans into Jack's neck and whispers something that makes Jack's breath hitch and his pupils dilate. Jack stands and pulls Cammie up with him. He's got her up and over his shoulder in a nanosecond. She shrieks in shock, and he playfully slaps her ass as her carries her up to his room.

Jack turns around so that Cammie can wave good-bye to us. She looks at me questioningly; there's concern on her face. "You sure you're okay to spend the night, Maddy? I could call you a cab if you want."

"No, it's okay, really, Cammie. I'll be fine." I smile back at her and return my attention to Logan.

"Sorry for the drama tonight, Maddy. I have no fucking clue what came over Reid. He can be such a tool sometimes. I'd offer to drive you home, but I am most definitely not in any shape to drive."

He leans in and seductively offers to let me sleep in his bed. I feel pretty strongly that if I go up there with him, he'll want to do anything but sleep.

"No, it's okay, Logan, really. I can't drive home, either—especially since my ride just got carried caveman-style up to a bedroom. If it's okay with you, I'm just going to make myself comfortable here on the couch."

"No, Maddy, I don't want you to have to sleep on the couch. Come on up to my room. I'll sleep on the floor. Really, it'll be okay. I'll keep my hands to myself." He holds his hand up in a "Scouts honor," gesture and

I recall my initial thought that the couch looked like it could transmit an STD. I quickly fire off a text to Melanie that I'm with Cammie and that we're staying at Jack's for the night. She says that she hopes I had fun, and I laugh at the inaccuracy of her assessment.

" Okay, fine. But you are definitely sleeping on the floor." I relent and just hope that he can keep his promise.

A true scout, Logan kept his promise and slept on the floor. He lent me a T-shirt and a pair of shorts to sleep in, and it is this outfit that Reid sees me wearing in the morning when we run into each other in the hallway.

"Nice shirt," he mumbles as he walks past me to the bathroom.

I murmur "douche," and that seems to catch his attention. He turns back around and gets in my face.

"What did you say?" His voice radiates anger.

"I said 'douche.' You're being a douche. Or maybe you prefer 'dick.' Pick one. You're doing a great job of being both, actually."

"What the fuck is *your* problem?"

Is he serious? Does he not see how childishly he's behaving? Does he think what he did last night was acceptable?

"My problem? Really, Reid!? What the fuck is your problem? You dance with me and flirt with me and there is definitely something there, and then you drop me like I'm disease-infested. You ignore me every morning at the gym, but I catch you staring at me, too. You almost knock me on my ass last night, and then you punch Logan because he's actually being nice to me. And you have the audacity to ask *me* what *my* problem is." I take this break in my berating to poke him in the chest. "You're the one with the fucking problem, and I have no clue what it is because in the time we've known each other, you haven't said more than two words to me. So, yeah, you're being a douche!"

I turn around to head back to Logan's room, but before I make it all that far, Reid grabs me by the wrist and pulls me back to him. His mouth crashes into mine before I even realize what he's doing. I open to him immediately, and it's not just because he's caught me off guard. I've wanted this kiss since the moment I saw him, and it is everything I hoped it would be. It's a heated and hard kiss full of all the angst we've been carrying around.

Our tongues lap at each other furiously, tasting, exploring. He gently nips at my lower lip and then soothes his bite with a tender lick. He grabs the back of my neck and pulls me closer, and I reach my hands around his waist up the back of his shirt. His skin feels hot under my fingertips—silky smooth and muscled. He tastes….so indescribable that words fail me. It is, hands down, the best kiss ever.

When he pulls away, my lips are swollen from his passion, and I want to ask him why he stopped, but he starts talking before I can get any words out.

"Douchey enough for you?" His voice is laced with venom, and I am beside myself with anger and humiliation.

I stand there, completely immobilized by his anger and utterly confused by the change in his demeanor. I choke on my tongue and can't manage to get anything out in response to his question.

He leans down to my ear and says, "Why don't you hurry back into Logan's bed now? I'm sure he'll be wondering where you are."

I understand what it looks like, me walking out of Logan's room in his clothes this early in the morning, but thanks to Reid's antics earlier in the evening, Logan didn't even have the chance to kiss me. Reid's words hit me like a fist to the stomach, and I can almost feel the bile rising in my throat. He scoffs a "whatever" at me as he continues on his earlier path to the bathroom.

I can't stop the tear that breaks free, and once that first one is out, the floodgates open. I stand there crying at his hurtful words, harsh tone, and slutty implication. In that moment, I hope I never see Reid Connely again.

Chapter 5

AFTER REID LEAVES ME CRYING in the hallway, I return to Logan's room and gather my things. He's still pretty out of it; he's definitely not a morning person, so he doesn't even realize that I'm upset when I wake him up to take me home. I think about knocking on Jack's door to get Cammie, but I don't want to interrupt them.

Honestly, I don't even care if Logan sees me upset. I just want to get home.

Melanie is in our room when I get back to the suite. She knows that I've been crying and opens her arms to me as soon as she sees me. After she's done squeezing all of the air out my lungs, she holds me at arm's length, almost as if she's checking me for injuries.

"What happened, Mad? When I got the text from you last night, I figured things had finally panned out for you and Reid. Why are you crying? You're scaring me a little here, Maddy."

I tell her all the gory details. Me dancing with Logan, Reid almost knocking me over, Reid punching Logan, Logan being a gentleman, Reid kissing me like I've never been kissed before, Reid being a complete asshole. She listens, gasping here and there at Reid's behavior. It's clear that he is not one of her favorite people right now.

"He is a huge asshole, Maddy. I don't get why he treated you like that. It makes no sense. And then to kiss you like that. What the freak?!"

I flop down on the bed and harrumph. What a shit show! Cammie's plan to push his buttons sure as hell backfired.

"So what do you want to do today?" Melanie asks, and there's a hopeful airiness to her voice. I know she's trying to bring me out of this funk, but a large part of me just wants to curl up and sulk. I feel sad all over again. I mean, I didn't really put myself out there with Reid. I'm not even sure how I really feel about him, but he treated me like dirt, and it hurts.

"Come on, let's not sit around and waste a perfectly nice fall day. How does shopping and lunch sound?" She's persistent; I'll give her that much.

"I could actually use some outdoor running shoes. I've been meaning to check out this trail that someone at the gym recommended. Want to hit Sports Authority, grab some sandwiches, and head out on the trail for a picnic?"

I can tell by her giddy smile that Melanie is in love with my plan. She's almost out the door before I get out of the bed.

Shopping is a success, and the trail is gorgeous. It's right behind the dorms and there are tons of other people taking advantage of it, which is great because now I don't have to use the treadmill at the gym and chance running into Reid. We follow the trail for about two miles, and it stops at a clearing that overlooks the lake. It's the perfect place to enjoy our lunch and catch up. I feel like I haven't had any time with Melanie since we've been here.

She tells me all about her job at the computer lab. For the most part it's deathly boring, but the one saving grace is the hot computer geek who works with her. I wasn't aware that computer geeks came in the "hot" variety, but apparently they do. His name is Bryan, and according to Melanie, who I'm sensing might be a little biased, he is not only gorgeous but funny, too. I am over-the-moon happy for her when she tells me that she has a date with him this Saturday night. They're going to this cute little mom-and-pop Italian restaurant in town.

I'd be lying if I said there isn't the tiniest twinge of jealousy. I know I could still be with Jay if I wanted, but I don't. There's Logan, who is apparently very interested. He is really sweet and a total gentleman, but I'd be lying if I said I wanted him. I have a feeling that if I get together with Logan, it would play out the same way things did with Jay. Both Jay and Logan are great guys, but there is just something missing. Some kind of understanding, some passion, some fire—I can't really put my finger on it, but I know in my heart that as sweet and kind as they might be, they are just not the men for me.

I hate that while Melanie is waxing poetic about Bryan, all I can think about is Reid. He's been nothing but a total jerk to me since the moment I met him, but I can't deny that I want him. There's some pull, some draw between us, and I just know that he feels it. He has to, or that kiss wouldn't have been what it was. I want to dig deeper; I want to know him better. I want to learn what put the pain in his eyes. I want to soothe it. I want to share my pain with him in the hopes that he can help me wash it away, because despite his anger, I've seen compassion in his eyes, too. I've heard the hope in his voice. I've seen him laughing with his friends, and I know there is a good guy in there somewhere.

Melanie and I finish our hike as the sun is setting on the horizon. When we get back to the dorm, we huddle up on the couch and watch some girly chick flick and give each other manicures. I've missed time with my best friend. It's light and airy and easy—everything that Reid and what I'm feeling for him are not. In short, it is the perfect cure for my shitty Friday night.

I spend the entire afternoon and most of the evening on Sunday in the library studying for a major psych exam on Monday. The class is by far my most difficult, but I'm starting to figure out how to survive it. Hopefully at some point in the semester, I'll actually come to enjoy it, but that's highly doubtful.

I rarely oversleep, but since I was up so late studying last night, I barely have time to brush my teeth and make myself presentable before the big test. I make it to class just as the T.A. is handing out the exam booklets. I take a deep breath and give it my best effort.

When the exam ends an hour and a half later, I feel good about it. It might not be my best grade ever, but I studied my ass off. My next class passes in a blur. By lunch time, I am famished and completely exhausted. I grab a sandwich from the to-go bar in the cafeteria and head back to my room for a nap.

It's four in the afternoon when I wake up, and I feel rested and energized. Since I missed the gym this morning, I get my new kicks on to go for a run outside today. Maybe my oversleeping was an attempt by my subconscious to avoid Reid at the gym. Yeah, I definitely spent too much time with my psych textbook this weekend.

Running on the trail is so much more exhilarating than the gym. The fresh air is cool and crisp against my skin. Rather than beating down on my back oppressively, the sun is gently kissing my shoulders and warming my muscles. I make it to the clearing where Melanie and I had lunch the other day and take a break to breathe in the beauty all around me. The

lake is pristine and so unbelievably calming. It's surrounded by evergreens, and the contrast between the
deep emerald color of the trees and the aqua blue of
the water is so stark that it looks almost unnatural. I
hear some birds chirping in the tree above me and look
up and see a pair of sparrows perched side-by-side like
two love birds.. I laugh a little at the cheesiness of the
scene, but it really is beautiful.

In honor of my promise to myself to see the beauty
in the world, I lie down and look up into the sky. Jay's
words about not being able to get over the death of my
parents until I let myself play back in my mind. Usually
I push down the memories I have of my parents; they're
just too painful to let get to the surface. But on this
occasion, I decide to just let go and feel them for once.

One of my favorite memories from my childhood is
when my dad and I used to go to the park on Saturday
mornings. It was his sweet way of giving mom some
time to herself. I think he just liked his weekly slice of
Maddy-time. We would lie on our backs and name the
shapes we saw in the clouds. I would put my head on
his chest and hear his heartbeat. I was safe and protected and loved. In this moment here on the ground,
staring up at the clouds, I can almost smell his cologne,
some spicy aftershave; I can almost feel his heart
against my cheek, a calming *thump-thump* in his chest.
I can hear him chuckling as I name some pretty ridiculous things—a starfish, a baby, a peanut butter and
Fluff sandwich. An unbidden tear rolls down my cheek,

and I can't help but smile at the memories. We would always go out to the diner after our park dates, and get pancakes and bacon for lunch. Some afternoons we'd come home and Mom would be napping on the couch, so we would sneak off to go catch a movie, or hang out down in the den and watch a baseball game.

Those days were the happiest in my life. I hope that maybe one day, it'll feel like that again, like heaven on earth. I might not be there yet, but for the first time ever, it doesn't feel like hell.

Chapter 6

Reid

Saturday Morning—Post Best Kiss Ever with Maddy

I SEE THE TEARS POURING DOWN HER FACE as I retreat to my room, but I am just too fucked up right now to go to her. I know I'm being exactly what she said I was—a dick—but I don't have it in me to hear from her sweet lips how much I've hurt her. I want to apologize for almost knocking her over, for insulting her, for being a huge douche, but I just can't own up to those feelings right now.

I will most definitely not apologize for kissing her, though. Since I first met her, I've wanted to kiss her—to do so much more with her. But that kiss—oh, God—what the fuck was that kiss? I have never felt anything

like that in my life, and well, to put it mildly, I've kissed
my share of girls.

Love 'em and leave 'em. Yeah that's always been how
I work, and it works for me. No attachment, no com-
mitment—perfect. I put up some pretty fucking sturdy
walls after Alex fucked me over, and no one has been
able to break them down. I won't let them. But there
was something in her eyes; I saw it when we were dancing. I could see into her soul, and it shook me to my
core. She knocked me totally off my game. She's sarcastic and snarky, but she's got so much sweetness, too. I
just cannot get her out of my head, and now I've gone
and really fucked things up.

She leaves shortly after our kiss, and I know she's
upset. Logan is sitting at the kitchen table, pouring milk
into his cereal. I stare him down, beyond pissed off that
he would do that to me—you know the whole "bros
over hos" thing, but then again, it's not like I made it
known that I want her.

*Why would anyone think that you actually want a
girl. You've done your best to push them all away.*

"I guess it's safe to say that you had a good night,
Logan," I remark; my voice is laced with angry sarcasm.

He leans back in his chair and folds his hands
behind his head. "Fucking fantastic, actually. Maddy's
fucking hot."

His words antagonize me, and I fist my hands at my
sides. I don't want to hit him again. Well, actually, I do
want to hit him, but I won't. I want some details, and

somehow punching him in the face might not help my mission.

"Is she? Hot, I mean? I hadn't noticed."

He sees straight through my bullshit, not that I tried that hard. Can't lie about how gorgeous Maddy is.

And sweet.

And sassy.

And perfect.

He straightens and glares at me. "You didn't notice? Seriously? Then what the fuck was your problem last night? You nearly took her out and came close to knocking me out, too."

"Close to knocking you out? No, I definitely got you good. Nice shiner, by the way." I can't hide my smirk. I got him pretty good.

As he walks past me to go watch some ESPN while he eats, he whispers, "Best lay of my life."

"You're a shit, Logan." I don't want to say more than that. I don't want to lay my cards on the table and give him more fuel, but I'm furious - at him for swooping in and looking like a knight in shining armor, at her for sleeping with Logan, at myself for being an asshole.

Definitely not pissed because I wanted to be the one sleeping with her. No, definitely not that.

I haven't seen Maddy since our kiss Saturday morning. She hasn't been to the gym. She hasn't been to the house. She hasn't been anywhere that I am. After a week of not seeing her anywhere, I'm getting the distinct feeling that she's avoiding me.

Now why would she want to avoid you, asshole? It's not like you kissed her like you meant it (which you did) and then all but called her a slut (which you did). Yeah, "asshole" pretty much sums it up.

Okay, she's definitely avoiding me, and I don't know what to do with it. After she left the house on Saturday morning, I tried to figure out my feelings. I was not successful. God, I sound like a pussy. Figure out my feelings. Logan bragging certainly didn't help me in the least.

My phone vibrates in my pocket, and for a minute I hope that it's Maddy.

Asshat, you never gave her your number, and at this point she wouldn't want it.

I slide my finger across the screen, opening up the text. It's from Jessa.

~ Wanna get together later?

"Get together" is her code for a booty call. Usually I jump at the chance. Sex with no strings—fucking sign me up. We've hooked up a bunch in the last few months. When most girls agree to the "no strings attached" fling, they usually do so with the hope that it'll eventually turn into more. They want to tame the untamable, but not Jessa. She's fine with the distance. She's crazy hot and is always up for a good fuck, but I'm just not in the mood tonight, though. I don't even bothering texting back. She'll find someone else to "get together" with her.

I need that distance when it comes to girls. I've always needed it and wanted it. I refuse to let anyone get close to me.

And it is in this moment of clarity that I realize why I've been such a prick to Maddy. She's been nothing but nice to me—okay, fine she's been sarcastic and on guard with me, too, but I make her feel that way. She hasn't been all over me like all these other girls, but there's something there that says she wants more. There's a vulnerability and openness that she's trying to guard, and I know it because I'm the same way.

I can't deny that I want more with her; it just scares the shit out of me.

The knocking on my door steals my attention away from my thoughts on Maddy.

"Hey, man," Jack calls from the doorway.

"What's up?"

"Me and some of the guys are heading out to Shooters tonight. Wanna come with?" At this point, Jack's offer sounds perfect. Some time with the guys, shooting pool, having a few beers—not thinking about Maddy—absolutely fucking perfect.

The pool hall is packed and loud and the perfect distraction. We're on our third game when I see her enter. My mouth goes dry, and my heart plummets in my chest. Gorgeous—simply stunning. Her hair is down in flowing waves; it looks sex-mussed—it looks perfect. Her tight jeans accentuate every single fucking curve of her perfect ass. Low-cut jeans and a midriff-baring top would look slutty on most women in here, but on Maddy it looks hot and oh, so inviting.

Jack nudges me with his pool cue, indicating that it's my turn to shoot. He chuckles a little when he realizes the cause of my distraction. When I'm done with my shot, he asks, "You've got it bad, huh?"

"What do you mean?" I retort.

"Maddy." He angles his head toward her direction. "You've got it bad. That's why you kicked Logan's ass and why you've been in a mood all week. I didn't put it together before now, but it's her. You want her, and you can't have her." He's wearing a smug look on his face, obviously proud of his newfound detective skills. Jerk.

A quick shrug of the shoulders, and the conversation is ended. I think Jack can tell that I just don't want to get into it. The fact that Cammie walks in right behind Maddy helps to distract him as well.

Lia, Melanie, and some other guy, who I later learn is Melanie's new computer-lab boyfriend Bryan, follow Maddy and Cammie. What the fuck. Jack didn't tell me this was a family reunion. I'm so not in the mood for this tonight.

I am in the mood for ripping Maddy's clothes off and hearing her scream my name. Now, that doesn't sound like a horrible plan.

"Hey, baby. Up for a real game?" Jack's words are laced with lust, and I know that he's just challenging Cammie to a game so he can look at her ass while she plays.

Hmmm, not a bad idea. Not a bad idea at all. Now, if I can only get Maddy to go along with the same plan.

Cammie sneaks a look in Maddy's direction, obviously unsure whether Maddy wants to play against us. I've really pushed this too far. Maybe it's time for me to give this a shot and see what happens. The chemistry between us is already off-the-charts hot. Maybe it's time to let some of those walls come down—not all the way, but just a little.

"C'mon, girls. It'll be fun," I chime in and wink, hoping that it will lure her in.

Cammie responds with a cheery "sure." All I get from Maddy is an exasperated sigh and a disinterested "whatever."

Really dug myself in deep with this one.

I walk up next to Maddy and lean in. I want her to play. I want her to see that I'm not always a jerk. Okay, fine, "jerk" is an understatement. But I have to make things better. It's time to turn on the charm.

"Please, Maddy? I promise I'll be a good boy," I coo into her ear.

"Oh, puuulease. Like you even know what that means!" she snaps.

"It'll be fine, Mad," Cammie interrupts. "Jack is here. He'll keep ass-face…um, I mean Reid in line." I have never liked Cammie more than I do right now.

"Oh, okay, fine." Maddy huffs. Well, she might not be happy about it, but at least she's staying.

Lia, Melanie, and Bryan set up at the table next to us, and we all start playing and laughing alongside each other. Maddy quickly forgets her anger at me and relaxes into the game.

Seeing carefree and fun Maddy lightens my spirits and only makes me want her more.

And oh, thank the gods who created low-rise, ass-hugging jeans. Watching her bend over the table for the last few hours has been quite the show, one that I catch some asshole at the next table enjoying as well. Maddy notices him, too, and adds an extra strut to her stuff; there's more sway in her hips. Damn her. She's flirting with him, and I'm right here.

When our game is over, he swaggers over and puts his arm around her waist. I can only catch snippets of the conversation, but I see her smiling and giggling like a little girl. She looks happy.

She's happy because he's not treating her like a piece of garbage.

"Cam, I'm going to go grab a drink with Mike," Maddy announces to the group, but I catch the sharp look in her eye as she walks past me.

She's been at the bar with him for two hours now. She hasn't had anything but a couple of sodas. They started out just talking, but that quickly grew into playful banter and flirtatious touching.

Part of me is seething in anger that she's doing this to get back at me. Part of me is enraged with jealousy because I want her to be like that with me. And part of me, a much larger part of me, is concerned for her. There's just something about this guy that I don't like.

Jack, Logan, and I have been coming here for years, and I've never seen him before. He doesn't look young enough to be a college student, either. I just don't like him.

He realizes I'm watching them and occasionally leers over at me; he then leans into Maddy's ear and whispers something. Her eyes widen in a state of shock, but she quickly recovers. She's shaking her head "no," and she points over to where Jack, Cammie, and I are still playing pool. Melanie and Bryan left a little while ago. Lia left with them, too. The pool hall has never been her scene.

Mike quickly recovers from her rejection and resumes his playful flirting. Maddy seems to welcome its return.

I can't watch any more. I need a break from this scene playing out in front of me. I suddenly realize that Maddy getting together with Logan would have been much better than her hooking up with this guy. Logan is one of the good ones—a fucker for sleeping with her, but a genuine good guy, nonetheless; Mike, not so much.

I hate to leave my watch post, but nature calls. As I walk past them on the way to the bathrooms, Mike leans in to kiss Maddy, even though she clearly said no to his advances earlier. She sees me and kisses him back. I think she sees the look of disgust on my face because her eyes seem to convey some sort of apology.

I push past the exit at the end of the long hallway where the bathrooms are located. I just need some fresh air. I need to clear my head. I need a few minutes to regain what little composure I thought I had.

I sit down on the curb of the sidewalk and hang my head down low. This is all so foreign to me. I feel like a gigantic pussy over all this, but one thing remains clear: I want her.

For the first time ever, I want a girl for more than just one night, for more than just sex. She's alive and vibrant. I just feel like she sees me, the real me. Scares the shit out of me, but I can't deny it any longer.

I don't know how long I've been out here, giving myself this little pep talk, but it has definitely strengthened my resolve with all things Maddy-related. The only way for her to know how I feel is to tell her. I have to stop being an asshole, stop being afraid, and just see what happens.

All that shit happened years ago, and Maddy is not Alex. She wouldn't hurt you like that. Plus, Shane's already dead, so it's not even possible for Maddy to hurt you like that.

I bury the sinking feeling of guilt over my dead brother and try to shake the vile thoughts of Alex out of mind. No matter how many times people tell me otherwise, I know I killed him. It was entirely my fault—and hers—Alex's. My blood goes cold just thinking about her and Shane.

But Maddy is different. I know she sees my pain; I see hers, and I can't help but wonder what put it there. It's been five years. Maybe now it's finally time to heal. Maybe Maddy can help me figure out how.

I push back through the exit, only to be greeted by Mike and Maddy. We're at opposite ends of the hall, but even from that distance I'm sure that Maddy can see the shock and disgust in my eyes.

She is leaving. With him? What the fuck!?

I stalk past them, and I turn on my heel the second that I make eye contact with Maddy.

Something's wrong. Really wrong.

Her eyes look all cloudy and faraway. She's stumbling, so much so that Mike is practically dragging her out.

"Maddy, are you okay?" I can't hide the genuine concern in my voice.

Mike answers for her. "She's fine, douchebag. We were just leaving. You can go back to your little friends now."

I grab her by the shoulders and pull her face up to meet mine. She is definitely not okay. I don't get it, though. She hasn't had anything but soda all night. Even if there was rum in those cokes, she wouldn't be this drunk after only three or four.

And then it hits me—the look he gave me when I walked past earlier. It was him. He did something to her drink. He waited for me to leave so he could get her out of here and alone.

"Maddy, please tell me you're okay. Come on, let's get out of here. I'll take you home." I'm practically begging her to come with me, but she won't leave his side. I realize at that point that it isn't so much that she won't leave his side, it's that she can't. She can't stand on her own. She's really fucked up.

"What the fuck do you care, Reid? You don' wan' me. Made that perfectly clear. I'm not hot 'nuff for you or whatever." Her words are slurred, and her eyes start to roll back in her head.

"Let go of her." My calm, even voice belies my boiling anger and frustration.

"No, fuck-face! You heard the lady. She's leaving with me. Now get out of my way." Mike pushes me back in an attempt to get past me.

I size him up. I've got a few inches on him and at least twenty pounds of muscle.

Nope—she's definitely leaving with me, and you're getting your ass kicked, too.

"Wrong move, asshole. I said, LET GO OF HER!" I push him on each word to accentuate the seriousness of my threat.

He drops his arm from around Maddy's waist. Thankfully, she is close to the wall and uses it for some support. The second he takes to recover his balance is all I need to knock him on his ass. I knock him further off balance with a quick left hook to the chin and a swift knee to the groin. While he's bent over in pain, I grab Maddy and run through the back exit.

Running my hands over her face and pushing her hair out of her eyes, I ask if she's okay. She can't even form a response. I can feel her slipping away from me into unconsciousness. I've got to get her home.

I carry her over to my Mustang and drop her in the front seat. I lean over and buckle her in, and she leans into my neck.

"Hmmm, you smell so good, Reid. You always smell good. Kiss me, please." She's obviously regained her voice and her bearings for a minute.

"Soon, baby. I'll do more than kiss you soon, but right now I just want to get you home and take care of you." She nods her "okay" and swiftly returns to her nearly comatose state.

I tuck her hair back behind her ear and kiss her forehead. I won't kiss her how she wants to be kissed right now. I will not take advantage of her, but, well, if she wants a kiss, then a kiss she'll have.

When I get into the driver's seat, I shoot off a quick text to Jack, telling him that I've got Maddy and that we're on our way back to the house. I also ask Jack for Melanie's number. I know she'll freak if Maddy doesn't come home. He sends me Mel's number and responds that he knew I had it bad. I'll deal with him later. My main concern is that everyone knows she's okay.

When we pull up to the house, Maddy is completely passed out. I lift her out of the car and carry her up the front steps. It's not an easy feat to open the door with her in my arms, but it's a welcome challenge. She's here with me, and she's safe. That's all that matters.

Walking through the living room, I consider letting her sleep on the couch, but I don't want her to wake up alone. I don't know what she'll remember, and I don't want her to get scared. I decide that her sleeping in my bed is the safest place for her. Upstairs it is, then.

No hidden motives at all.

I lay her down in the middle of the bed and pull off her strappy black sandals. I decide to leave her in her clothes. Not that I don't want to take them off—oh, God, I want that more than anything—but I want her to be conscious when I undress her.

I crawl in next to her, pull the covers up over us, and fold my arms behind my head. I won't be able to sleep a wink tonight with her soft, warm body next to mine. I need to stay awake anyway to make sure that she's okay.

I lean into her ear and whisper, "Goodnight, sweetheart. Don't worry—I'll take care of everything."

She mumbles something, hopefully not in protest, and returns to her deep slumber.

I stare wide-eyed at the ceiling, chuckling on the inside. I wanted Maddy in my bed, that's for certain, but definitely not like this.

Chapter 7

Maddy

My head is pounding. My mouth is dry. My body is weak. I try to blink the sleep from my eyes, but even that requires monumental effort. I have never felt like this before. What the hell happened to me?

As consciousness slowly returns, I stare up at the ceiling and realize I'm not in my own bed. Where the hell am I?

Panic sets in. I can feel my body start to tremble as the panic morphs into fear. I take a deep breath to try to calm myself, and in that moment I know exactly where I am.

Inhaling the scent from the pillow arouses more than my sense of awareness. I'm with Reid. I would know that smell anywhere. It smells like home.

The panic of not knowing where I am retreats, and a new one surfaces. Did I sleep with him? Did he take advantage of me? I don't even remember hanging out with him last night. How the fuck did I end up here?

He senses that I'm awake and rolls over to face me. His hair is all sleep-mussed, and his eyes are still drowsy. He looks innocent and sweet—two words I never thought I would ever use to describe Reid Connely.

He reaches out to cup my cheek when he sees what I can only imagine is shock in my eyes.

"Good morning, beautiful," he croons.

His words and soft endearment make my belly clench in a good way—a deliciously good way. He moves his hand from my cheek to brush back a piece of hair that has fallen in my eyes.

"Um, did we…" I move my hand back and forth between the two of us, "…you know? Did we…um… do it?"

Well, that was articulate.

He chuckles a soft laugh at my question and continues stroking my cheek with the pad of his thumb.

"No, Maddy. We most definitely did not 'do it.' Believe me, when we 'do it,' you'll remember." He pauses for a beat and looks like he's searching for the right words before he continues. "So, what do you remember from last night?" he asks.

He sits up and leans back against his headboard. I join him and pull the covers up as I do. I chance a peek under them. Thank God! I'm still clothed.

Not that being naked with Reid isn't on the top of my current bucket list.

I swallow past the choking feeling in my throat. Wait a second! He said *when*. He *wants* to sleep with me? He hates me, though? My brain can't handle much this morning. Maybe I just heard him wrong.

"Did you just say *when* we sleep together?" I can't hide my shocked tone.

"Yes, I did," he replies bluntly.

Okay—not really sure what to do with that. I'll just have to file it away for later, but it's definitely nice to know.

He repeats his earlier question. "So, Maddy, what do you remember?"

"Um, well, I remember being at the pool hall with everyone. And then I remember Mike and I hanging out at the bar for a little bit. After that things get a little fuzzy."

His brow furrows as if he's trying to figure something out. He looks worried, but he's not saying anything.

"What, Reid? What happened? What aren't you telling me?" His silence is scaring me a little.

"You got most of that right. You were with Mike, and you had a few drinks at the bar, but from what I saw, it was just soda." He leaves that last part hanging in the air between us—loaded and heavy.

Realization dawns—I didn't drink last night. This is not a hangover.

Reid catches the look of overwhelming panic in my eyes, and he immediately reaches to comfort me.

"Don't worry, Maddy. Nothing happened. I was walking back into Shooters when Mike was trying to leave with you. You guys walked past me, and I saw that something was off. Your eyes weren't clear. They were all glassy, and you just didn't seem with it. I had been watching you all night, so I knew you weren't drunk. That's when I realized that he must have slipped you something. I knocked him on his ass and then brought you here. I know you probably didn't want to wake up next to me, but I didn't want you to be alone and scared when you woke up."

As reality starts to settle in, I realize that Melanie doesn't know where the hell I am. I gasp and cover my mouth with my hand. "Oh, God, Mel! I need to call Mel. She must be worried sick. I never stay out without telling her." I fumble a bit in a half-assed attempt to get out of the bed. My head is still foggy, and I immediately feel dizzy when I try to move.

"Shh. Don't freak out. It's okay. I texted her last night and let her know that you were here. Don't worry. It's all taken care of." His voice is calming and soothing, as are his fingers, which are still delicately tracing lines over my eyes, cheeks, and lips.

I lean back against the headboard and take a few more calming breaths.

"You were watching me?" My question catches him off guard.

He doesn't answer right away. I can tell he's searching for the right words. He stops stroking my face and runs his hands through his own hair. I can see him internally battling over what to say. He's really struggling here, and if I wasn't on the edge of my seat for his answer, I might actually find this pretty funny.

He finally decides to speak.

"Um… Yeah. I guess you could say that. It's just that…well…I didn't trust that guy. I'd never seen him there, and he was staring at you while you were leaning over the pool table like a wolf eyeing up a lamb. I wanted to make sure that you were okay, that's all."

I can't manage more than an "oh" in response. The silence stretches. Unsaid words are hanging heavy between us. I can't take it any longer, so I say, "Thank you."

"For what, Maddy?" His eyes are wide and clear now, all traces of sleepiness gone.

"For saving me from him. For bringing me here and knowing that I would be scared if I woke up alone, for texting Mel, for not taking advantage of me. I know you don't really like me and all, so I just wanted to say thank you for helping me despite that."

He visibly flinches at my words. He looks offended and pissed—he looks more like the Reid with whom I'm familiar.

"That's what you think? You think I hate you?"

I pull back from the harsh tone of his cold words. "Well, I know I'm not your favorite person, that's for certain. I'd like to think you don't *hate* me, Reid, but I don't think you like me very much."

He inches toward me, closing the distance I just created.

"I definitely do not hate you." His hand returns to my cheek, and his eyes meet mine. He gazes intently and I'm mesmerized, completely glued to the honesty shining through their blue depths.

"Then what is it, Reid? What is going on here?" I throw my hands up in frustration. "I'm exhausted from all of this. You antagonize me and all but treat me like shit, and then you run in like some kind of knight in shining armor to rescue me from some big bad wolf. I...I...don't know what to do or how to feel. I can't keep running away from you. Avoiding you is draining me." I inhale a shaking breath before admitting this next part. "Since the moment I met you, I've wanted to be here in your arms, but you've done nothing but push me away. So tell me how I was supposed to think that you felt anything other than hatred for me."

"So you think I'm a knight in shining armor huh?" His lips quirk up into a gorgeous little smile, and I roll my eyes. I slap him playfully on the chest—his broad, muscular, perfect chest that I just seem to now be noticing is not covered in a shirt.

God, I hope he's not naked under here.

Yes, I do.

No, I don't.

Yes, I do.

Silence again permeates the room, but he's the one to break it this time.

"I've been an ass, Maddy." His confession gets a small chuckle from me.

"That's an understatement, Reid."

" Okay, fine! I've been a huge ass. Like, off-the-charts ass. I'm pretty sure Sir Mix-a-lot wrote a song about me." His words are playful and mocking, but he knows that there is truth in them.

"That sounds more like it. You can proceed now," I quip, and stick my tongue out at him, hoping to keep the mood light. I want him to keep opening up. I'm dying to know what he feels.

He reaches out with his other hand so that he's cupping both of my cheeks. He lines my face up with his and stares even deeper, if that's even possible, into my green eyes.

"I'm so sorry I've acted that way, Maddy. I know it sounds cliché and dumb, but I never meant to hurt you. I…well, you…I mean…. Oh, God I can't even speak right now. What I mean to say is…um…well…." His incoherent ramblings trail off as I lean my face in closer to his.

I stare patiently up into his crystal-blue eyes and whisper, "What, Reid? What do you want to say?"

He takes a deep breath and lets it out slowly, his gaze never wavering from mine.

"You've completely knocked me off my game. I've never met anyone like you, and it scares the shit out of me. It's like you don't see me." My brow furrows in confusion and I move to interrupt, but he continues before

I get the chance. "You don't see me—you see straight through me. You see beyond the outside, and it's like you see the me that no one else sees. I saw it in your eyes that first night I met you, and it knocked me on my ass. I was a goner, and since then I guess I've just been trying to push you away."

Wow, now that's a confession.

He shushes me and continues.

"You're a smart-ass, and I love that you keep me on my toes. You are most definitely not like the other girls, and I love that, but it also scares me like nothing else. I haven't let anyone in for years and, well, with you I feel like I want to give it a chance."

Did he just say love?

Twice?

It's all so much to take in. My brain is still in a fog, and all of this new information is not processing very quickly. Reid must see me trying to make sense of it all, and even under his scrutinizing stare, I can't form any words.

"It's a lot, Maddy—I know. And I know I have no right to ask you to share how you're feeling, but can you give me something? I'm dying here."

"I've never let anyone in, either." My words are barely a whisper, but I continue, "I've kept so many walls up my whole life. The only one who has ever gotten through is Mel, and that's mostly because I've known her since middle school. I keep people at such a distance that I even broke up with the only boyfriend

I've ever had before I came here because I didn't want us to get close."

His response is a laugh. He asks me to open up and then laughs.

Fucker.

"Seriously! You're going to laugh at me, Reid? Well, thanks for this heart-to-heart, but I think I'm done." I cross my arms over my chest and huff at him. He's such an ass.

"I'm sorry. It's just that you said you've only had one boyfriend, and I find that fucking hilarious. Seriously—just one. You mean to tell me that your dad didn't have to beat the boys away with a stick?"

Suddenly, I'm frozen. I don't know what to say. I don't know what to feel. With everything that's been going on with Reid, with everything that happened last night, with this morning's revelations, the mention of my father, as unintentional as it is, it's all just too much to take in.

A tear rolls down my cheek as I think about my dad never having the chance to grill prospective boyfriends. Another tear follows as I think about how he'll never be waiting up for me to come home from a date, how he'll never be asked for my hand in marriage, how he'll never walk me down the aisle.

Reid pulls me into his arms when he sees my tears. We slink down from the headboard, and he leans on his side. I lie on mine, and we're facing each other still entangled in one another's arms.

"What, Maddy? Please tell me what I said. I hate that I've already made you cry once. I hate seeing you like this. I'm so sorry if I upset you." His eyes are sincere and genuine. He's offering me everything I've ever wanted—a chance to let someone in and share my pain, to lighten my heaviness. I take a deep, cleansing breath and decide to take him up on his offer.

His hands are lightly combing through my hair and tickling my scalp. It's so comforting and soothing that I almost forget to speak. His lips touch down lightly upon my head, and he prompts me to say something.

"Please, Maddy. I want to be here for you. I know that I've been a dick, but I'm really sorry for that and I want to make it up to you, if you'll let me. Please."

He brushes my hair behind my ear and looks pleadingly into my eyes.

I try to come up with the right words, but there aren't any, so I go for bluntness.

"My parents are dead. Both of them. They died when I was ten, so he never had the chance to chase the boys away. Not that I've ever had a real date anyway."

I hate telling people this part of me. It's always met with a pathetic "I'm so sorry for your loss"—what does that even mean? I hate the stares of sympathy and the inadequate words. For the most part, I've learned to stifle the urge to yell and scream when someone acts that way toward me, but there have been a few times I couldn't. So naturally Reid's reaction cuts me to the quick.

"Makes sense, then," he says.

I stare at him blankly. "What makes sense, Reid?"

"The walls you've put up. Losing someone you love is fucking hard. Losing the two people you love the most and who love you more than life itself must fucking hurt so much that you've got no choice but to keep everyone away." He puts his fingers under my chin and angles my face up to meet his eyes. "Just so you know, your dad would probably have bought stock in Nike with the amount of chasing away he would have done."

I smile as I think about what my dad would have been like. I never really let my mind go to how things would have been if they were still alive. There's no point in it. They're dead, but being here in Reid's arms makes me feel safe and secure, so I let my mind explore the possibility for a minute.

Reid's voice interrupts my dreamlike state. "Tell me about them."

I'm taken back—no, wait, that's an understatement. I'm shocked and rendered speechless for a minute.

"No one's ever asked me that. It's always some pathetic attempt at an apology. But by not asking about them, it's like saying they never existed. I guess after a while it was easier for me to feel that way, too. It's been so long since I've even let myself think about them. It's just too painful. But lately I've been letting some of the memories come back, and they're nice in a way." I smile up at him. My emotions are a little more in check, so I continue,

"My dad was amazing. He always wanted to spend time with me. Not like those dads who work and come home and can't be bothered. He was always helping me with homework and whatever wacky science project I had to do. He was funny, too. Not like cheesy funny, though—I guess I get a lot of my sense of humor from him." Reid shoots me a wry look, but I ignore it and go on, "He just looked at life in a different way from most people. A lighter, easier way that just made him seem carefree most of the time, but he was serious, too. And oh, my God did he love my mom. She was beautiful."

"Well, one look at you, and I can only imagine," he interrupts, and kisses my forehead again.

"Thank you, but no, she was gorgeous. I can't remember too many specifics, but I know we have the same eyes. She was just flawless, but what little girl doesn't think her mom is perfect and that her dad is some kind of super-hero? I'm sure in reality they were far from it, but in my memories they were simply amazing together. I don't ever remember them fighting. They would dance—like out of nowhere with no music. Dad would just swoop in behind her and twirl her around, and I thought it was the most romantic thing ever. They looked at each other with such love and tenderness. I'll always remember that about them. So yeah, I guess that's why I put those walls up. It's easier to keep people away than it is to have them look at you like that and then be ripped away from you."

We lie in each other's arms for what feels like an eternity. I feel as if a weight has been lifted from my shoulders, having shared about my parents. I won't lie; it hurts to think about them, but the pain is a dull ache instead of the excruciating knife to the heart it usually is. Reid is tracing lazy circles on my back, and I feel sleep claiming me again.

To keep myself from nodding off completely, I say, "I should get going. I don't want to keep you all day. I'm sure you've got better things to do than listen to me gab about my dead parents all day. Plus, I'm still pretty groggy from last night, so I think I'm just going to crash and sleep the day away." I start to get up, and he pulls me back to his chest.

"How about this instead? I get you some sweats and a T-shirt. You can shower if you want, and while you do, I'll make you something to eat, and then we can relax all day if you want. I like having you here. If you want, I mean. I can drive you home if you want. It's up to you, sweetheart. Just promise me one thing?"

His words floor me. I'll give him anything when he's being this heartfelt.

"Of course, Reid."

"Well, two things, actually." He quirks his eyes up playfully as he adds more to his initial request.

I pretend to be debating his request, but he sees through it. I love when he's all playful and fun like this; it's so easy and natural. So of course I nod that I'll agree to his promises.

He lays his cards on the table.

"One—go out on one date with me. You said you've never been on a real date, and I would be honored if you'd let me be your first."

"And the second thing?"

He laughs as he realizes I'm not going to answer his first question without hearing the second.

"Well, I guess the second thing is more for both of us. We'll both promise to not put up so many walls. I'm not saying that what's already there needs to come down right now, but just that we should both be open to the possibility that this thing --" He gestures his hands between the two of us, "—might actually be good."

Again, I'm floored by his honesty. It's as if he is reading my mind about letting him in. I've wanted to since I met him, but I guess he just took a little longer in coming around. He says he's got his own walls, too, and I want to push a little to get him to open up, but I don't have the energy, and I don't want to change how it feels right now.

Another thing to file away for later.

"I think I can agree to those terms. So you really want to take me out on a date? You don't have to, you know? If it's out of sympathy, I mean. I'm a big girl. I can take it if you really don't like me."

I'd be crushed and eat my way through a few pints of ice cream to get over it.

But I would eventually.

Like when I'm sixty.

He cups my face in his palms, looks me square in the eye, and says, "I like you. A lot. If I didn't, I wouldn't be asking you out. I don't take anyone out, like, ever, so please know that my offer is for real. Will you please go on a date with me? Just one, and if you absolutely hate it, I'll leave you alone. I promise." He crosses his heart and looks at me with what can only be characterized as puppy-dog eyes. Damn, he's adorable.

His face is so close to mine that I can feel his warm breath on my lips. I whisper a "yes" in response, and the second I do, his lips are on mine.

It's not hard and fast like our first kiss. Rather, it's sweet and erotic. His tongue dances around mine, and when mine strokes his in return, I'm rewarded with a sexy groan. He picks up the intensity and gently nips and bites at my lips, quickly laving over the tender spots with his tongue. He pulls his lips away from mine, and I groan in protest. The protest stops immediately as I realize that he's kissing a path from my lips across my jaw and down to my neck. His tongue is tracing wet, hot patterns right below my ear, and I can't keep the whimper from escaping my lips. His hand is tangled in my hair, and he pulls me close to him so there is no space between us. Every single part of us is touching—chests, hips, legs, toes.

Souls.

Our legs are entangled, and I can feel how aroused he is. I wrap my arms around his waist and let my hands roam all over his chest and back. His lips are back on my mine, and he is no longer just kissing me. He is devouring me. This time I break the kiss and move for his neck. I lick the outer shell of his ear and bite at his lobe, and he pushes his erection into me in return.

"Oh, God, Reid! God, please do that again."

He does, and I nearly shriek in return. He feels amazing, and I want to kiss every inch of him.

Before I have the chance to, he pulls back, and I immediately feel self-conscious that I've done something wrong.

"What's wrong, Reid? Did I do something wrong?"

"Fuck no, Maddy. You did nothing wrong at all. A few more minutes of what you were doing, and you would have unmanned me. God, I want you. You have to know that." He nudges his arousal into me one more time just to prove his point before he continues, "It's just with everything that happened last night, I don't want to take advantage. I want to try to do this right. So please know that it kills me to stop this, but I have to."

He gets out of bed, and I can't help but stare at just how much he was enjoying himself. The proof is tented in his sexy-as-sin tight-as-hell black boxer briefs. He shakes his head and laughs at me as he catches me staring.

"I need a shower—a fucking cold one." He turns and walks out the room, and I can't help but laugh at his frustration.

My laughter subsides when I realize that I'm going to need a cold shower, too.

I lie back and take stock of my current situation. I'm in Reid's bed after one seriously steamy makeout session, and he said he wants to take me out on a proper date. He likes me, and he's openly admitted to being an ass these last few weeks.

Hmmm, maybe I should play the lottery. Today seems like my lucky day or something.

He comes back into the room after his shower with nothing but a towel wrapped around his waist. He notices me staring and laughs at me again.

"Like what you see, huh?" He chuckles.

I flush a furious shade of red, and he sits down next to me.

"It's okay, Maddy. It's perfectly fine to like what you see. I like what I see, too. Hands down, you're the hottest girl I've ever seen. So there, we're even." He leans down and gives me a sweet chaste kiss on the lips before gathering a pair of shorts and T-shirt. Thank God he goes into the bathroom to get dressed, because I'm pretty certain I would spontaneously combust if he got naked in front of me right now.

When he comes back out, he's fully clothed, sadly. "I left you out a clean towel and some clean clothes, too. I don't have any of that girly shower shit, but there's soap and hot water, which I'm sure is just what you need after last night. I'll go make us something to eat while you get cleaned up. Sound okay?"

"Sounds perfect, Reid. Thank you again."

"Shhh—no need to thank me. You're the one I should be thanking." He kisses my cheek and then continues, "I'll bring your food up here so you don't have to deal with the guys. See you in a few minutes."

He was right. A hot shower has definitely helped clear my head, and I feel refreshed when I'm all done. His clothes are huge on me, but I don't care. I roll the sweats up a few times and tie the string as tight as I can, but there's really no point; they will not stay up. The T-shirt he's left out is huge as well. It comes to the middle of my thighs. I take a peek in the bedroom to see that he's still downstairs. I go to the drawer I saw him pull the boxers out of before and steal a pair. Even though the shirt is long, there's no need to go around flashing everyone the goods.

He comes in a few minutes later with some coffee and a bagel with cream cheese. He's just taken a sip of coffee when I tell him that I'm wearing a pair of his underwear. When he all but chokes on it, I realize I should have waited to share that sexy tidbit.

He regains his composure and goes to take a bite of his bagel. Before he does, he says, "Have you got anything else to share with me before I take this bite? Because more information like that, and I might just stop breathing all together." I laugh and scrunch my face, pretending to think about anything else that might throw him off his game.

"No, I think that's it, but I'll let you know if I think of anything else that might make you want to swallow your tongue."

"Thanks for the heads-up, babe." He smiles and playfully elbows me in the side.

We eat in companionable silence, and when we're done he piles the dishes up on his nightstand. Between the shower and the full belly and basically everything else that's transpired over the last twelve hours, sleep is claiming me quickly.

Reid pulls me into his arms. I rest my head on his chest and close my eyes. He kisses me sweetly and whispers in my ear, "Close your eyes, sweetheart. You've had one hell of a morning. Let's take a little nap, and I'll take you home later."

I nuzzle in closer to him and, before I can say anything in response, feeling safe and warm and secure, my lids close, and sleep washes over me.

Chapter 8

Reid

I wake up to the most beautiful thing ever—
Maddy curled into my side, sleeping peacefully. I can't
help but smile at the scene. Who the fuck would have
thought that cuddling—hell, intimacy of any kind—
would make me smile?

It's only 2:30 in the afternoon, so I've got a little
time before I need to wake Maddy up to get her home.
I shoot out a quick text to Melanie to let her know that
everything is okay. Her response is immediate.

**Melanie: What the hell happened, Reid? I've been
trying to call Maddy all morning. It just goes straight
to voicemail. What did you do?**

**Me: Nothing bad. I swear. I'm sure she'll fill you in
when she gets home. I'll have her back by 4ish. She's
sleeping now.**

Melanie: "Nothing bad," really? Like you know anything else?

Me: Yeah, I know, but I'm trying to change that. I promise.

Melanie: Whatever. Maddy seems to like you. Have no clue why, so I'll try to be nice for her, I guess.

Me: Can you do me a favor? It's for Maddy.

Melanie: Ummm—sure, but as long as it's really for her, and not some backhanded way for you to get what you want. You're on thin ice as it is.

Me: Can I buy you lunch tomorrow?

Melanie: What? You realize that's my best friend there with you. You're a sleazeball, you know that?

Me: No!! Not like that. I want to get to know her better, and you're her best friend, so I'd like to get to know you, too.

Melanie: Oh, okay. I guess so, but it doesn't mean that you're forgiven, though. My last class ends at 1:30. I'll meet you at the student union right after that.

Me: Thanks. I'll see you later.

Maddy might not have her dad to chase the boys away, but Melanie sure is a close second. I know that if I have any chance at winning Maddy over, I'm going to have to win Melanie over as well.

I feel Maddy start to wake up, and I smile down at her warmly. I can't help but laugh a little at how far out of my comfort zone this is, yet it feels so natural at the same time. I feel a piece of that wall around my heart crack a little. I want to share why the walls are there in the first place with her, but how can I lay that at her feet? She's already lost so much and dealt with a ton of pain. I know for certain if she finds out what a horrible person I am on the inside that she'd never give me a chance. No matter how close she gets, she can't ever know that part of me. If my own family doesn't want me, why would she want me? I know it'll push her away for good, and I was already burned once, horribly, irreparably. I can't chance that again.

She's fully awake now, and looking up at me all dreamily and sexy as fuck.

"Hey, sleepyhead. Feeling a little better?"

"Much better. What time is it? How long have I been out for?" Her voice is so sultry when she's sleepy. I'll have to make a conscious effort to wake up next to her more often.

"It's almost three. I just got done texting Melanie. She thinks I kidnapped you."

Maddy chuckles. I guess Melanie is partly right; I did kind of kidnap Maddy. "She would think that! Let's just say with all the shit that's been going on with us, you haven't been her favorite person." Her arched eyebrow is so fucking snarky. I love it.

"That's completely deserved on my part. I'll make it up to her and to you. I promise." Winking an eye at her, I hope that she'll let me make it up to her.

I kiss her lightly on the lips and slip out of bed, fearing that if I stay next to her any longer we'll never get out of here. Don't get me wrong—I'd love to spend the day and night in bed with her, but I'm going to do this right. She deserves it.

As I'm pulling a T-shirt over my head, Maddy comes behind me, and wraps her arms around my waist and presses her cheek against my back.

"Can I ask you something?" She sounds uncertain, and I immediately wonder what I've done wrong.

"Anything, sweetness, you can ask me anything."

Anything except why I hurt. I'm not ready for that yet.

"What do you think happened with me and Logan?" Her voice is a bit uncertain. This is a raw nerve for her, and I know I acted like a fool with her and Logan. Her business is hers. God knows I've got no right to be judgmental.

"He told me you guys slept together. And that's fine, Maddy. I'm in no position to judge what you've done." Suddenly, I regret every sexual encounter I've ever had.

The atmosphere in the room shifts as she gathers her words. "And you believed him? Did you ever think to ask me what happened?"

She's hurt. We're two minutes into this relationship—or whatever the hell we are—and I've already gone and fucked it up.

"I'm sorry, Maddy. It's just that when I saw you in his clothes coming out of his room, well, what was I supposed to think? Then when I talked to him later he told me that he'd fucked you, so what was I supposed to do?"

So much for avoiding heavy conversation.

"For starters, you could have called me, gotten my side of the story, rather than jump to conclusions."

She puts things so simply. I am an ass.

I'm definitely going to set Logan straight on this one. Lying to me is one thing, but talking shit about Maddy is just not fucking cool.

I try to lighten the mood and say, "Well, I don't have your number, so I couldn't do that, now, could I?"

She rolls her eyes at me and storms off to get her purse. God, she's adorable when she's in a frenzy. I love it.

I hear my phone buzz on my nightstand. She's holding her phone up in the air and wiggling it around. "There. Now you have it. If you ever want to know any-thing, call me. Ask me. Don't just blindly assume the worst. And for the record, I did not sleep with Logan." A blush creeps up her neck and face with the last piece of information, but she continues, "I've never slept with anyone, actually." The last part is barely a whisper.

So that's what it feels like to have the wind knocked out of you.

She sees that I'm taken back by her revelation. Is she serious? She's never slept with anyone? She's gor-geous. How has she not been snatched up by this point?

"Reid, say something, anything. Please." Her face is still a bright red at her embarrassment, and I just can't seem to get over my shock.

She continues trying to defend something that needs no defense at all. "I told you I've never let anyone in. I've never allowed myself to get that close. I understand if you'd rather not take me out now. I know I've got nowhere near as much experience as you. That's why I thought you should know before things got too serious. Ugh, listen to me. 'Before things get too serious'—we haven't even gone out, and I'm talking about getting serious."

My lips silence her rant. She is so damn cute I can't help it.

"Maddy. Stop it. Listen to me. I'm sorry I didn't go to you to find out what really happened. I promise to talk to you before I jump to conclusions. As far as you being a virgin—well, I'm just a little shocked. That's all. You're beautiful and funny and smart and, well, just plain amazing."

She smiles at my list of compliments. "So it's not a big red 'X' for you? Me being a virgin, I mean?"

She's fucking adorable.

"Are you fucking kidding me—of course not. Not at all. We'll take things slowly. It'll kill me, but we will. I told you I want to do things right. Don't take this the wrong way, but I've had lots of sex." Oh, my fucking God, could I sound more like an ass right now? I try to backtrack. "What I mean is that I've had lots of *just* sex. That's all it's ever been—just sex. There's never been any intimacy, any connection, any desire for more." Okay, that's a little better.

"And you want those things? Intimacy? Connection? More? With me?" She has every right to be skeptical, but I can't deny that her disbelief stings a little.

"Yes, Maddy. I'd like for you to give me a chance to earn those things with you. I'm not going to say that it'll be perfect all the time. I've never done this before, but I want to try with you. And hell, if the physical stuff comes as part of that package, then that's fucking fantastic." I wink to try and lighten the mood before I continue in a more serious vein, "And if it doesn't, then that's fine, but after this morning I have a pretty good feeling that it won't be a problem. Just know that I'm not pushing you. I want to be with you, and when you're ready, well, we'll just take it one step at a time. Okay?"

" Okay—that definitely sounds like a plan." She wraps her arms around me again this time, pressing her face to my chest. I can feel the stress leave her body.

"Can I ask you something now?" I prod.

"Of course, Reid."

"How'd you get my number?" I waggle an eyebrow, and she all but chokes on her words.

"Umm...well.... I asked Cammie for it. You know, just in case."

That crazy adorable blush is back, and I can't help but kiss her.

"It's okay, Maddy. I'm glad you had it. You know, 'just in case.'"

She playfully slaps my chest and rolls her eyes.

" Okay, so if we're done with the Q&A, I'd like to get you home now."

"Kicking me out already, huh? You got the next girl out in the hall or something?" She's trying to be sarcastic about it, but I can hear the real worry.

I grab her shoulders firmly and look in her eyes. "Listen to me carefully, Madeleine. I told you I wanted to do this right. I promise you that I will not go behind your back. It's just you. There's no one else. I've wanted you since I first saw you, and I'm going to try my hardest not to fuck that up. So stop this nonsense of me being with other girls. It's just you. Got it? I want to get you home because I know Melanie is worried sick about you, and I told her I would have you back by four. By the way, you'd better check your voicemail—she said she's been trying to get in touch with you since early this morning."

At the end of my little speech, I kiss her firmly and passionately to get my point across. When I pull back, her eyes are wide and she's out of breath.

"Got it. Yup, definitely got it," she stammers as she lightly traces her fingers over her swollen lips.

I drive her back to the dorms and walk her to her door. She protests, saying that I don't need to escort her to her door, and I just shoot her a knowing glare.

"I told you that I'm doing this right. Now, shush."

She just rolls her eyes in response.

"Will you be back at the gym now that we've made up?" God, I hope so. Those spandex running shorts are so worth getting up at the crack of dawn.

"Do you want me there? I don't want to make you feel like I'm cramping you or anything, but it is getting a little cold to run the trails anyway."

"You've been running the trails by yourself? That's not safe, babe. What if something happened to you? Please say you'll come back to the gym."

" Okay, then. I'll see you tomorrow morning. Thank you again, Reid, for everything. I know you said to stop saying that, but thank you. Being drugged aside, this morning was the best I've ever had."

She reaches up and gives me a sweet kiss before she disappears into her suite. As I watch her walk away, I feel another piece of that wall I once thought so impenetrable crack open.

I'm excited as hell to get to the gym the next morning. If I said it was all about this new MMA class I enrolled in, I'd be lying my ass off. Maddy's back today, and I love that I get to start my day with her. I meet her at the door.

"Good morning, beautiful." I lean down to kiss her, and she seems hesitant. "What? Don't want to be seen in public with me?" I ask, partially kidding, but I really hope she's okay with me kissing her, because being without her for the last twelve hours has been a killer.

Definitely needed a cold shower to make it through the night.

"No, that's not it at all. I just thought you didn't want to be seen with me. I figured the date was one thing. We didn't really set any boundaries or anything yesterday, so I didn't know what to expect this morning."

"I guess saying that I want you isn't enough, huh?" I arch an eyebrow at her. "Let me clarify, Maddy. I not only want to go on your first official date with you, but I'd like to date you, exclusively. If that's okay with you, I mean. I don't want to be to presumptuous or anything." Did those words just come out of my mouth? Exclusively? I am in deep here.

"So what would that make me? What would that make us?"

She really doesn't get it, and her uncertainty makes me wonder if I'm not being clear enough.

"Well, I'd like for you to be my girlfriend. When I thought you had been with Logan, I was beside myself with rage. Logan's face can attest to that." I snicker, and she shoots me a stern look.

Okay, not funny yet.

"And then when you were flirting with that guy at Shooters, well, I lost it then, too. I can't say I'll be any good at it—fuck, I've never done it before—but I'd like to have a real relationship with you. Something about you makes me want to try at least."

Her shocked silence has me teetering on the edge of sanity for a moment. I want to ask her what she thinks. I want to make some wiseass remark, but I don't want to scare her away, and I don't want to make her think I'm not serious. I'm very serious, so much so that it scares me, but I've never been more willing to try. So try I will.

She still hasn't said anything, so I break the silence.

"Look, maybe that's a bit too soon. I'm sorry. Maybe you'd feel more comfortable waiting to see how our date goes and then we'll take it from there? Does that sound more reasonable?" I'll wait a week for her. Might take a lot of cold showers, but I'll wait.

"No."

What the fuck did I do wrong? Why is she saying no?

She catches my wounded look. In a split second her arms are around me, and she's reaching up on her toes to kiss me. She tastes minty-fresh and steaming hot at the same time. Her tongue dances around mine passionately. God, I love her kisses. When she pulls back, I can't help the confused look that creeps across my face.

She sees it and begins her explanation.

"What I mean, Reid, is that waiting until our date is most definitely not more reasonable. I'll be honest. When you left me hanging on the dance floor that first time we met to go make out with the Barbie look-alike, I lost it, too. I do not like the idea of you with anyone else, either. So if you'd like to be my boyfriend, then nothing would make me happier than to be your girl-friend." She smiles sweetly and reaches up on her toes again to plant a soft, innocent kiss on my lips and adds,

"And just so you know, Reid, I'm scared, too. Maybe more than I let on. I am so scared of being hurt, but I feel safe with you. I believe you when you say that you're going to try your hardest. I'm not certain that either one of us isn't going to screw things up and that we won't get hurt, but I know, or at least I hope, that we won't hurt each other on purpose."

She feels safe with me.

I have never felt as content as I do right now. She gets it. She's just as scared as me, and she's still willing to give it a try.

"Maddy, I hope one day that I have half as much strength as you do. You amaze me. You know that, right?"

"Me? Strong? Nah, you must be mistaking me for my kickass boyfriend who," She glances down at her watch before she continues, "is going to be late to his little 'fight club' if he doesn't get his ass in gear."

"Oh, shit, you're right. I'll catch you when we're done, and I'll walk you to the library." I kiss her lightly and slap her playfully on the ass as she saunters into the gym ahead of me. She peers back at me and gives me an "I can't believe you just did that" look. I just shrug my shoulders and smile back.

My world feels more alive with her in it, and it's nothing short of an act of God that she wants me in hers as well.

Another reason I'm stoked to start this class is because Logan signed up with me. If that little shit thinks he's going to get away with lying about sleeping with Maddy, then he's got another thing coming to him. He was out last night after I brought Maddy home, so I haven't even had a chance to lay into him. This actually works out perfectly. He has no idea how pissed I am, and we're in a situation where I'm actually encouraged to beat the crap out of him.

We're both running a few minutes late, so there's no one in the hallway when he greets me at the door to the wrestling room.

"Hey, man. How was the rest of your weekend? I heard Maddy spent the night. Never knew you were the kind for sloppy seconds." He moves to playfully elbow me in the side—like any of this is a fucking joke.

I've got my forearm shoved up under his chin in a second flat. I can feel him struggling to swallow beneath my arm. His eyes are wide; I've got the added element of surprise on my side.

"Fucker. You want to say that again?" I push harder against his throat. "You're a real shit, Logan. So when were you going to tell me that you lied to me?"

His face pales and I can see his eyes start to drift closed. Realizing that maybe I'm pushing just a little too hard, I pull my arm back away from his throat. Logan slides down the wall that is holding him up, gasping for air along the way.

When he catches his breath, I grab him by the collar of his T-shirt and pull him back up into my face.

He's regained his composure. "What the fuck is your problem, Reid? Did you all of a sudden learn how to respect women overnight or something? And was that before or after you fucked her?"

Through a clenched jaw, I growl, "Take it back. Now, Logan."

"Take what back? You're fucking crazy. I don't even know what the fuck you're talking about."

"You do, and I'm going to give you until the count of three to realize what I'm talking about and for you to apologize before I beat the shit out of you."

Logan is trying to process everything, but he's just not doing it quickly enough for my liking. I begin counting. Maybe that'll motivate him to eat his fucking words.

"One."

"Reid, you're out of your mind. You're really going to hit a friend over a piece of ass?"

He's deflecting, trying to make me relent; it's so not going to work here.

"Two."

"She must've been really good, then. I mean, for you to go all ape-shit like this. Just remember I had her first, bro."

"Three." I don't even give him the chance to respond to my counting this time. I punch him in the gut, and he crumples in pain.

Trying to catch his breath once again, he can barely get any words out. I bend down so my whispered words can only be heard by him.

"Last chance, asshole. Take it back, or I'll really make you pay."

He straightens up and looks me in the eyes; I see defeat in his, so I wait on his words.

"Seriously, Reid? You're going to beat the shit out of your friend over some girl."

"She is not just *some* girl. She is *my* girl, and I will not have you talking shit about my girl. She's mine now, and you owe me an explanation, asshole. So either you start talking, or I keep hitting."

"She's your girl? Should I expect an apocalypse next?" He's trying to be funny, but I'm not in the mood at all.

"Not that it's any of your fucking business, but yes, she's my girlfriend now."

"Well, then. You're a lucky son of a bitch, because she's a great lay!"

" Okay. Fine. We'll do this your way, Logan."

I'm not going to give him the satisfaction of telling him what I want him to say. I'll beat it out of him if that's what he wants. I step to the door and hold it open for him. Extending my arm into the weight room in an "after you" gesture, I watch as he steps through the doors. I notice the caution with which he walks past me. Good, he's scared. The fucker should be.

After a brief warm-up and stretch, the instructor tells us to partner up for some sparring. I immediately move next to Logan. Keeping my voice low so only he can hear me, I say, "Your ass is mine, Logan."

Ben, the instructor, blows the whistle, and I've got Logan knocked down on the floor in about two seconds flat. He's face down on the mat; my knee is shoved up into his kidney and I've got his right arm twisted up the center of his back. He twists his body to try to get out from under me, but I'm not about to let him up just yet. I push on my knee a little harder and pull his arm up further. His face contorts in pain, and I release him. He made his choice before. He could have come clean, but now I'm going to draw this out as much as possible.

We both stand and start dancing around each other, lunging and making attempts at punches. He swings at me a few times, but I'm quicker on my feet, so he never lands a single one. In quick succession, I land several punches to his face. His cheek splits under his eye, and he must feel the blood trickling down his face. He wipes it away and looks down at his hand.

"What the fuck?" he says.

My response is simple—a punch to the other side of his face. I land a heel in his side and one more kick to his upper thigh before the instructor realizes what's going on. Everyone else is standing around us, shocked at the ferocity with which I'm beating his ass.

I'm enraged, and logical reasoning has completely left my mind. I get him down on the ground and start pounding him—his face, his stomach, his sides. He's curled up into a fetal position. Forsaking all fronts at defending himself, he's in preservation mode at this point.

My voice is feral and beast-like. "I said take it back, now!"

I feel someone pull me off Logan. Ben is between us as some of the other students work to pull us apart. Out of the corner of my eye, I see Maddy looking in through the glass wall that separates the wrestling room from the rest of the gym.

I break free from their hold and storm out of the room to go to Maddy. She looks afraid and wide-eyed. I'm covered in sweat, and I'm fairly certain some of Logan's blood is on my shirt. She tries to step back from me, but I just step closer.

"Shh. It's okay, Maddy. I'm not going to hurt you. I promise." I extend my hand to her, hoping that she'll reach back for mine. When our fingers interlock, I pull her with me into the wrestling room. My little spat with Logan has pretty much cleared the place out. Only Logan and Ben remain at this point.

Ben speaks first. "You all cooled off now, Reid?"

"Yeah, I'm good." I speak to Ben, but my eyes are shooting daggers at Logan.

"Good, because any more outbursts like that, and you'll be kicked out of the class. You got it?"

"Of course. This is the last time. I promise. Can the three of us just have a minute? Some things need to be said."

Ben looks among the three of us, and I can see the pieces fall into place in his head.

"Sure, just try not to beat the shit out of him again. Okay?" Ben walks out of the room and the door clicks behind him.

Maddy breaks the tension-filled silence. "Reid, what's going on? You're kind of scaring me here."

"Logan has something to say to you." I shoot him a knowing glare.

He doesn't want to get beat up again, so he finally gives in. He faces Maddy and clears his throat nervously. "I'm sorry about lying to Reid about us."

Maddy looks shocked. She probably thought I would just let it go. Doesn't she understand that I won't stand for anyone talking shit about her?

I nudge Logan with my elbow. He's going to have to say more than that to make this okay.

"I wanted to get under Reid's skin after he punched me that night. I never should have dragged you into it. It was wrong to say that we slept together just to piss him off. I hope you can forgive me."

Maddy just nods in his direction and Logan then turns his attention to me.

Holding out his hand as a means of a truce, he starts talking to me. "I'm sorry. If I would have known that you were serious about her, I wouldn't have said those things. You're just not the girlfriend type. Sorry for pissing you off and for talking shit about your girl. Friends?"

I'm not ready to forgive him and a few "I'm sorrys," no matter how sincere they might seem, are not going to be enough to make things better, but it's a start. I do have to live with the guy, after all, so I shake his hand and say, "Yeah, we're good. Just keep your fucking mouth shut from now on."

With that, Logan stalks out of the gym intent on licking his wounds.

Maddy turns to me, and she looks like she doesn't know what to say. After a few minutes of silence, she finally finds her voice.

"You beat him up? For me?"

I can't tell if she's impressed or appalled. "He lied about you. That's not cool. I won't stand for that. You're mine, Maddy, and I won't let him get away with it. So yeah, I beat him up for you." She has to realize that I will never let anyone hurt her.

"Yours?" Her voice is barely above a whisper.

"Yes, Maddy. Mine. You're mine. Please tell me you're okay with that?"

"And you get to be mine?" I hear the disbelief in her voice. Hell, even I find it hard to believe that I've turned over this new leaf so quickly.

"Yes, babe. I get to be yours and you get to be mine. Deal?"

She holds out her hand to shake on it, and I chuckle at her. I grab her hand, and my body zings to life under the heat of her stare. A simple touch from her is more exhilarating than any physical contact I've ever had before. We shake and she says, "Yes, it's a deal. Under one condition."

Our hands are still locked together, and I lean in to kiss her softly on her quivering lips.

"Anything for you, Maddy. Name your terms."

"First, stop beating up your friends for me." She arches her eyebrow at me, indicating that she's not pleased with my antics.

"As long as they keep their mouths shut, we're good on that front." I kiss her again and prompt her for her next term.

"And second, next time you have class, can you promise not to wear a shirt? You're freaking hot!" She places her hands on my chest and stretches up on her toes to kiss me.

I can't hold down the smile that creeps across my face.

"I can definitely work with those terms, love. Now, let's hit the showers and get ready for class."

We kiss briefly before heading our separate ways. If she didn't believe me earlier that I was in this relationship 100 percent, then she sure as hell believes me now.

Walking Maddy around campus after we leave the gym feels like walking on a cloud. While I would love to spend all day with her, she's in class until after three, which gives me the perfect opportunity to have lunch with Melanie without Maddy knowing.

I know. I know. Honesty and openness and all that, but my intentions are good. I fully intend to tell Maddy about my lunch with Mel tonight. I just didn't want her to be all worried about it beforehand. Plus, after my "open mouth, insert foot" comment yesterday morning about her father, I want to make sure that I don't say anything else stupid.

The other part of my plan is to win Melanie over. I already know that I am not her favorite person, but Melanie is the only person Maddy has ever let in. I need to be on her good side.

I get to the student union before Melanie and figure the nice thing to do is to buy her lunch. I get her a grilled chicken salad and a bottle of water. My new MMA class kicked my ass this morning—quite literally—and I am starving. Like, plate me up an entire horse—I'm that hungry. So I opt for a cheeseburger and fries. Not the healthiest choice, but a boy's gotta eat.

When I see Melanie walk in, I stand up and wave her over to my table. It's an awkward meeting. We're not quite at the hug stage. She's not a dude, so a fist bump seems weird. And we're not interviewing for a job, so a handshake is ridiculous. So I just stand there and wave hi. Yup, I wave. I am such a dork.

She laughs and takes a seat.

"Hi, Melanie. Thanks for meeting up with me."

"No problem, Reid. Anything for Maddy, you know that. And call me Mel. I'm going to grab something to eat. I'll be right back."

I stop her before she can walk away. "No wait, Mel. I already got you lunch. It was the least I could do for your help."

She literally looks like she just saw a unicorn or something.

"Um, okay. Thanks. That was really nice of you. I had to study before class today, so I totally missed breakfast and I am so freaking hungry." Her eyes land on my burger and she looks at it like she's never seen food before in her entire life.

"Well, then you're in luck. I wasn't sure what you'd like, so I figured what college student doesn't like a burger and fries." My stomach protests as I slide my plate in front of her.

"Omigod. Thank you, thank you, thank you. This is amazing." She manages all of that around the gigantic T-Rex-sized bite she just took out of the burger. "You're so good. I could never survive eating salad, but Maddy says you work out every day, so I'm sure a burger would just undo everything you've already done today."

If I wasn't here for Maddy, I'd be lunging across the table to rip that burger out of your mouth. You're lucky you're a girl.

I figure I can just grab another burger after she leaves, so I just dig into my salad—fucking rabbit food. Swallowing back my bitter mood, I tell her about my new class.

"Yeah, I work out every morning. I won't lie—it's gotten a lot easier to get up every morning now that I get to see a certain someone there as well. But I just started this new MMA class. That's mixed martial arts," I explain.

"No need to explain that. Gorgeously ripped guys wrestling around getting all sweaty. Yeah, I'm familiar with the sport." Her clarification gets a chuckle out of me.

"Anyway, I'm sure Maddy told you about how I lost my shit a few times with her and Logan. I guess I've always had anger issues, so I figured it was time for me to be constructive about it. When I saw the sign-up sheet at the gym last week, it was the perfect opportunity."

"That's great, Reid, but I don't get why you're telling me this. I mean, I know you want us to be friends and all, but what's really going on here? I'm still not buying your 'nice guy' routine."

"I need to do some digging—"

Mel stops me mid-sentence and glares angrily at me. "I am NOT here to tell you about Maddy. Anything you want to know, you need to get from her. Maddy and I do not keep secrets from each other, and I refuse to start now just because you want to know something. I knew you were up to no good."

"No, Mel, please listen. I opened my stupid-ass mouth the other day about her dad having to chase away all of her prospective boyfriends. Needless to say, it upset her a lot. And then when I was texting with you about where she was, it struck me that you're her protector in a way." I shrug, as if that helps to clarify my little story. "I just wanted you to know that I am trying to work on my anger, and I promise that I'll never hurt her. As angry as I was about the Logan thing, I would never touch Maddy. Never. And I just wanted you to know that. Besides, I think we worked that whole situation out this morning."

"Um, yeah, about that, you basically called her a whore for being with Logan. You see the irony there, right? Even if she had slept with him, you calling her a slut was epically stupid." She pauses her rant of insults and I don't say anything, because she's right. It seems as if she's weighing her options here—trying to figure out what to do with me.

She finally decides and says, "All of that aside, Reid, you saving her from that asshole who drugged her drink is proof that you would never want any harm to come her way. But it's really good to know that you're not only aware of your issues, but that you're willing to work on them, too. Well, that's just a bonus." She smiles brightly and sincerely.

I feel like I've won her over at least a little. "Thanks, Mel. So I know you don't keep secrets from her, and I don't want to know anything about her that she wouldn't tell me herself, but please tell me if there are any other landmines that I need to avoid. It really hurt for me to bring up her parents, and I would go a long distance to avoid making her feel like that again."

"Her parents are definitely a raw nerve. But if you lost both of your parents when you were ten and had to move away from the only home you've ever known to live with someone you've never met before, I'm pretty sure you would be raw over it, too. It's been getting better, though. She's really been working on it. I think she's just tired of being sad, and she's making a conscious effort of letting herself be happy. I think you play a part in that happiness, Reid, so don't go do anything stupid to fuck it up." She points her finger at me while arching an eyebrow. Her face is a mix of genuine concern and playfulness.

I can definitely understand raw. Raw and numb, that's how I've felt for the last five years. Losing your entire family will definitely do that to you. I only wish I could deal with my pain the way Maddy does hers. Maybe someday.

Instead of those intense revelations—ones that I'm not ready to share with anyone—I just smile and nod. "I promise. I will try my hardest not to fuck it up. So can you tell me one more thing?" I bat her my "pretty please" eyes.

"Sure, but hurry up about it. I've got class in fifteen minutes across campus."

"So come on. I'll walk you there. I'll even carry your books for you," I offer, and she just smiles a sarcastic little impish grin.

"Yes, I'm trying to be a gentleman. Can I get a little credit?" I pinch my fingers together, indicating how much credit I might actually deserve at this point.

" Okay, fine. It is definitely sweet of you to do this for Maddy. And for us, for that matter. I have a feeling that if you hold true to your word, I'll be seeing a lot more of you. And it would suck to have to be mean to you all the time." She elbows me in the side and starts gathering up our trash. I grab her books, and she walks away, laughing a little. I can see why she's Maddy's best friend. They're so alike in so many ways.

" Okay, so dish, Connely. What else do you want to know?" she asks as we leave the cafeteria.

"Well, I'm taking her on a date Friday night, and I want it to be special. So I thought maybe you could tell me something, without breaking your 'no secrets' promise to Maddy, of course. Home-cooked meal and rent a movie? Or am I better with a fancy restaurant and an art show, or some shit like that?"

Please, whatever you say, please do not say art show. Please please please!!!

"Definitely not an art show, that's so not her scene. But there is this stupid video arcade she's been trying to drag me to."

"Are you telling me that Maddy likes video games? Maddy, tall, hot, blonde Maddy, loves gaming? Holy fucking hell—that's awesome!"

"Yeah, she used to love video games when we were kids. I hated them, so unless I wanted to play, she never had the chance. Bryan told her about it the other day, and she was practically drooling over it, but I so don't want to go. I think she'd like the arcade. Plus, you'll earn bonus points with me. If you take her, then I don't have to."

I can't help but smile and laugh at that. It's obvious that Melanie loves Maddy like a sister, just not enough to suffer through video games.

"She'd like to chill and watch a movie, too. That's right up her alley. She's a huge fan of all those John Hughes films from the '80s. Pick any one of those, and you're good to go."

"Thank you so much, Mel. I mean that. I know it's her first 'real' date, so I want to make it special for her. I want her to really enjoy it."

"Reid, in all honesty, the way she talks about you lately, as long as she's with you, she'll be enjoying it. Just keep that in mind, and have fun. That's all Maddy really wants. I have to go. Class is going to start in a few minutes. Thanks for lunch again. I'll see you soon." She waves over her shoulder as she turns away from me.

She walks into the building, and I feel like I can breathe again. It went well, really well, in fact. I made friends with Mel, and I got some dirt on Maddy—in a non-scumbag sort of way, of course.

A quick look at my watch tells me that I've got about an hour before I pick Maddy up from her last class of the day.

It also gives me one hour to figure out who the fuck John Hughes is and go download every one of his movies before Friday night.

Chapter 9

Maddy

I'm meeting Reid in an hour for our first date, and I am beside myself with excitement and anxiety. It's pretty silly, actually. I mean, I'm almost finished with my first semester of college and I'm getting ready for my first date like some nervous, giddy sixteen-year-old. Melanie is having a field day, however. She told me that she met with Reid earlier in the week to discuss plans for this date. She's been teasing me relentlessly about where I think we're going, what I think I should wear—stuff like that. I have to admit, I thought it was weird that they went out to lunch. I was even a little mad at Reid for not coming to me first, but when he was all nervous that night that he "had to tell me something" and that he "didn't want me to be upset with him," I couldn't help but go easy on him. He just wants to make tonight special, and it makes my heart skip a beat knowing that he's really and truly trying to make this work.

Even though we go to the gym together every morning and he walks me to pretty much every class he can, and he texts or calls every night before I go to bed, Reid hasn't told me anything about this date. We've talked about pretty much everything else, but as far as tonight goes, it's top secret. So as I stand in front of my closet, trying to figure out what to wear, I am completely stumped. I hold up countless outfits, and while they all look presentable, I don't want to wear jeans if we're going somewhere fancy. Nothing about Reid screams "fancy," but I just don't know.

I suddenly have visions of Julia Roberts shooting snails across some classy restaurant. I really hope it's more of a laid-back night. I'm supposed to be meeting him at his house in an hour, and I really can't figure this out. I'm going to text him. Screw it.

Me: Hey :)

Reid: Hi, beautiful. You excited for tonight?

Me: Very ;) I know you're being all "mystery man" about tonight, but can you at least drop me a hint about what to wear? I'm stressing here!

Reid: Babe, you could wear a potato sack and you'd still look gorgeous ;) but if you must know, jeans and a T-shirt will be fine for what I have planned.

Me: Great, thanks—see you in a bit. xxx

Jeans. Perfect. I feel like I can breathe again. I choose my sexy black skinny jeans and a red babydoll T-shirt. A pair of black Chuck Taylor Converse sneakers finish off the casual look perfectly. I keep my makeup simple as usual and leave my hair down in long waves, also as usual. I decide to ramp up the sex appeal of the outfit with a black leather motorcycle jacket. Perfect. I look hot, and when I walk out into the living room, the girls agree. Of course all three of them are home tonight. I don't think the four of us have been in the same room all week, but they all wanted to be here to send me off.

Sticking her fingers in between her lips, Lia lets out a sharp whistle. "Maddy, you clean up something fierce. How have you kept that jacket hidden from me all this time? I so want to borrow that." She's practically ripping it off my body as she speaks.

"I kept it hidden because I knew I would never get it back from you. You know, like my pink top and my black heels and my silver hoops and my Guess sunglasses. Do you see the pattern here, little miss Lia?" I stick my tongue out as I finish my teasing. I love her to death, but she loses shit.

"Reid's going to go crazy over you." This is from Mel.

"I freaking hope so. This not knowing what we're doing is torturing me." I eye Mel suspiciously because she does know where we're going, but all she does is make a zipping motion across her lips. I tell her, "Payback's a bitch, Mel. Just remember that."

Cammie is up in the kitchen, popping some pop-corn for their movie. "Whatever you're doing to him, keep it up," she chimes in. "I've known him for a while now, and he's a completely different person with you, Maddy. I actually like him now!" Even she sounds surprised by her new opinion of him.

Lia bounces into the kitchen to pour everyone some sodas. "Yeah, he's totally different. I actually don't hate him."

I can't help but glare over at Lia. I know he's acted like a real ass in the past, but it still hurts to hear them talking about him so flippantly.

"Thanks, guys. It means a lot that you see him changing. It's hard to believe that he's the same guy I met when I first got here." I shrug. "I believe him, though, and he makes me happy, so I guess I'll have to take it one day at a time."

The girls nod back at me in agreement. If they see the change in him, they most definitely see the change in me.

Cammie walks over to the door when she hears a knock. "I'll get it," she says cheerfully. Seriously, is she ever not happy?

She opens the door to what I can only describe as the most beautiful man ever. Reid is at the threshold, looking downright edible. He's wearing an outfit similar to mine, casual and laidback, but there's something very "bad boy from the wrong side of the tracks" about it that makes my insides quiver. His dark jeans are ripped at the knee, but not because they're from some expensive designer. I'm pretty sure Reid wouldn't be caught dead in a pair of jeans that cost more than twenty bucks. The navy blue henley accentuates every sinew on his chest and arms. He is so yummy, and I can't believe he's mine.

His face is chiseled and hard—the definition of male beauty. But his lips, oh, my God, his lips are heavenly. I can personally attest to their heavenliness. To call his eyes blue is a gross understatement. Up close, they're like waves of the ocean, powerful and stormy, but calming and just breathtaking. There are little flecks of gold in the outer rim of their dark blue depths. I could gaze into them for hours.

I take so long drinking him in that I almost completely miss the gigantic bunch of flowers in his hand. My mouth is dry, both from his scorching hotness and the simple sweetness of the flowers, that I can barely get any words out. When my feet finally start to function, I walk over to him and reach up on my toes to plant a sweet kiss on his cheek.

"You got me flowers?" My voice is a breathy whisper at best.

Who else would they be for?

He just nods his head as he drinks in the sight of me. It's nice to know that I affect him the same way he does me.

"No one has ever gotten me flowers before. Ever. They're beautiful, Reid. And calla lilies are my absolute favorite. How did you know?" My voice is starting to regain some volume, but I'm still in awe of his gesture.

"I had a little help." And with that he shoots Mel a wink across the room. She walks over to us and takes the flowers from me.

"I'll put these in some water for you. Go out and have fun. I'll see you guys later." Mel gives me a light squeeze of a hug and ushers me to the door. She holds Reid back and mumbles something into his ear. I roll my eyes at their thick-as-thieves routine.

When she's done giving him what I can only imagine is the "be on your best behavior and don't fuck this up" speech, Reid leans down and kisses me, and asks me if I'm ready. I grab my bag quickly, and we're gone.

Reid reaches his hand down and laces our fingers together. Whenever we walk anywhere together, he has to be holding my hand. I love it. I have to say that I really thought Reid was going to be weird about being public with our relationship. But the more time we spend walking around campus, the more I realize that my original assumption about him being less than serious about us is more about my insecurities than anything that he's ever said or done. And tonight, with the flowers and his sweet texts from earlier, I know that he really is something special. In the midst of all these mushy-gushy thoughts, something dawns on me.

"Hey, I thought I was supposed to meet you at your place? Did I miss something?" I ask. He really did distract me before with his utter delectableness.

Before he can answer, we reach his car, and he walks me to the passenger side. He presses me against the door so that every inch of our bodies are touching. He puts his fingers under my chin to tip my head back so that I can gaze into his stunning sapphire eyes. With his other hand, he runs his knuckles gently across my cheek before saying, "Now, what fun would it have been if I did what you expected? It's your first date and I want to do it right, so that means I get to chauffeur you around and buy you pretty flowers and tell you how damn sexy you look."

He leans his face into mine and lightly brushes his lips against mine. His tongue flicks out and licks my lips, begging for entrance. He bites my lower lip and sucks on it almost to the point of being painful, and I open to him immediately. I reach my arms around his neck and twist my fingers into his silky, chocolate brown hair. He moves his hands so that one is around my waist and the other is fisted at the nape of my neck.

We kiss wildly and passionately for what seems like forever. Our hands are roaming and exploring. His hand at my waist spans my entire rib cage and grazes dangerously close to the underside of my breast. My nipples harden at the thought of him touching them, playing with them, nibbling on them. I feel his hardened arousal at my hip, and I press into it. I want him more than I have ever wanted anyone, and it's fairly clear that he wants me. I bite his lip at that thought, and he nearly growls at me in response.

When we hear the group of rowdy, drunken partygoers yell, "Dude, get a room," we break the kiss.
Reid stares at me from under his lustfully lowered lids.
"Beautiful, Maddy. You are so damn beautiful, and one
fucking outrageously good kisser." He winks and then
opens my door for me. I see him try to readjust himself
as he walks in front of the car.

*Probably wishes he could take another cold shower
right about now.*

When he takes his seat, he reaches across the center
console and gearshift to hold my hand. Once our fingers are intertwined, he raises my hand up to his lips
and sweetly kisses it.

"So, Maddy, are you ready for the best date ever?"
he asks, smiling a ridiculously goofy grin.

It's a grin that I can't help but send back his way.
"Yes, Reid, I'm ready. I'm ready for whatever you've got
up those sexy sleeves of yours."

"I can't believe you kicked my ass like that.
Seriously, who would have known you were such a
gamer. Smoking hot, sweet as fuck, and a gamer? I hit
the girlfriend lottery with you!"

I love that he calls me his girlfriend. I mean, I know
we said that's what we are, but it's still sinking in.

"Well, now, what fun would it be if I did what you
expected?" He laughs as I mirror his words from earlier, and I plant a kiss on his cheek. "So what's the plan
now? Or was me kicking your ass at every video game

imaginable your master plan?" I smirk at him, and he rolls his eyes in return.

"Would you just get in the car already and stop rubbing it in my face?" He quickly swats my ass and he pretends to be wounded, but I know he's being playful.

I get in, and he turns the radio on as we start driving toward our next location. The Foo Fighters' acoustic version of "Everlong" starts up, and I tell him how much I love this song. I turn it up and start singing along loudly—very loudly, and off key, I might add. He just laughs at my antics. When Dave Grohl sings about breathing each other in, Reid leans in close and whispers the lyrics into my ear, sending shivers down my spine and heating my blood. I've always wanted someone to say things like that to me, to want me beyond reason, to make me feel loved and in one sweet whispered sentence, he has done just that. In that moment, I realize I am falling hard and fast for this gor-geous man beside me.

We pull up to a large open park area. There are couples walking their dogs and groups of kids playing Frisbee. I have to admit, I'm a bit confused by his plans. Nothing about hanging out at a park screams "date." Hesitant to rain on his parade, I opt to keep my mouth shut.

We keep walking, hand in hand, of course, and it's a comfortable silence. But there's so much that I want to know about him that I can't hold back my questions.

"So tell me about your family. You already know about mine. Not that there's much to know."

His reaction to my seemingly simple question is palpable. He is no longer calm and laid-back. I can feel his palm sweat in mine; his shoulders stiffen and I see him clench his jaw. I immediately regret my question.

His words are curt and cold. "There's not much to say. No family to speak of."

He's not going to share; that much is clear. I don't want to push and ruin our night, so I drop it, but not before saying, "It's okay, Reid. You don't have to talk about them. I was just trying to get to know you better, that's all." I reach my hand up to cup his cheek and kiss him to reinforce my words. He relaxes instantly and I try for a less sensitive topic.

"So…" I drag out the word to try and lighten the mood, "are you excited to be graduating this semester? I can't believe you've finished early and you're starting an internship. That's so cool, Reid. Tell me about it."

He smiles.

Okay, school is a safe topic. Good to know.

"I'm really excited about it, and anxious, too. It took me a little while to settle on a major, but once I finished my first counseling class, I knew I'd really found something I loved. Kids don't always have someone to turn to when they're dealing with shit—and they've got more shit to deal with than people think, so I just always wanted to help. The internship is at a local school working with the psychologists, social workers, and guidance counselors. I'm going to have to go to grad school no matter which career I choose, so it's a great opportunity to try each of them out and see which I like best."

I'm in awe of how enthusiastic he is about helping kids. My first impressions of him were definitely that he couldn't care less about other people—him being a dick and all—but I obviously judged the book by its cover. Reid is kind and caring, and obviously wants to help out kids who need it. I wonder if there's some kind of personal motivation for him. But, based on his earlier reaction about his family, I won't push that right now, either.

"Reid, that's amazing. I'm so excited for you. You're going to be awesome at whatever you choose."

He smiles down at me, and I melt. He is gorgeous and sweet. I have definitely caught myself a winner; I have no clue how, but I have.

"Here we are." He stops in front of, well, in front of nothing. It's just an open patch of grass up on a hill. He sees that I'm just not getting it, and he chuckles at me. He tells me to stay where I am and that he'll be right back. He disappears into some trees that are behind us, and when he comes out, I can't help the smile that splits my face. He's got a small cooler, a blanket, and some pillows to sit on.

"You are so sweet. This is awesome, Reid. Thank you."

We hold the blanket out by the corners and set everything up. He opens the cooler and pulls out a few bottles of water, and plates and utensils, but there's no food.

I offer a look of sympathy. I don't want him to be embarrassed that he forgot the main course. It's the thought that counts, right?

And just as I am about to tell him as much, he looks beyond me and smiles. He stands up and walks past me without saying a word. I turn to look over my shoulder in time to see him paying the delivery man.

When he sits back down, he smirks at me and says, "You didn't think I was going to cook, did you? I'd like to keep you around for a while, and cooking for you would be a surefire way to make you leave." He starts pulling the containers out of the bag.

"Did you order Chinese food? Oh, my goodness!! Mel and I have tried every Chinese place in town since we got here, and they all suck. I've been dying for some shrimp lo mein. Please tell me there is some in there." I am astonished by his thoughtfulness.

"I had to call a place two towns over and pay double for delivery, but seeing you get all excited about it is worth every penny. So you see, me being friends with Mel is worth it, right? I might even have to make a weekly date with her to dish about you." He passes me my plate.

"If it means you plan more stuff like tonight, then hell yeah. Go for it!"

His laughter at my comments does funny things to my insides. I've never felt like about anyone. And it's certain that no one else has ever made me feel like this.

As we eat our meal, we get lost in conversation. I'm not all too surprised to see that we have very similar tastes in pretty much everything—from books to television to music. It's so easy and carefree being with him here like this. We laugh and smile nonstop; it's surprising that we are actually getting any eating done.

He pulls me in to his side after he's put his plate down and kisses the top of my head. "I'm having the best time, Maddy. I know that you've never done this before, but neither have I, really. I'm really happy to see you happy. I spent too long pissing you off and making you cry."

"Stop, that's all in the past. Besides, I'm having a great time because I'm with you, so all that shit that happened already doesn't matter anymore. Okay?" I lean into him a little closer and kiss his chest, inhaling as I do; he smells divine.

"So what's your favorite movie?" he asks, continuing our conversation from earlier about our favorite things.

"My all-time favorite has to be *Pretty in Pink*." The look on his face suggests that he's never even heard of it, though that's not too shocking. Reid doesn't seem like a guy who would watch a movie with the words "pretty" *and* "pink" in the title.

"Huh, never heard of it. What's it about?" At least he's feigning interest.

"It's about this quirky but beyond cool girl, Andie, who really only has one friend. Her mom leaves and her dad has mentally checked out, so she's essentially on her own."

He smiles knowingly at me, instantly recognizing the personal connection I feel to the movie. I smile back but continue,

"She falls in love with this guy, Blane, and he's totally gorgeous and rich—pretty much everything she's not. Anyway, his friends hate her because she's not part of 'the cool gang,' and they essentially talk him out of taking her to prom. So her best friend, Duckie, this guy who is totally and senselessly in love with Andie, comes to the rescue and takes her to prom. When Blane sees her, he realizes he's made a huge mistake and he apologizes."

"So what happens in the end? Does the guy get the girl?" He seems genuinely interested, but I have a feeling he isn't asking about the movie.

"Yes. Even with everything that should keep them apart, they end up making it work." I hope he sees that my answer isn't about the movie, either.

We sit for a few more minutes, and as dusk settles in, he suggests that we should leave before it gets too dark. He packs everything up, and we walk through the park. Assuming that we are walking back to the car, I am completely caught off guard when we turn a corner and see that a huge crowd has gathered in the clearing. They're all settled on pillows and blankets in front of a huge movie screen.

When I look up at him for some sort of explanation, he says, "Expect the unexpected, babe." He just laughs and proceeds to spread the blanket back out on the ground. He pats the spot next to him, and I willingly comply.

When I'm all cozied up next to him, I ask, "So what are they showing tonight? I've heard about these movie in the park nights, but I didn't realize they still did them."

"Actually, I think this is the last one for the fall. It's starting to get a little too cold for them, but it's a good thing you've got me to keep you warm." He looks at me seductively and chuckles. When he says, "I'm not sure what they're playing, though. I guess we'll have to wait and see," I see the mischievous glint in his eyes. He's up to something.

When the movie starts, I immediately recognize it as the one I described earlier—*Pretty in Pink*—my favorite movie *EVER*!

"What the hell? What are the chances? Did you set this up?" I glare at him. "There's no way that of all the movies in the world, they'd play this one." My questions are rapid-fire. He just shrugs his shoulders and laughs at me a little.

It had to have been Mel, that little stinker. I can't be mad, though. This really is amazing.

"Well, Mel told me about your favorite movies, and when I found out that this was the last 'movies in the park' for the fall, I *might* have convinced the operator to show this particular film."

I'm in complete and utter shock. I wrap my arms tightly around his waist and tell him, "Reid, you have been simply amazing. Thank you so much. Tonight is a night I will never forget."

We watch the movie cuddled together on our blanket, and when he drives me home later, he walks me to the door and kisses me goodnight. I physically have to restrain myself from turning into a puddle of mush when he tells me, "Goodnight, Maddy, and sweet dreams. Make sure you dream of me. I know I'll be dreaming of you."

Chapter 10

Reid

Maddy's face hovers over mine seductively. I'm on my back in my bed and she is sprawled, naked and beautiful, on top of me. Her breasts crush into my chest—so soft and supple, I can't help but sit up with her on my lap and touch her. It's an instinct—a magnetism like one I've never experienced. I reach out and graze my palms over her pebbled nipples. She moans and arches into my hands. Holding their weight in my hands, I brush over her nipples with my thumbs and pull on them slightly. She grinds her pelvis down onto mine. She likes it, so I pull just a little harder, extending her already elongated peaks between my forefinger and thumb.

Leaning closer to her, I kiss the expanse of creamy porcelain skin between her breasts before pulling her pink *nipple in my mouth. She nearly shrieks in response, and when I take it between my teeth and nibble lightly, she all but convulses on top of me. She is grinding into me, and I can tell she's on fire. I can feel her heat; it's scorching me. I kiss a path up from her breast to her neck. I kiss and lick every inch that I can reach. She leans her head to the side to give me better access. Burying her face in my neck, I can feel her hot breath at my ear. She's mumbling incoherently, though occasionally I hear something that slightly resembles my own name.*

She pulls herself back up to a straddling position and rocks back and forth over my arousal. I almost lose it. She's so fucking sexy and so turned on. She can barely control herself. Placing her hands on my chest, she lightly traces her nails over my pecs and across my nipples. My eyes roll back. She moves her way down my body and grabs my cock, stroking with an intensity that I can't endure much longer. Lying next to me on her side, my length firmly in her grasp, she whispers in my ear, "I want to do this with my mouth, Reid. I want to lick and taste every inch of you. Will you let me do that?" At that, all thought processes elude me.

She's moving down the length of my body now and settling between my legs. I can feel her warm breath on me. I can't take much more. She pulls me up to her mouth and leans down. Her golden, silky hair creates a veil around us. I reach down to move it out of the way. I want to see her mouth wrap around me, see myself disappear in between those sweet, hot lips.

When I have her hair pulled back and fisted in my hand, she licks at my tip before taking the first few inches in, and in that instant I know this is what heaven on earth feels like. She's tentative at first, unsure—so I guide her with my hand, never forcing her to go further than she can. She catches her own rhythm, and I am lost to it. My back arches off the bed, and my head falls back. I try to open my eyes, but I can't. The pleasure is too intense. My heart swells with joy having Maddy love me like this. It's a feeling I've never known, one that I never want to go away.

But when Maddy lifts her head, my bliss evaporates instantaneously. Maddy's face is replaced with one I had hoped never to see again. Her silky yellow locks are replaced with a short, severe black bob. Green depths with shimmering, vibrant flecks vanish, and cold, empty almost black pools of pure evil stare back at me.

Alex.

I shoot upright in bed. Oxygen will not enter my lungs. I gasp and nearly scream at the image that ended my nightmare—or was it just the beginning? I am sweat drenched and shaking at the thought of her mouth on me, of her body touching mine. Bile rises in my throat, and I have to sprint to the bathroom before I empty the contents of my stomach onto the carpet. Purged though I may be of this vomit, I will never be clean of *her*.

Alex is the last person who ever got close to me, and she's the reason my family is gone. She's the reason my world fell to a million pieces at my feet. Five years should be long enough to erase her from my memory, to absolve myself of this overwhelming guilt. Yet occasionally she makes an appearance in my dreams, which promptly turn into nightmares.

This one is different, though. Images of Maddy morphing into Alex aren't just haunting; they're terrifying. On some level, I know this is my brain's way of telling me I need to share my past with Maddy. In all honesty, it's killing me to keep it hidden. Part of me wants to tell her, wants to open up to her, wants her to help ease my pain. The other part of me is scared shitless. If Maddy knows the truth, if she learns about Alex and how fucked up I am, she'll leave me. Of this, I'm certain. No one as sweet, loving, kind, and caring as Madeleine Becker would ever stay with someone who killed his own brother, all because of a girl. The world just doesn't work that way.

The night after our first date, Maddy has plans with the girls, so the guys and I order some pizza and grab some beer. It hasn't been just the guys in a long time. There always seems to be a party going on or a revolving door of girls set up for the weekend. Well, now that I've got Maddy, the number of girls strutting through here has diminished considerably.

Jack tosses me a beer as he sets himself up on the other end of the couch. He props his legs up on the coffee table and takes a bite of his pizza.

Egging me on, he asks, "So how was your date with Maddy?" His tone mimics that of a middle-school student. Jerk.

"Tread carefully there, Jack. You don't want to end up looking like me," Logan warns Jack as he points to the yellow bruise on his cheek.

"It was good, great, actually." I'm not going to lie about my feelings for her. I really, really like her, so fuck whatever anyone else thinks.

"Seriously? You, Reid Connely, the man who has never spent more than one night with the same girl, not only went on a date, but actually enjoyed it?" Jack is nearly beside himself with shock.

I'm pretty shocked myself, but it's the truth. "Yeah, I know. But Maddy's different. I really like her, and I don't want to fuck it up." I look over at Logan on that last part. He knows I mean business, so he just holds his hands up in defense.

"Hmm. Never would have thought it, but I understand. It's like that with Cammie." Jack may be a guy's guy through and through, but he's also been with Cammie forever, and he loves her more than life itself.

"Maddy will probably be around here more often, so I would appreciate it if you guys could hold back on the 'Reid used to be a ladies man' routine around her. I'm sure Cammie and Lia have already filled her in on all the gory details of my past. She shouldn't have to come face to face with them every time she's here. I don't want her to feel uncomfortable."

Logan surprises me when he speaks up instead of Jack. "Of course, man. Listen, I know I was an ass for what I did. I just wanted to say that I'm really sorry for the other day, and not just because you kicked my ass—again. I just honestly never saw you as more than a 'hit it and quit it' kind of guy."

"Well, things change. Maddy makes me want to change. So cut the shit, and we'll be good from here on out." I do want to move past this with Logan, but I'd be lying if I said I'd already forgiven him.

"All right, you two. Can you kiss and make up already? I'd like to actually watch some of this game. Logan's sorry, and you're in love. Are we good now?" Jack has always had this fatherly air about him. It's shining through right now.

Logan and I eye each other up, and we both speak almost simultaneously. "Yeah, we're good."

"Great, now quit your bitching, hand me another slice of pizza and another beer, and watch the freaking game." Jack looks at us expectantly, and we hand over his demands.

The guys spend the night busting my balls. I don't care, though. They can make fun of me for how I feel about Maddy all they want.

I'm happy for the first time in a very long time, and no one is going to take that away from me.

The weeks pass, and the nightmares continue. I wonder if their occurrence, coinciding with the daily calls from a phone number with my hometown area code that I don't recognize, have anything to do with one another. I push those thoughts into the depths of my brain, though. I have more important things to think about, more beautiful things—like Maddy and our relationship.

Things have been going beyond amazing with us. She's fun and carefree, and we spend as much time as possible with one another. She spends most nights here, but I've also stayed at her place, too. We still haven't taken it to the next level physically, and oddly, I'm okay with that. We stay up late into the night talking and getting to know each other. Falling asleep with her cuddled up in my arms, her cheek nuzzled against my heart, is pure perfection. I've fallen for her hard and fast, and I know it. I'm fairly certain that I fell in love with her that first time we danced, but over the last six weeks those feelings have definitely solidified and rocked me to my core. We've become so attuned to one another, and the closeness I once feared to be crippling and horrifying is now my life force, my next breath. I would do anything for this girl, and I know that she feels the same about me. We haven't actually said the words yet, but it's there in how she looks at me, in how I hold her close to my side in bed every night, in how her eyes crinkle in the corners when she's laughing at me, in how I know that I would do anything to make her happy and to keep her safe.

So when she brings up her plans for Thanksgiving, which is in three days, I catch the sadness in her emerald eyes.

"What's the matter, sweetness? Not a fan of Thanksgiving? How can you be sad over cranberry sauce and turkey?"

She sighs and pours her heart out. "It's just that I never really got to do the holidays right. I know that my parents must have gone out of their way to make things special for me when I was a kid. I've seen the pictures, but it's like when they died, they took my happy memories with them. They're gone physically, and when they left, everything good associated with them went away, too. Looking at the pictures is like looking at someone else's life. And then when I lived with Aunt Maggie, it was just her and me. There was no need to make a huge meal. There was no family to gather around the table and to share stories with."

My heart hurts for her, and I wish I could give that all back to her. I would hang the moon for her if I could.

"Aw, baby. I wish I could change that for you, I really do. Come here." We're sprawled out on her couch at her suite, studying for finals, which start next week after the holiday. She moves in to my side and cuddles up against my chest.

"Aren't you going home with Mel, though?" I ask.

"That's the plan, but it just reminds me of how temporary everything is in my life. I mean, how many years am I going to go to Mel's before something changes, before that's no longer my home, either? Before we left to come here, I just had this distinct feeling that I was going to be on my own. So as much as Mel and Momma would love to have me there, I just feel alone." She wipes a lone tear off her cheek and says, "The holidays are always rough for me, so I guess I'm just being emotional. It's not really a big deal."

A plan blossoms in my head. It'll take some legwork and some cash, both of which I'm willing to spend on my sweet Maddy. As I'm lost in my planning, the girls stumble through the door, overloaded with shopping bags. You would think between the four of them, they would have all the clothes and girly shit they would ever need.

Melanie sees us on the couch and smiles warmly at us. We've been having lunch together every Monday since that first time and I really like her, and not just because she's helped me with Maddy, but because she's a genuinely nice person. Maddy's grown used to our covert operations and more often than not, she just laughs at us, knowing full well that she'll benefit somehow from our plotting. So when I ask to talk to Mel in her bedroom, no one bats an eyelash.

"What do you have going on in that pretty little head of yours now, Reid? You've got that scheming look in your eyes."

Damn, she knows me too well. "Oh, this one's a good one, though, Mel, and you're definitely going to want to help me out."

Please, please, please with a cherry on top!

She glares at me, but it's a playful glare. I know she can't say no to me.

" Okay, what do you need me to do?" she sighs.

"When were you planning on leaving for Thanksgiving?"

"Maddy and I are done with class at 1 p.m. on Wednesday. Then we we're stopping here to grab our bags before the three-hour drive home. Why do you ask?" She arches a conspiratorial eyebrow at me. She knows I'm up to something.

"We were just talking about it, and she sounded like she was really disappointed that she's never had a huge family gathering for the holidays, and I want to give that to her. I know that Jack is already planning on staying here for the holiday because he's got too much work to do."

"Which means that Cammie is staying, too. And if Cammie is staying, then Lia is staying," she chimes in, as awareness of my plan dawns on her.

"Right. So I can talk to Logan tonight and you can invite Bryan, and it'll be the eight of us, which is more than she would ever expect."

" Okay, but where are we going to do this? We can't fit that many people in the suite. We don't even have a dining room table."

My phone buzzes in my pocket, momentarily distracting me. It's the same number that's been calling for weeks. I hit "ignore" and return to my conversation with Mel.

"Well, we could do it at my house." A look of disgust creeps across Mel's face. She's trying to be tactful in searching for the right words, but I know what she wants to say, so I beat her to the punch.

"I know. I know. The house is disgusting. But…" I drag the word out, trying to convince her, "what if I cleaned the place top to bottom?"

"Reid, you guys would need a power washer and a steam cleaner to even begin to scratch the surface on the filth in that place."

Damn, she's right. I guess three college-age men don't make for good housekeepers. Then the idea dawns on me.

"I'll hire someone. I call a maid service and have them come in while we're all out, and it'll all be good." See? Simple.

" Okay, but where on earth are you going to get that kind of money? You're going to need a couple hundred bucks for the maid alone. Add in the cost for food and everything else—you guys don't even have real silverware or plates! I doubt you even have any pots and pans to cook with, do you? And I'm sure Logan and Jack aren't going to be keen on coughing up that kind of money for your girl. Can you even cook?"

"If I cover all of the expenses, will you help? I've got the money. Believe me, I've got more than I know what to do with, and I just want to make this special for Maddy. Help me write out a list of everything I'll need, and I'll go buy it all. Fuck, I'll hire the most expensive caterer in town if it means that I can give her the Thanksgiving she's always wanted." My words are sincere, and Mel knows it. I've got her hook, line and sinker.

It's about time all that money went to a good cause.

"But what about my mom, Reid? I can't just leave her all alone. She doesn't have anyone, either, and, as much as I love Maddy, I can't do that to her."

My phone buzzes again—the same damn number—at the same time that Maddy gently knocks on the door and through it says, "Now, I know I'm okay with you guys being friends and all, but you've been in there forever. We're going to grab something to eat. Want to come with us? Or are you guys too busy plotting to take over the world in there?"

I quickly answer Mel's concerns about her mom, wanting to end this conversation before Maddy gets too suspicious. "I'll take care of that, too. I promise. We can work out the details later. I also want this to be a surprise, so don't tell Maddy, either."

" Okay. I'm in. Let's do this." She claps her hands and jumps up and down a little. She's just as devious as I am; she just hides it a little better, that's all.

She responds to Maddy, saying that we'll be right there, to which I'm certain Maddy just rolled her eyes and scoffed out a "whatever." I put part one of my plan in motion and sneak Maddy's psych textbook into my bag. As we're walking out the door, my phone buzzes again, and I immediately hit "ignore." I can't be bothered with it now. I've got way more important things to do than figure out who is calling me from that god-awful place I used to call home. That place hasn't been home in forever.

Here is my home because Maddy is here - she is my home. If things go according to plan, here will finally feel like home for her, too.

Chapter 11

Maddy

I STAND IN MEL'S DOORWAY AND YELL, "Melanie Elizabeth Crane," in the hopes of getting her to move her ass. We're already supposed to be on the road to go home for Thanksgiving. She knows I hate driving in the dark down those winding, narrow mountain roads. And as much as I love her, the girl has a serious problem with getting anywhere on time. "Come on, Mel! We're going to be late."

"Would you just relax, Maddy? We're just driving home. You can't be late when you're going to your own house, silly. Besides, I'm almost done. Do you have everything you need? What about your psych textbook? I know that's your first final when we get back."

"Oh, crap! You're right. I don't think I packed that." I retreat to the living room, where I've been waiting patiently for over an hour for her to get ready. I rifle through my bag, and my book is not in there. I scan my desk, only to find that it's not there, either. I could've sworn I had it the other night when Reid and I were studying. Where the hell is it? Shit, maybe I left it at Reid's house. I text him quickly just to be sure.

Me: Hey, baby—I can't find my psych book anywhere. Is it at your place?

Reid: Yeah, it's right here. Want me to bring it over?

Me: No, it's okay. We'll stop on our way and I'll pick it up.

Reid: You mean I get to see that sexy body and kiss those sweet lips one more time before you leave me here all alone all weekend?

Me: Quit making me feel guilty. I said you could come with us.

Reid: Okay, fine, you win. I'll see you in a bit xx

Me: k xx

There is just something about him texting me kisses that makes my knees go weak. I knew I was falling hard for him pretty much since the first time I saw him, but now I know for sure—I love him. He is everything I originally thought he wasn't. He's kind and sweet and so loving. I have a very distinct feeling that he loves me, too, but I guess we're both just too afraid to be the first to say it. I know that my walls have come down where he's concerned. He's in my heart, and even though it can be crazy scary at times, it's pretty much everything I've ever wanted. I just wish he would let his guard down a little more. I know he loves me, but he's still hiding something. There's some wound that hasn't healed, and he's keeping me from it. I can't push him to share it, though; it's his to share. I'm sitting on my bed, lost in my musings about Reid, when Mel comes in to tell me she's ready to go.

"Finally!" I huff at her.

We load up the car with our bags and tons of snacks, and then head over to Reid's to grab my book. It's not a long drive at all, so we just listen to some music and sing along for the ten minutes that we're in the car. As we park in front of the house, I notice a change in Mel. She's extra bubbly—if it's even possible to be bubblier than she already is on a daily basis.

"What are you up to, Mel?" I ask, leering my eyes in her direction.

She just shrugs in return and says nothing. She hops out of the car, and I follow right behind. She knocks on the door, which is so odd; we never knock here. As the door opens, she steps to the side so that my view is unobstructed. I am stunned at what I see. Reid holds out his hand to grasp mine, and he brings me into the house.

"It's…it's so clean. What the hell? What is going on, Reid?"

They're definitely up to something, but neither Melanie nor Reid is saying anything. They're just sharing glances with each other, laughing secretly. Shock is giving way to frustration at this point, and I nearly yell, "What the hell is going on, guys? I've put up with your little secrets for almost two months now and it's getting a little old."

Why not stomp your feet and huff and puff while you're at it, Maddy?

They look at each other once more, and Reid pulls something out from his back pocket. "Trust me?" he asks. I'm confused by his question, but when I see that he's holding a blindfold, I understand.

"Of course I trust you, Reid, but if you don't start talking soon, I'm going to freak out a little."

He just laughs and moves to tie the blindfold over my eyes. He pulls my hair out of the way as he does so, and I can feel his breath, hot and sweet on my neck. He kisses me gently right under my ear before nibbling lightly. Shivers course over my entire body, and my nipples harden. He knows he has this effect on me, and I can feel him smiling against my neck.

"I hope you like your surprise, Maddy." And with that he finishes his assault on my neck. I have to squeeze my thighs together to try to tame the inferno that he causes in me.

I nod, and he leads me into what I believe is the direction of the living room, which was hidden from my view by the wall of the entryway. It smells of cleaning solution—some fresh pine scent. I can sense other people in the room; I can feel their collective nervousness, and I'm jittery to take this blindfold off and see what the hell is going on.

"Can I take this thing off now, Reid? I feel like an ass."

His response is a chuckle and an "okay." He is standing behind me, and as he unties the blindfold, he wraps his arms around my waist. Tears fall from my eyes at the scene before me. That pine scent wasn't from the cleanliness of the room. It was from a Christmas tree, a huge, real, gorgeous tree. My eyes go to that first because it takes up the majority of the large living room, but eventually I catch people in my periphery. Jack and Cammie are here, fingers interlaced at their side; Lia's here, too, smiling away as usual. I'm surprised to see Logan and Bryan as well.

"What are you guys doing here? Aren't you all supposed to be traveling today?" I can't hide the shock in my voice. I really don't understand what is going on.

Lia pipes up for the entire group. "Well, your sweet boyfriend here talked us all into changing our plans so that we can spend the weekend together." She pauses a beat before adding, "Here at home." She wraps her arms around me and squeezes tightly, and then looks up at me. Unshed tears are shimmering in her chocolate eyes. "We all wanted to be here together, like a family, for you."

Big, fat crocodile tears fall from my eyes. I turn to look at Reid and smile. "You did this for me?" My voice is shaking with emotion. I am in love with this dear, sweet man before me.

"Well, I had some help, as usual." He winks at Melanie, and I can't help but swell with love for her, too.

"You guys, all of you," I make brief eye contact with everyone in the room, "are amazing. You'll never know how much this means to me. I've never had a big family holiday…" My words trail off behind my thick emotion. I can't speak past the lump in my throat. When I finally rein in my emotions, I look at Reid. "What's with the tree, though? You know Christmas isn't for another month. Did you get your holidays mixed up or something?" My sarcasm always gets the best of me.

Logan responds rather than Reid. "Well, I couldn't be here for Christmas, and Bryan has to fly home, too, so I thought we could all do both holidays together now, start a new tradition. You know?" He stands next to me while he's saying all of this. When he's done, he pulls me into a platonic hug and says, low enough so that no one else can hear, "Plus, I was a real jerk for lying to Reid about us, and I really wanted to make it up to you."

I've been really angry with him about that whole situation even though he's said he's sorry a bunch of times—even though Reid's already kicked his ass. This gesture of thoughtfulness causes me to soften toward him. I can't stay mad at him when he's played a part in all of this, so I hug him back and tell him thank you.

"So here's the plan," Cammie chimes in. "Tonight we're going to trim this monster of a tree and drink cheap wine and eat pizza. That was always the tradition at my house, so now I'm sharing that with you. Come on," she says to Mel and Lia, "and help me in the kitchen with some drinks, and we'll order for delivery while the boys bring in all of the decorations from the car."

At that everyone scurries off to their task. Reid stays behind, though, and sweeps me into his arms, and he starts dancing with me, just like I remember my parents doing—no music, no beat, no dance floor. Just us. I am most definitely in love.

I rest my head on his chest and inhale his perfectly masculine scent. He is my home, and I feel so safe in his warm arms. He kisses the top of my head, and I look up into his ocean-blue eyes, which are shining with emotion.

"You're not mad at me, are you? I wanted to surprise you and give you something that you've always wanted."

His question catches me off guard. Mad? Is he kidding? I'm beyond elated at his loving gesture. "Reid, how can I possibly be mad at you? This is all so amazing. I feel so loved and cherished. That could never make me mad. You are the sweetest," I plant a kiss on his lips, "kindest," another kiss, "hottest," another kiss, this one deeper, "boyfriend ever, and I am so unbelievably lucky to have you in my life."

He kisses me deeply, passionately, lovingly, and then holds my face in his large but gentle hands. "Yeah, I guess I am quite the catch, huh?" Sweet and playful—God, he's amazing. He continues in a more serious tone, "You're the one who's the catch, Maddy." He cups my face gently and strokes his thumbs over my cheeks. I lean into him once more and kiss him with the sudden wave of love that I feel for him.

My curiosity finally gets the better of me, and I have to start on my truth-seeking quest. I pull back from him and ask, "So how did all of this come together? I mean, aside from the obvious answer that you and Mel did it all." I arch my eyebrows at him.

His lips quirk up into a playful smile as he pulls us over to the couch, which, I'm just now realizing, is new. "You got a new couch! Oh, thank God! I felt like I needed a shower after sitting on the old one."

He just laughs at me and says, "It was pretty gross, huh?"

"Gross? Reid, that thing was beyond filthy. I get the creeps just thinking about what might have happened on that couch over the years." I actually shudder a little at that thought. "So dish. How did this all go down, and how on earth did you afford all of this? I mean, a tree, decorations, a new couch—I'm dying here!"

"Well, when you said you wanted a big family dinner, I couldn't help but get Mel in on it. Everyone was more than willing to change their plans for you. They all love you, you know that, right?" He kisses me chastely on the lips before continuing, "Your suite was definitely the cleaner option, but it wasn't big enough. So I hired a maid service to clean the place up, and I spent most of yesterday and today while you were in class at Target and at the food market getting everything else. I didn't realize how much we didn't have until Mel pointed it out to me. We didn't even have plates. And food—the fucking cabinets were bare. So I stocked up on everything, and when I came home and saw how clean the place was, I couldn't imagine keeping the furniture. I was lucky enough to talk the sales guy in to letting me buy the floor samples. I threw in a pretty large tip, and wouldn't you know it, they were able to deliver it all this morning."

He makes it all seem so simple, but where on earth is all of this money coming from?

"But the money, Reid, that's a shitload of dough to spend on one person."

"You're right. It's a lot to spend on one person, but, Maddy, you are not *just* one person. You are everything to me. I just wanted to do something nice for you. The money is no big deal, please believe me."

I want to believe him that it's really not a big deal, but he's a twenty-one-year-old college student; this is way too much for him to spend on me.

"But, Reid, this is crazy! Please let me pay you back. My tuition and room are mostly covered by scholarships, and the rest is taken care of by my parents' life insurance policy. I can pay you back out of there."

He looks angry—like, really pissed—at the suggestion that I pay him back.

"No." His voice is hard and stone cold. Even he hears it, so he lets the anger recede before saying more. "You will not pay me back. You will not use money from your parents on me doing something nice for you. I've got it covered. The money is from a lawsuit from when I was a teenager. It settled out of court, and I never really touched it. I never had any reason to use it, so it just sat there and grew. Now I have you, and doing shit like this makes me happy, so it's the perfect reason to finally spend it. Believe me, all of this is a drop in the bucket where that money is concerned. Plus, if I didn't have that money, how else would I have been able to pay off that movie operator and have him play your favorite movie of all time on our first date?"

I can't help but melt into him and his thoughtfulness. I stare into his eyes and tell him, sincerely, "Thank you, Reid. For all of this—not the material stuff—but for the family I never had, for giving me the chance to finally open up to somebody. You make me so happy, and I only hope that I make you half as happy."

"Happy? Are you kidding? Maddy, you are the reason I breathe. Without you, my life would have no meaning at all, so saying that you 'make me happy' is a huge fucking understatement. You bring more happiness into my life than I ever thought I deserved." His lips crush into mine, and he kisses me with all the emotion that he's trying to convey in his words. These feelings of love and joy are so overwhelming that I feel like my heart might explode.

Our kiss is broken when we hear the guys barging through the door, carrying all the bags from Reid's shopping excursions. "Reid, get your ass in here, man! This shit's heavy."

Jack's words are strained under the weight of the bags he's trying to lug through the door. I move to help him, but he tells me stay right where I am. I lean my head back on the couch and revel in the idea that I'm not going to need to scrub my skin clean when I get up.

I hear the door slam shut and bags hit the floor. The girls come back into the living room with a tray full of snacks and some drinks. Lia passes everyone a glass of wine and proposes a toast. "To our first Thanksgiving together as a family." Everyone raises their glasses, saying "hear, hear," and takes a sip.

When Lia says "family," realization dawns. "Oh, no, Mel, we have to call Momma and tell her about all of this. She'll be worried to pieces over us." I glance down at my watch and realize that we should have been there two hours ago. "She's probably got the search-and-rescue team out already!"

I bend down to get my phone out of my purse, which fell to the floor when Reid took my blindfold off. When I'm upright again, I can't help the shriek of shock that comes out of my mouth.

"Momma C!" I scream so loudly that everyone actually has to cover their ears. I run into her open arms and bask in her motherliness. She must have been hiding behind the wall in the entryway. "But…how…when…what are you doing here? How did you even know we would be here? I didn't see your car up front." I stutter over my words, but I'm just so surprised to see her.

Mel walks up next to her mom and wraps an arm around her waist so that it's the three of us linked together before all our friends.

I see Momma wipe a stray tear from her cheek before she starts talking. "Well, Maddy, your boyfriend over there," she smiles warmly at him, and I know that he's won her over, "he called me the other day and asked if I wouldn't mind changing my plans to be here with you and all of your friends. And then he promised that I wouldn't have to lift a finger, that he would take care of everything. I couldn't turn him down. A weekend with my girls and their best friends and…" she stretches out the last "and" for emphasis, almost as if to remind Reid of his promise, "I don't have to cook or clean or do anything but enjoy all of you—how could I turn that down? Reid sent a car for me this afternoon so that I wouldn't have to drive myself and, well, here I am."

Reid steps over to Mel, Momma, and me, and he reaches out his hand to Momma. "It's an absolute pleasure to finally meet you, Mrs. Crane. I'm so thrilled that you could help me do all of this for Maddy."

She releases us and looks at his hand as if it's a foreign object protruding from his arm. She's a hugger, not a hand-shaker, so she pulls him into a soft hug. When she whispers something into his ear, a small smile curves up at the corner of his mouth. She says, this time loud enough for everyone to hear, "It's my pleasure, Reid. Anyone who would go through all this trouble for my Maddy deserves at least a little effort on my part."

And at that, we all return to our drinks, and the conversation carries through the room. We begin unpacking all the decorations and immediately go to decorate the tree. The evening passes by quickly because we're all having so much fun. We eat pizza off paper plates on the living room floor while we all share memories of holidays past. Reid looks concerned for me, and I understand why; I don't have all that many memories to share, but I just smile warmly at him.

"You doing okay, baby? I don't want you to be sad." He's so cute when he's worried about me.

"I'm perfect, actually. This is all so perfect." I kiss his cheek, place my hand on his chest, and whisper, "And later I plan on giving you the *perfect* payback." His breath hitches, and I can feel his heartbeat quicken in excitement.

Everyone has left, and it's just Reid and me standing in front of the newly, and beautifully, decorated Christmas tree. Momma is going to stay with Melanie at the suite. I could tell that she wanted to say something about me staying here with Reid, but she didn't. I know she sees what I feel for him, and I'm pretty certain she sees what he feels for me, even though neither of us will admit it to one another. So she kept her comments to herself, and for that, and so many other reasons, I love her.

"I hope you had a good night, baby."

His uncertainty is endearing, but he has got to be kidding me. This was the best night ever and it's about to get a lot better. "Reid, it was amazing. I loved every minute of it."

He interrupts me before I can continue on my promise to give him the best night ever in return. "I have one more surprise in store for you. Do you think you can wait down here for a few minutes while I set it up?"

He's looking at me all wide-eyed and lovingly, so I can't refuse even though I can't think of anything else he can do to make this night more special. He kisses me quickly before he struts upstairs to his room.

I sit on the couch and try to sort through my emotions. I smile at the memories from today and from the last two months that I've known Reid. I know for certain that I love him. I want to tell him so badly, but I fear that it'll scare him away. Even though I have a gut feeling that he loves me in return, I don't know if me loving him is enough to make him own his feelings for me. Despite the love I feel for him, there's still a part of me that's afraid to give myself to him completely until I know that he feels as safe with me as I do with him.

I can't let myself love him completely for fear that he'll pull away because he's scared. I have to know that his walls have crumbled like mine before I can give him all of me.

Reid comes back down to the living room and ambles toward me. He looks different—more sensual, lustful, hungry. He laces his fingers with mine and pulls me up from the couch. We walk up the stairs, hand in hand. My heart is thudding in my chest. The desire I have felt for him since the moment I met him is pulsing wildly through my veins. I want him. I want him more than I have ever wanted anyone or anything in my life. With my earlier realizations that I love him, I know that I am ready to give into my desires. Yes, I have some reservations, but I'm ready for this. For him. For us.

We stop outside his bedroom door, and he says, "There's no pressure to do anything. I just wanted to make tonight," and I know by "tonight" he means whatever is about to happen, "just as special as the rest of the night has been."

"Reid, I know you would never make me do anything I don't want to. So shut up and take me to bed." I reach up on my toes and lick my tongue across his heavenly soft lips. He opens the door, and once again I am blown away by what is in front of me.

His room has been completely transformed. Where there once was a full-sized mattress with a rickety frame and an old beat-up comforter is a gorgeous four-post bed with some kind of silky fabric draped across the top as a makeshift canopy now sits. It's covered in the most beautiful cream and white fabrics that I have ever seen. As light and airy as it is, it is still completely masculine and beautiful. He's repainted the walls, too, a soft blue gray shade that matches his eyes. There are candles on every surface that's safe, and some where it's not. He's got his iPod plugged into the speakers on his dresser, and my attention is drawn to it as I hear David Gray's sultry voice croon across the room. Next to the iPod sits a huge bouquet of white calla lilies in a large crystal vase. He's rendered me completely speechless, but words are not needed now. There's just Reid and me in this sensual heaven that he's created.

He spins me around and pulls me close to him. He places his hands at the nape of my neck and pulls the hair tie out of my hair so that it falls softly around my face. Gently sweeping the hair that has fallen in my eyes out of the way, he brings his face closer to mine and kisses me. This kiss is different from the rest we've shared. It's full of the promise of pleasure.

His tongue brushes up against mine. He's tentative and slow at first. I can tell he's trying to control himself, but that's not what I want. I want to dive into his depths and get lost there, to give myself over completely to this man I love. I know in this moment that I need to tell him that. Despite my earlier reservations about being scared, he needs to know that I love him. Whatever walls he's keeping up, whatever secrets he's got from me, can't possibly be enough to change my love for him, and he needs to know that.

I break the kiss and look up into his piercing blue depths. "Reid, I have to tell you something."

He looks at me questioningly before saying, "Maddy, you can tell me anything." He brushes his knuckles softly across my cheek and says, "Is it something I did? Talk to me—tell me what's on your mind."

I pull him across the room to sit on the bed. My insides are trembling with nervousness over what I'm about to say and over what I know I'm finally going to let happen. He's sitting on the edge of the bed, his feet touching the floor. I straddle his lap so my legs are wrapped around him and so I can look at his cool cerulean pools of love when I speak. I cup my hand around his cheek tenderly and take a deep breath, bracing for the words that are about to come out.

"Reid, I love you." I pause to register the shock in his eyes, but there is none. He just smiles adoringly at me and traces slow, soft patterns across my back. There's silence for a moment, and I need to fill it. "I know that you might feel like it's too soon, and I know we each have our own boatload of issues, but I can't help how I feel. You're amazing, and you've broken through every barrier I've ever put in place to keep people out. There's no one I want more than you, and I know that we'll be able to overcome whatever is thrown at us. I feel that strongly about us. It's scary, terrifying, actually, but I just needed you to know that I love you. I love you so, so much." I say all of this so quickly that I need to inhale deeply just to get some air back into my lungs.

His lips tip up into a devilishly beautiful smile, and he says, "Are you done? Can I have my turn?"

I nod and say "uh-huh" in return. Normal language function has completely left my brain.

"Madeleine, I love you, too." I move to say something, but he silences me with a kiss. "No, you got your turn—now it's mine." He kisses me again before saying the rest. "I love you more than anything. I would move heaven and earth to make you realize how much I love you. And I don't want you to think I'm saying this just because you've said it. I've been thinking about it a lot lately, and yeah, I've got some fucked-up shit in my head, the same shit that made me build those sky-high walls in the first place, but around you, they just vanish. That's why I did all of this up here tonight. I wanted to create a beautiful memory of the first time I told you that I loved you. When we do decide to take things to the next level physically, I wanted the bed to be ours and ours alone. I wanted it to just be me and you in there—no other memories except this one right now, of you glowing beautifully by the candlelight, sitting in my arms, listening to me carry on and on about how much I love you." He kisses me on the tip of my nose and brushes the pads of his thumbs under my eyes, where a few stray tears have fallen.

His confession of love ignites a fire low in my belly. If I thought I wanted him before, I was sadly mistaken.

I reach for the hem of his shirt and pull it over his head, our eyes only breaking contact when the fabric brushes over his head. I push him back onto the bed so he's lying down and I'm still straddled on top of him. His hands are at my waist, but they're so big that they nearly span it entirely. He moves them down a little to where my hips flow into the upper swell of my ass, and he squeezes gently. His thumbs begin tracing sensual circles dangerously close to my core.

I lean down and kiss his chest. It's broad and muscled, yet warm and soft to the touch. The sprinkling of chest hair tickles my face. I kiss over his heart and say "I love you" before descending to follow the thin line of hair that disappears behind the snap of his jeans. Before I can unbutton his pants and have my way with him, he's got both of my wrists in one of his hands and he's sitting up with me still on his lap.

"No, Maddy. Let me love you. Please."

My mouth goes dry, and my insides clench deliciously at the thought of what he wants to do to me. I nod, almost imperceptibly, but he sees it. He reaches for the hem of my shirt and relieves me of its weighty presence. His pupils dilate when he sees my pink lacy bra. It's nearly see-through and my nipples pressing against the fabric leave little to the imagination.

He goes to unsnap it. I beat him to it and grab for the hooks behind my back, undoing each of them slowly, seductively. My breasts fall free from their cups and I toss my bra on the floor where our other clothes lie. He doesn't reach for me like he usually does—we've gone this far before. No, instead of touching me, he just stares. He stares so long that goosebumps start to pimple my flesh, and my nipples harden even more under his lust-filled gaze.

"Beautiful. You are so damned beautiful, Maddy."

He wraps his arms around my waist and swiftly changes our position so I'm beneath him. He's supporting his weight on his arms, and he's half lying on top of me. He begins kissing my neck, and I groan in appreciation of his sensual assault. His tongue is hot against my skin, and my breasts are begging for his touch. He begins tracing his fingers across my chest, but he doesn't touch my now painfully aroused tips. Shifting so he is completely on top of me, he lowers his mouth to my left breast, but he doesn't do more than breathe a hot, steamy breath on it, making it more erect than I thought possible.

He kisses every part of my breast, every part except where I want him the most. Moving across to the other one, he continues his torture, and I'm nearly squirming with need under him.

"Please, Reid. Oh, God, please."

"What, baby? Tell me what you want. I want to give you everything you want." His eyes are hooded and sexy as fuck.

"I want you, Reid. I want you now. Please." My voice is no more than a breathless, lusty whisper.

He obeys my command and pulls a nipple into his mouth, and I feel my insides spasm at the feel of his hot, wet tongue gliding across my chest to the other nipple. He pulls the pink tip deep into his mouth and grazes it gently with his teeth. I arch my back off the bed and moan in ecstasy. He does it again and again and again until I can't take it anymore. I'm right on the sharp edge of my control; one more flick of his tongue anywhere on my body, and I'll fall into the abyss of pleasure that his mouth promises.

He must sense how close I am, because he pulls back and searches my eyes, looking for permission to go further. He sees submission in my eyes, so he bends down to kiss a path from between my breasts down to my stomach. When he dips his tongue into my belly button, I call out his name. "Reid…please…more…I need more of you…please."

He doesn't respond; he just continues kissing me everywhere. He moves to unbutton my jeans, and I lift my hips to help him as he pulls them off. He adds them to the ever-growing pile on the floor. He stares down again at me, but this time I feel self-conscious. We've never gone this far; I've never been this exposed.

He must see my inner turmoil, because he says, "You are the most beautiful woman I have ever seen before, Maddy. I want you more than you know, but if you're not ready, then that's fine, too. I just want to let you feel how much I love you. I want you to feel as amazing as you make me feel every single day." His words soothe my nervousness, and suddenly I no longer feel concerned about my nudity.

He leaves my lacy pink thong on as he kisses a path down each of my legs. When he returns to my center, I am burning with need. He licks over my hot core through the fabric of my panties, and I gush with even more wet heat.

Inhaling deeply, he says, "You smell fucking amazing, Maddy. You are so sweet. I can't wait to lick every inch of you."

All ability to say or do anything is gone, and I am at his mercy. He hooks his thumbs into my panties and pulls them slowly down my legs. "Open for me. Let me love you, sweet Maddy."

I let my knees fall to my sides and eagerly await the pleasure that I know his mouth will bring me.

With simply one broad stroke of the flat of his tongue across my molten core, he brings me right back to that razor edge of pleasure. When he swirls his tongue around my pulsing clit, I can't hold back the scream on my lips.

"Reid…so…close… please…"

But in that moment I'm not sure what I'm asking for. To stop? To keep going? I'm totally incoherent. He stops with his tongue and slowly slides a finger inside me.

"Oh, my fucking god, Maddy. You're drenched." His voice is full of awe, and when he removes his finger, I whimper. My emptiness doesn't last long, because he swiftly continues by adding a second finger. When he finds the soft patch of flesh in my trembling sex, he moves his fingers over it relentlessly. His tongue returns to my clit in a soft, delicate figure-eight pattern.

That edge is right there within my reach, and he doesn't stop this time. He laves and flicks my clit with his magical tongue and massages my inner walls with his large callused fingers until I'm coming loudly against his lips. My body is no more than a pool of liquid desire for him. If it's possible, I want him more now than I did before.

He moves up my body and kisses me. I taste myself on his tongue, and it is by far the most erotic thing I have ever experienced.

"Tell me to stop, Maddy, and I will. Tell me that's all you want tonight, and it will be fine. We'll go to sleep now."

"I know you're just saying those things to try to ease my fears, and I love you so much for even thinking them, but I'm ready, Reid. I love you, and I want to be with you. It's just that simple." I kiss him deeply so he can feel my words to his core.

"God, Maddy, I have wanted to make love to you for so long. You're making my dreams come true."

I know we're being all serious right now, but I can't help but say, "You're just glad you won't need cold showers anymore."

He chuckles lightly, but immediately resumes his serious tone. "I'd take three cold showers a day, if you weren't ready. Hell, there were some days I *did* take three."

We share a sweet laugh, and then the silence stretches. I'm lying naked in his arms, sated and hungry at the same time. He looks at me with the same ravenous gaze.

I kiss him hard before I say, "I'm yours, Reid. I don't want to wait any longer. Take me, please."

Whatever thread of self-control he had remaining is cut in that instant. He crushes me with his weight, and his tongue plunders my mouth. His hands are everywhere, fueling the fire burning in my core.

I fumble for the button on his jeans, but my fingers are jittering with nervousness. He stills them and helps me with the snap.

I trace over his bulging erection and gulp at the feel of him in my palm. "Now it's my turn. Let me love you, Reid, please. Will you let me do that?"

He cocks his eyebrows and shoots me a "like you even have to ask" look. I take that as my cue and shift so that I'm above him.

I pull his jeans down, and he lifts his hips, as I did mine earlier. One more item joins the others on the floor, but my attention is drawn to the only item of clothing remaining between us—his heather-gray, skintight, signature sexy-as-sin boxer briefs. He is straining against the waistband, almost peeking out of it. I kiss him softly over the fabric.

"Fuck, Maddy," he hisses at the feel of my tongue gliding up his length. "You're going to kill me, you know that, right?"

"Not yet. I haven't even tasted you yet."

I pull his boxers off and let him spring free. The pile is now complete, and we are fully bared to one another. He is the most beautiful man I have ever seen with clothes on, but naked like this, at the mercy of my desires, he is utterly gorgeous. Every single inch of him is perfect. I trace over his length with my finger-tips—some cheesy line about steel encased in velvet from some Harlequin romance dances in my head. Yet he is—both hard and soft at the same time. His skin is aflame under my fingers, and I lean my head down to lick at the tip.

He pulls my hair out of the way. "I want to see you, Maddy. I want to see myself disappear into your mouth." I take the first few inches in, and he bucks his hips and arches his back. "Oh…God…Maddy…" His words are a long, garbled moan.

I've never done this before, so it's good to know that he's enjoying it. Encouraged, I take more of him into my mouth, relaxing my throat as I do so. He wraps my other hand around what I can't fit in and works it up and down. We keep at that pace for long, heated moments before he pulls out of my mouth. A loud audible pop echoes in the room. Shit, I've done something wrong. I hurt him, or it doesn't feel good anymore. He must see my emotions, because he's sitting up next to me in an instant.

His hands are in my hair, smoothing it back out of my face. He wipes his thumb across my swollen bottom lip and pulls it out from between my teeth, where I'm worrying the hell out of it. "Before you even think for another minute that you did something wrong, stop it now. That was fucking perfect, Maddy—*you're* fucking perfect. In fact, another second of that, and I would have lost it. Okay?" His voice washes over me and reassures me that I did nothing wrong.

" Okay. I believe you." There's a part of me that doesn't believe him, that feels like I might be doing the wrong thing, saying the wrong words, acting the wrong way. It's all so new to me, and I'm just letting my need for him take over.

"Good, sweet Maddy." He pulls me down with him so that he's lying partially on top of me again. I feel him reaching over to his nightstand for what I assume is a condom. I grab his hand and stop his blind, one-handed search.

"It's okay, Reid."

His brows knit together tightly in thorough confusion.

"What do you mean, 'it's okay,' Maddy? I don't understand." The moment has turned awkward, but I guess that's to be expected.

"I'm on the pill. I knew it would be you, that it was only just a matter of time. So, what I'm saying is that, if you're okay with nothing between us, then there's no need for that." I indicate the condom with my eyes.

"I...uhh...Maddy...I've never ever had sex without a condom before, and I had to have blood work done before I started that MMA class at the gym, so I'm clean."

Yup—awkward. I'm kicking myself for not having brought all of this up beforehand, but, well, it never really came up.

"You've never had sex without a condom? Really?" I don't mean to sound so shocked, but well, to be honest, he's had a lot of sex, more than I care to think about. Despite all of that, I trust him; I know he wouldn't lie to me.

"Never. I promise. I'll use one if you want, but I swear I'm clean, and if you're on the pill, there is nothing I'd rather do right now than feel you completely bare as I bury myself inside you."

Not awkward anymore.

Just hot.

Fucking smoking hot.

"Reid," I look him in the eyes intently, hoping to convey the seriousness of the words I'm about to say, "I love you, and I want you. Now. With nothing between us. Make love to me, please."

He's over me in a heartbeat, and my legs are wrapped around his waist. He leans down and kisses me with all the love I know he has for me. I can feel him prodding at my entrance, and he sinks little by little into me. It's a full and stretched feeling like I've never felt before. My eyes roll back in pleasure, and I thrash my head from side to side at the feel of him entering me.

"My God, Reid. You feel amazing."

"Fuck, Maddy. So do you. God, you're so tight." He pauses for a moment before asking, "Can you take more now?"

"You mean you're not all the way in?" I didn't think it could feel better than this, but my insides spasm at the thought of taking more of him, all of him.

"Shit, I can feel you tightening around me. I'm going to move now. Look at me, please. I want to look at you." His eyes are huge in his face. The blue is only a thin rim at the edge of his irises; his pupils are black pools of lust and love for me.

I look up at him, and he sinks all the way into me. I only feel a brief, sharp pinch, and he stops at the resistance. Once it's no longer there, he asks, "Are you okay, baby? I'm so sorry if I hurt you. I promise I'll never hurt you again."

I can't form words; there is nothing in my brain except the pleasure he's giving me right now. I wrap my hands around his neck and pull his luscious mouth to mine to kiss away his concerns. He starts moving—a slow, sensual pace. His tongue mates with mine as our bodies grind against one another. His jaw is clenched, and I see the sinews of his shoulders and biceps strain. He's holding back; I can feel it.

"Don't hold back, Reid. I want all of you. Now."

We've been holding back with each other long enough, and right now I just want him to give me everything he's got. I want his wild passion and heated lust. I would have never pegged myself as this wanton, shameless creature, but he brings it out in me.

At my request, he starts moving at a furious rhythm. When he's filling me completely, it's like I can feel him hitting my soul. I cry and shriek his name as my body writhes with the pleasure of a million lightning bolts. He moves a few more times, hard and fast, before he shudders and stills above me.

He is covered in sweat and shaking. I pull him down to me and revel in the feel of his weight on top of me. I wrap my arms around him, and he cradles me in his. We catch our breath eventually. I am boneless and completely satisfied here in his arms, his heart thudding against my chest. My lids are getting heavy, and just as they are about to close, I feel him shift on the bed. He's up and moving into the bathroom. He's got a warm wash cloth in one hand and Advil in the other. I move to sit up, but he stills me; he is moving between my legs to clean me. I knew he was sweet, but this, this melts my soul. It also causes me to blush furiously. I know. It's crazy silly after what we've just shared, but it's just so intimate. I love him for it, though.

When he's done with his ministrations, he hands me the pills and a glass of water.

"But I don't have a headache. What are these for?"

"Well...you...umm... you might be a little sore tomorrow, so I thought these might help. Plus, if I'm being totally honest, I can't wait to do that again, so the less time you're out of commission, the better."

His lopsided grin is so freaking adorable; I can't help but kiss him some more.

He pulls me to him so that my back is to his front and whispers sweet nothings in my ear. He tells me he loves me and pulls the covers up around us. Warmth envelops me, and I can no longer keep my eyes opened.

I drift off to the tingle of Reid playing with my hair, to the huff of his sweet breath against my neck, to the feeling of complete and utter "wholeness" I possess at having let him in.

Chapter 12

Reid

I'm running as fast as my sixteen-year-old legs will carry me. My lungs burn and my eyes tear as the frigid wind whips across my face. Dread overwhelms me and only makes me run faster. The world is closing in around me, drowning me, burying me. There is no light; darkness engulfs me.

I toss and turn in bed, rousing myself from my impending nightmare. Not tonight. Not with Maddy here. Not with everything that's happened between us. I force the horrors of my past away and breathe deeply, counting backward from one hundred. I drift off somewhere around fifty-five, marginally hopeful that it will be a peaceful sleep.

I barge through the door of my house. No one is home. I call frantically for Mom and Dad, but I know they're at work. My throat is raw from the futile screams, but I keep yelling. The one person I want to answer me never will. The sound of my voice pierces even my own ears. I take the stairs two at a time. My toe clips the underside of one step, and I fall on my face. My chin is split open where I crashed with a loud, painful thud against the cold, hardwood floor.

My chest is pounding. My ears are rushing with blood. My face is soaked in sweat. Instinctively, I run my thumb across the scar on my chin. It's nothing more than a thin, white raised vein of flesh. It's superficial, but the real scars lurk far beneath the surface. Buried. Cold and dead, just like Shane.

I look to my side and see sweet Maddy still sleeping peacefully, curled in a ball. I spoon up behind her, and she wiggles her ass into my groin. I wrap my arms around her tightly, but not so tight as to wake her. Inhaling the coconut scent of her shampoo, a smell that I've come to associate with all things peaceful and beautiful, I try to calm my racing heart and paralytic anxiety. I count back from one hundred again. When I get to zero, sleep still eludes me, so I start again. On the third countdown, a fitful sleep overtakes me.

I finally make it to the top of the stairs, and I hear the water running in the bathroom. Fear freezes me. My feet remained glued to the floor beneath me. I can't move. I can't speak. The world tilts off its axis. I call for him.

"Shane. You home?" He doesn't answer. He can't answer. I call for him more loudly, as if that will rouse him from his eternal slumber. Still no answer. I knock timidly on the bathroom door, where I still hear the water flowing from the tub faucet. "Shane? Dude? You in there?" No answer. There will never be an answer. I try to open the door, but it's locked. I bang harder. I pound my fists into the white wooden door until the frame starts to splinter and my knuckles start to bleed. I change tactics as the panic crushes me. I drop my shoulder and ram it into the door. Still nothing. It just will not budge. I ram again and again. The pain is blinding. I'm pretty sure I've dislocated my shoulder, but I can't stop. I won't stop until I get to the other side.

The door cracks; I hit it once more, knowing that it will crumble if I put all my strength behind the next blow. My shoulder crashes into the door one last time and I fall through it, landing on the frigid, blood-covered tile floor. Shakes rack my body, and the scream that escapes my mouth is feral; it's the sound of a beast. I crawl clumsily; the blood-tinted water causes me to fall on my stomach. There's blood everywhere. I try to convince myself that it's my blood—from my chin, from my knuckles, from the splinter of wood that's stuck in my shoulder. I know it's not, though. It's his. It's Shane's.

I make it to the edge of the bathtub, where his arm dangles lifelessly. Blood is no longer dripping from the severed vein at his wrist. I grab him by the shoulders and try to shake him, try to pull him out of the water, try to save him. His head just lolls to the side. His eyes are fixed in a dead stare. He's so cold, gone already. I'm too late.

I crumple to the floor and vomit. I can't save him. I was too late. It's my fault. If I would have gotten here sooner, he'd still be here. Sobs overpower my body, and I thrash out in anger.

"Reid! Oh, my God! Reid, baby, wake up. You're having a bad dream. Please, baby, wake up. You're scaring me. Please!" Her panicked voice pulls me from the bowels of hell. Maddy frantically runs her hands over my face, my chest. She pulls me close into her so my cheek rests against her heart. It takes forever for me to calm down, to regain a sense of here and now, but her fingers stroking gently in my hair, her palm rubbing circles on my back, and her sweet voice telling me that "everything will be all right" eventually work.

I crane my neck up to look at her, and that small movement cause my insides to churn. I feel it coming on, so I sprint out of bed, race to the toilet. She's next to me in an instant—calming, soothing. There's nothing left in my stomach, and I'm just heaving above the bowl. Maddy gets up and busies herself by the sink. She's back by my side in an instant, wiping a cool, damp rag across my forehead and cheeks. I can't look at her. I'll break; I know it.

When the heaves subside, she wipes my mouth with the washcloth and hands me a glass of water. "Here, baby. Have a sip. What else can I get you?"

She looks so fragile, so innocent, so concerned. I still haven't said a word, and I'm not sure that I can. I know if I tell her this shit, that she'll leave. I can't lose her and deal with this shit on my own. The floodgates open at the thought of losing her.

She goes into the bedroom and slips on a T-shirt, and hands me a pair of shorts. I slide them on as I remain seated on the floor. I already feel so vulnerable, so I'm grateful that we're at least covered by our clothing.

After everything we shared last night, I can't lose her. I'm crying uncontrollably now, and I can't imagine what I must look like—the word "pussy" comes to mind, but with Maddy, I just don't care.

"Reid, baby, please talk to me. You haven't said anything, and I'm really worried about you. Please, whatever it is, you can talk to me. I'm here for you. We're in this together. You're my rock and my strength all of the time. Let me be yours now. Please, sweetie, let me take the pain away."

That just makes me sob harder. She pulls me into her arms, her warm softness surrounding me, enveloping me. I feel safe. It's a sharp realization, and with it the massive wall that used to guard my heart comes crashing down.

I feel safe. In her arms, I am safe and protected. She's already shared so much of herself with me. She's so damn strong, and I am in awe of her. Maybe I can do this. Maybe she won't leave. I take a deep breath and mentally try to prepare myself for sharing my darkest secret.

"I…Maddy…I've never…" I don't know where to start. It's something I've never told anyone. A "fuck" grumbles out of my chest before I regain my composure and start over.

We're still sitting on the bathroom floor, the cold tile chilling my legs. I can't tell her this in here, so I stand above her and pull her into my arms. I hug her tightly and try to pull whatever strength I can from her.

I walk her over to the bed and sink down onto it with her. My phone buzzes on my nightstand, and I just ignore it. The only person in the world I want to talk to is here in my arms.

She cups my face and looks deeply, affectionately, into my eyes. "Reid. I'm here for you, but if you can't talk, or don't want to, I understand that, too. Just please let me know that you're okay."

I can finally manage a few words. "You're here. I'm okay. It's that simple." She lets out a breath that I'm not sure she even knew she was holding. "If it's okay with you, there are some things I would like to tell you about. I want to ask you not to leave me when I tell them to you, but I know that's not possible. I just can't keep them buried anymore."

"I love you. I'm not leaving. It's just that simple, too."

She nuzzles into my chest and wraps her arms around my waist, and for that moment all is right with the world. I kiss the top of her head and realize I need to brush my teeth. What I have to tell her is vile enough; I can't do it with the wretched taste of vomit in my mouth.

When I come back to the bed, she is staring at me, wide-eyed and eager to hear what I have to tell her. It's not an eagerness born out of wanting the details, though, like that of a gossiping teenage girl; it's an eagerness rising out of concern for what I'm dealing with. She knows what it's like to feel pain and to not have anyone to unload it on. Those thoughts fortify whatever resolve I had.

We sit cross-legged on the bed facing one another, hands interlocked in a show of solidarity against the ghosts of my past.

"There's really no easy way to say any of this, so just let me get it all out. Okay? I'm not sure I'll be able to get through it all if I have to stop."

She nods. Knowing that she won't interrupt gives me the final push to get started.

"Shane was my older brother." I see a look of shock widen her eyes at my confession. "I know I said I had no family, and that's the truth." She just looks at me knowingly—a shared pain at losing a family member kind of look.

I close my eyes, and for the first time in a long time, I allow myself to think about my brother and my best friend.

"He was everything I ever wanted to be. The sun practically rose and set over his head in my eyes. He was two years older than me, so we were more than brothers—he was my best friend. We did everything together. We shared a room and would stay up all night together. When we were young, it would drive my parents crazy. I'm sure there were times they thought we were going to crash through the ceiling. As we got older, we'd horse around less—never stopped entirely—but the goofing-off changed into late-night talks. I know it sounds girly and shit, but we really were best friends. I always thought it was so fucking cool that when all of my friends had to go home at night, they had to leave all their friends behind, but not me—Shane was always by my side.

"When I got to high school, he would take me to the weight room with him after school. He was the one who turned me into a gym rat. We would spend hours each day working out together, and after a while, his friends became my friends. Things changed a little within the group when he graduated, but only in the sense that Shane wasn't at school during the day. We would all still hang out together on the weekend, and since Shane stayed home to go to a local community college, we still shared a room together.

"One night, I woke to the sound of him trying to stifle a cry. He was keeping it in, but this high-pitched whining sound still escaped his mouth, and I could tell something was wrong. He was shaking uncontrollably, and I was scared shitless. He was like a superhero to me. But there he was, broken and crumpled over, obviously dealing with something serious. I told him I should get Mom and Dad, but he said no. There was no way they could know. I tried to calm him down, and eventually he did. I told him that if he couldn't tell Mom and Dad, then he needed to tell someone. Whatever his secret was, it was enough to cause him this pain and anguish, so he had to tell someone. He said he would tell me, but only if I promised on my life that I would never tell anyone. That he would die if anyone ever found out.

"So of course I promised I wouldn't ever tell another living soul, and when I said it, when I vowed to him that my lips were permanently sealed, I honestly meant it." The sobs creep back up in my throat at the knowledge that I broke my promise. That it is my fault he's dead.

Maddy just shushes me and pulls me close to her chest as I cry. She doesn't say anything, and I love her for it. She just lets me hurt; she lets my pain bleed out. Holding back my tears, I continue my story.

"He told me he was gay, and honestly, I wasn't shocked. I mean, I never would have asked him, but there was always a part of me that suspected as much. It didn't change how I felt about him. He was my brother. I loved him no matter what, but I totally understood his fear of other people finding out. My parents are ultra-conservative, and our small town is narrow-minded. He would be shunned immediately by his friends and more than likely disowned by our parents. I was only sixteen at the time, so I couldn't fully wrap my head around the enormity of his confession, but I knew it was a big deal. In our town, in our family, it was huge. So I never told anyone.

"Until I met *her*. You see, Shane started dating this girl named Alex. He met her in his freshman English seminar. She was all flirty and darkly beautiful. He figured it was a good cover, but I think there was a part of him that was hoping he wasn't gay. As sad as it is, it would have been easier for him if he wasn't. I can't imagine the thoughts that went through his mind—how he must have felt with the knowledge that he would never be accepted for the person he was.

"They dated for a while -- I would say about three or four months before she approached me. She was leaning up against her car outside the batting cages where I worked. I knew who she was immediately. I had met her a handful of times. Shane was mindful to bring her home to meet Mom and Dad and to be seen out in town with her. I mostly laughed at his antics, and I just wished there was a place where he felt safe enough to just be himself. The real Shane was fucking awesome, but I knew that as long as our mom and dad were still his parents, that as long as our town was still his home, that the real Shane would be someone only I knew.

"So anyway, she wanted to know if I wanted to hang out, which struck me as odd. She told me she was waiting for Shane to get done with something—homework or something like that—and she just wanted to kill some time. I didn't trust her entirely, but she was Shane's girlfriend, and she was pretty hot. She had a bottle of Jack in the front seat, and she asked if I wanted a drink. I didn't want to be a pussy. I mean, I'd been drunk before, but something was screaming at me to keep my defenses sharp with her. We drove out to some hilly overlook and sat on the hood of her car, sipping the Jack. The conversation was innocent enough to start. You know, shit like how's school? Was I excited for baseball season in the spring? Before I could realize it, I was fucking wrecked. Jack sneaks up on you quick, especially when you're not used to hard liquor.

"Once she saw that I was drunk, she made her move on me. She started kissing me and pressing her body up against mine. I was a scumbag for hooking up with my brother's girlfriend, but I couldn't help but react. I was a fucking horny sixteen-year-old with a college girl's tongue down my throat. She had my pants down and my dick in her mouth before I could even realize what was happening. In the next heartbeat, she was straddled on top of me, fucking me like there was no tomorrow."

I stop and register the look of unadulterated shock on Maddy's face. She doesn't deserve this. She doesn't deserve me. I know I'm being such a shit for unloading this on her after last night. I know what it meant for her to let me in like that. It fucking meant the world to me, too. And here I am telling her about fucking Alex, but she has to know. So I brace myself and steel my resolve, and just hope that she'll still love me when all is said and done.

"It was my first time, so it didn't last long. As she climbed off me, she said that 'it was about fucking time that someone fucked her good.' She must have seen the look of confusion on my face. I asked if her and Shane had had sex. It came out more shocked than I meant for it to, but I was drunk. My shock and confusion must have been enough for her to push forward on her original intentions. I could see the cruelty in her eyes. I saw the evil boiling beneath the surface, but alcohol and lust clouded my vision so much that when she said she knew he was gay, my acknowledgment of the truth must have been clearly written on my face. I didn't come right out and tell her, and I never meant to, but it was because of me that she found out. It was because of me that they all found out."

My head has been down pretty much the entire time I've been talking. I've been avoiding eye contact with Maddy, knowing that I'll see judgment and anger in her beautiful moss-colored eyes.

When I finally do meet her gaze, there is shock there. I guess she wouldn't be human if she wasn't somewhat shocked. That's a lot to take in; hell, it's a lot to let out. I have to try to convince her that I'm not that person anymore. "Maddy, you have to believe that I never would have told her any of that. Please believe me. It's why I never drink. It's why I've never let anyone in, except you."

She still doesn't say anything.

"Maddy, please. Tell me that we're okay. That you're okay." I reach out to cup her cheek, and I gasp when she leans into it tenderly.

She doesn't hate me.

"Can I say something now, Reid? I don't want to interrupt you if you've got more to get out." Her concern for me just makes me love her even more.

"No, go ahead, please say something," I plead with her. I do have more to share, but I need to catch my breath and wrap my head around it all. I also need to hear her say that she doesn't hate me for who I used to be, for what I did.

"I'm trying to find the right words. I know you don't want to hear 'it's okay' or 'it wasn't your fault,' because I know it's not okay. You threw up at the nightmare about all of this—that's definitely not okay. And I could swear up and down that it's not your fault, and it's not, but I know that is not going to change how you feel about it."

I nod my head 'yes' at her line of reasoning. I know deep down that if I hadn't slept with Alex, and exposed Shane's secret, then he would still be here.

"I never blamed myself for my parents dying. I mean, there really was nothing anyone could've done."

I huff a sarcastic laugh at her. If she's trying to make me feel better about my guilt, then she's failing miserably.

She backtracks and says, "What I mean is that even though I never felt responsible for them dying, I still felt the pain of their death. I know that all-encompassing grief you've felt, that you're feeling right now—the kind of grief that keeps you up at night, threatening to eat you whole. So you do your best to protect yourself, to keep the world at bay, and everyone at arm's length. You learn to protect whatever is left of your heart because you can't even begin to fathom what it would feel like to have the small piece that remains broken along with the rest. I don't know how to begin telling you to forgive yourself, but I do know that you are a good man I love more than anything. I'm here for you. I want to help you figure out your past and figure out how to move on, just like you've helped me figure mine out, just like how you're helping me move forward."

She pauses, and I see her trying to piece together the rather lengthy story I've laid before her.

"Will you tell me the rest?" she asks timidly.

I've never been forthcoming about my family, and I know she can tell that there's something I'm keeping from her. Feeling emboldened by her inner strength, I tell the rest.

"Well, after Alex found out what she wanted, she drove me home and promised not to tell a soul. Fucking bullshit. I could see it in her face. She was embarrassed that she had been duped, that her boyfriend had tried to fool her. She was most definitely a woman scorned, and she was on a mission to destroy Shane for making her look bad. It was five years ago, and I was still in high school, so I didn't know much about Facebook and MySpace and all those social networking sites. Alex did, though, and she used them to make Shane's life a living hell. She made a video of snapshots that she had taken of the two of them throughout their relationship and used it to out his sexuality. It was mean and cruel and just downright vindictive.

"Like I said, we lived in a small, close-minded town. Denning, that's where I grew up—a small rural upstate New York town—is only about five hundred people. They're mostly farmers, blue-collar workers. People who live there have had roots there for generations, and they don't take well to anything that isn't *normal*. People down the road knew when you farted, so word of Shane being gay spread quickly. When he came home from class one night, a few days after my encounter with Alex, my parents were waiting on the couch to confront him. They told him that he had to leave. No son of theirs was gay. They wouldn't house 'that kind of person.' He stopped being their son in an instant. They stopped loving him. They made him leave. I couldn't believe how cruel and callous they were treating their own son. But Shane, he didn't fight or yell and scream or anything. He just walked away, head hung low. I know they're not really dead, but in that moment, the people I thought were my parents died right before my eyes.

"I can't imagine how bad the bullying online and in school must have been for him, either. When he walked past me on the stairs, his eyes were sad, dejected, pained, but somewhere in there I saw relief, too—relief that the truth was out. A small fleck of hope sprang from that shimmer of relief. I started to think that maybe things would be okay, that maybe he would figure things out and that all of this shit would just go away in the morning.

"But it didn't. When I woke up the next morning, Shane was gone. When I went downstairs to find him, my parents were sitting at the table, eating their breakfast and sipping their coffee like nothing happened. I yelled and screamed at them. Told them they'd lost their fucking minds, that they were heartless and fucking worthless if they could just disown their own flesh and blood for being gay. They told me that if I felt that way, I should leave, too. I felt like I was looking at strangers. They were my parents. I had obviously known them my entire life, but when they told me that, I felt like I was in some kind of twilight zone or some shit like that.

"So that afternoon when I knew they would be at work, I cut out of school early to come home and pack my bags. I was going to find Shane and leave with him. Wherever he was going, I didn't want him to be alone, and I most certainly didn't want to be in my own house any longer. As I was walking home, I had this gnawing feeling in my gut that something was wrong. I ran and ran and ran to get home as quickly as I could."

I pause, trying to gather whatever strength I can for this next part. The deep breath that I take racks my lungs, like that of a child who has sobbed itself to sleep.

"He was in the tub, wrists slit, blood everywhere. I was too late. There was nothing I could do. He killed himself because of me and my fucking mistake. He left a note, but all it said was that he was sorry that he couldn't be who they wanted him to be. I killed him. It's all my fault that my brother is dead." The tears claim me full force now.

Maddy just pulls me closer to her side and sinks down onto the bed with me in her arms. After long moments pass in silence, and I finally calm myself down, she asks, "That's why you want to work with kids, isn't it?"

I smile before saying, "Yes. Sixteen-year-old me blames myself for everything that happened with Shane, but twenty-one-year-old me knows that maybe if he had someone to turn to, he might still be here. I couldn't be there for him like that, but maybe I can be there for someone else."

She smiles at me lovingly and then just holds me. We don't say anything for a while; we just bask in the feel of one another, reveling in the comfort of having someone who understands your pain.

I get lost thinking about how happy things were before Shane died, about how much I loved my life and my family. That all came crashing down in an instant. I know Maddy understands that; she had no warning where her parents' deaths were concerned. Her world shattered instantly, just like mine.

She must have some kind of ability to read my thoughts, because as I'm thinking about how my parents are essentially dead to me, she asks about them. "So what happened with you and your parents, then?"

I can't help but sigh and laugh flippantly. "Well, they essentially kicked me out, and I was ready to leave with Shane. But after he died, I lost the will to do much of anything. I lived in a numb fog for the last year and a half of high school. I just existed. We passed each other in the kitchen or in the hallway that connected our bedrooms, but never said a word. When I graduated, I packed up and never looked back. I haven't heard from them since. They never tried to contact me, and I never bothered with them."

If she thinks less of me for cutting my parents out of my life when hers are really and truly gone, she's hiding it well.

"So, then how do you pay for school? And this house? I mean, I know it's not the Ritz, but you don't have a job or anything. So without your parents helping out, how do you afford all of this? And the money that you spent on yesterday, too -- where is all of that coming from if you're on your own?"

"This is where they earn their 'Parents of the Year' award," I quip angrily. "After Shane killed himself, and my parents learned of all the online shit, they went after Alex for something like defamation of character or wrongful death or something like that. I stopped paying attention to anything that they did, and they left me alone. They wanted nothing to do with me because I was mourning Shane. I just couldn't understand how they could act like he never even existed. Anyway, they wanted all traces of him being gay erased. They wanted Alex to take her words back, even though they were true. They had no interest in the money, really—it was tainted with Shane's homosexuality. They just wanted to save face. So when they settled out of court, they put the money in a college fund for me. I'm pretty sure they'd flip if they knew that I was using the money to invest in a career to help kids who were like Shane. But really, I never wanted to touch the money, and aside from tuition, rent, and the basic living expenses, I've never spent a dime of it. Until you, that is." I get lost in reminiscing about how much happiness I've been able to share with her because of that money. "Shane would have loved you, you know." The silence stretches again, and this time my fear is what causes me to break it. "So where does this leave us, Maddy?"

She looks lost at my question, and I can't tell if that's a good or a bad thing. "What do you mean, 'where does that leave us'?" She situates us so that we're lying next to each other, face to face, looking in each other's eyes.

"I've been holding all this back because I just had this feeling that you would leave me if you knew. You're too good for me, for my past, and between everything that happened with Alex and essentially killing my brother…"

She doesn't let me finish my train of thought. Her lips silence me, and I feel like I can breathe again. She wouldn't be kissing me if she was leaving me.

"Reid, I said I love you. Now, this may come as a shock to you," she's trying to be playful, arching her eyebrows—God, I love her, "but I don't throw those words around lightly. That's some really serious stuff you've been carrying around with you, and I hate that you felt like you couldn't tell me. I'm here for you, baby. I love you, and nothing you did, even though none of that was really your fault…"

I try to interrupt her, but she just shoots me a stern "shut up" look.

"It wasn't, Reid—none of it was your fault at all. Alex seduced you. She raped you, essentially. Sure, you weren't held down or violently beaten, but she got you drunk and seduced a sixteen-year-old to get a piece of information that she didn't have a right to know in the first place. You were a kid, for God's sake. Your brother trusted you, and she played you. You didn't deliberately betray him. You didn't disown him like your parents did. You were actually going to leave with him, to be there for him and support him. And you most certainly didn't hold the blade to his arm. Think of how much pain and suffering he must have dealt with to make that decision. That wasn't your fault, baby. You're even dedicating your career to helping other kids like Shane. I'd say that's pretty fucking awesome. You have to forgive yourself. Otherwise, the guilt and anger will eat you alive."

I am in awe of this beautiful and compassionate woman. How the fuck did I get so lucky to have her in my life? "Maddy, you make everything sound so simple. God, I love you. I can't forgive myself completely, and I can't swallow the anger and pain entirely, but for the first time since it all happened, I'm willing to try. You make me want to try."

I kiss her and pour as much emotion as I can into it. She fucking amazes me. She doesn't run; she doesn't turn her back on me; she doesn't pity me. She is just there for me, holding me when I need to be held, listening to me when I need to be heard, wiping the tears away when they stain my cheek.

Maddy breaks the kiss to say, "I love you, Reid." She inhales a huge, cleansing breath—a cue to change the subject - and when she huffs it out, she says, "So I'm going to shower now and get that monster of a bird in the oven. Did you guys put a hit out on Big Bird or something, because it's abnormally huge?"

"Oh, shit, Maddy! I completely forgot that today was Thanksgiving and that we have to make dinner for nine people in," I reach for my phone to see what time it is and see that I have five missed calls, all from the same fucking unknown number, "like six hours."

"It's okay, baby. I got this under control. You just have to sit there and look pretty." She smirks a sarcastic grin in my direction. "I'm going to shower and then start cooking."

As she walks away from the bed, I slap her ass playfully. I love that she brings that out in me—that light playfulness. God, if she wasn't here today, after that nightmare, I'm not really sure what I would be doing. I definitely wouldn't be laughing and smiling. I've never been more thankful for anything in my life.

I hear the water turn on and join her in the bathroom. I can use at least one of those six hours showing her just how thankful I am.

She's already under the hot spray, rinsing the soapy lather out of her long, luxurious mane. Water sluices down her perfect body. I could watch the scene before me for hours. Her long, lean legs go on forever, and when they do end, they are topped with the most glorious ass I have ever seen in my life. It's full, round, and firm; I could sink my teeth into it. Her hips and waist are soft and full, perfectly feminine. She is a far cry from those skin-and-bones models out there that everyone says are perfect. Well, if they think that is perfect, then it's clear they've never seen Maddy.

She's still facing away from me as I strip out of my boxers and slide in behind her. She gasps in audible shock, "You scared the crap out of me, Reid! What are you doing in here?"

She's trying to cover up—silly girl. I wrap my arms around her waist and pull her so that her back slides up against my front; the water makes our bodies glide together in a perfectly delicious way. I kiss her neck softly before biting it more than a little lightly. She shivers and leans into my lips.

"Did you really think I could stay in the other room, knowing that you were in here all hot and soapy and wet?" I kiss her neck again, this time on the other side. I kiss from where her long, graceful neck meets her shoulder up to her ear and suck the lobe into my mouth. Her breath is becoming shallow; I know she's losing it. Thinking about how wet she is, not just from the shower, makes my cock twitch. She feels me hardening behind her and she reaches behind to touch me.

My knees buckle slightly. She has that kind of power over me. The feel of love, the power of all of her emotion, travels through each and every touch of her fingers on my skin, and I am rendered weak by it. I can't help but lean in to her touch and buck my hips up into her hand. The water flowing down around us makes my movements effortless. She turns around to face me to make the angle less awkward.

As I gaze down into her gorgeous green eyes, they are hooded with lust and filled with love and passion. I know the same look is present in my eyes. My hands glide wetly up her waist and graze the underside of her full, round breasts. Those are perfect, too. Her nipples pucker under my soft touches. I pinch them between my forefingers and thumbs and pull lightly. She groans and rolls her hips into mine. Bending my head down to them, I take her right nipple deep into my mouth and suck.

"Ahhh, Reid. That feels amazing." She wraps her hand around my neck and twists her fingers into my hair, holding me in place.

I pull away, sucking air back into my lungs, and say, "You are so fucking beautiful, Maddy. Every inch of you is perfect." I trace my hands over her body to emphasize my point. "And up here," I run my short nails through her scalp, forcing another shiver and causing her pert nipples to harden further, "my God, you're the smartest and funniest person I have ever known." I place my hands over her heart. "And here. My God, in here is the kindest, most compassionate heart. I can't believe I have the privilege of being inside it, of being a part of your world and your life. I love you, Maddy, more than you can possibly know."

Her lips crash into mine before I can say anything else. Not that there are words that even exist to convey how much I love her, especially now that she knows everything, now that I've laid my heart, my black heart, open and bare at her feet, and she still wants to be with me. Never in a million years did I ever think I would be this lucky.

She deepens the kiss, taking it to a feverish pace. Our teeth crash together. We nip and bite at each other's lips. Tongues dance wildly. We are lost in each other, lost in this moment of unbridled passion. I reach down and caress between her legs, and this time it's her turn for her knees to buckle under the touch of pleasure.

"Spread your legs for me, baby. Let me touch you."

"Oh…God…yes…Reid…"

Her voice fades away into incoherent moans of ecstasy. I swirl my fingers around her hardened nub, pressing ever so softly. She could be sore from last night, and I most definitely do not want to cause her pain. When she grinds herself down onto my hand, I know that pain is the furthest thing from her mind. Two fingers glide through her silky folds, and she is completely lost to me. Her head rolls back onto her shoulders, and she can barely hold herself up. I wrap my other arm around her waist to support her weight.

My hand pumps into her; my thumb circles her clit. My name on her lips as she comes is the most beautiful thing I've ever heard. It breaks the chains I placed long ago around my heart and causes it to swell with love.

Finally able to hold her own weight again, she wraps her arms around me and leans her head into my pecs. "Reid, that was amazing. You make me feel… oh, God…I can't even put words to it. I love you." She reaches down to grab me once again and resumes her stroking from earlier, but after touching her and feeling her come against me, I can't take more than a few strokes before I'm already on the edge of coming myself.

"Maddy, your hands are fantastic. I love the way you touch me. Ahhh…baby…I'm close…" I'm in complete oblivion, so I don't even realize that she has shifted and is now kneeling down in front of me. The sight of her alone pushes me even closer to my climax, and I throb in her hand. She takes me into her mouth, and I am gone. Her tongue, her lips, they are my undoing.

I try to pull away from her; I wasn't expecting her to use her mouth. I don't want her to think she has to do anything she doesn't want to. She just grabs my ass and pulls me back to her, deeper into her mouth. I want to tell her that she doesn't have to, but I'm coming before I can even get the words out.

She doesn't flinch, doesn't move an inch. She just takes all of me—body and soul—she takes everything and turns it into something beautiful. I cup my hands under her shoulders and pull her up into my arms. Kissing the top of her head, I say, "You know, you didn't have to do…well…you know." Something about her just makes me want to be a little more discreet, a little less vulgar about all of this.

"Reid, do you really think I would have done anything I didn't want to? I love you, and I wanted to show you just how much I love you. Unless…did I do something wrong? Oh, God, I did something wrong? I must look like an ass."

Her insecurities are so fucking adorable. She had me coming in her mouth in less than a minute, and she thinks she did something wrong.

I chuckle lightly at her misunderstanding of the situation. "Maddy, believe me. You did absolutely nothing wrong." We stand under the water, just holding one another, basking in the bliss we've just shared. When the water turns cold, we rush to finish getting cleaned up.

I wrap a towel around my waist and drape one over her shoulders. Pulling her into my embrace and resting my chin on the top of her head, I realize that, while last night was a rather obvious first for her, this morning was a first for me, too. It was the first time I've told someone that I loved them; it was the first time I ever told anyone about Shane and Alex; it was the first time I felt love in return, despite all of the demons of my past.

I can't help but feel that the shower did more than wash my body. With Maddy at my side, I feel like my soul has been cleansed and my heart has been given a second chance.

When a smile curves my lips at these thoughts, for the first time in a long time, I don't try to push it down.

Chapter 13

Maddy

I AM IN AWE OF EVERYTHING before me, and not just
because the girls and I put together a pretty impressive
spread for Thanksgiving dinner. It's the love and feeling of family that makes my insides get all mushy. The
boys have been in the living room watching football all
day. A bit sexist, sure, but I'd be lying if I said my heart
doesn't melt a little each time I hear them yell at the
television. My dad used to get like that about football,
well, any sport, really. What is it about men and yelling
at a game on television? Don't they realize they can't
change the outcome, no matter how loudly they yell?

Silly boys.

" Okay, so the table is all set and all the side dishes
are all ready. I think we're good to go." Melanie informs

me of the status in the dining room. I honestly couldn't have done any of this without her and the girls. I've never really cooked more than mac and cheese. God, I hope I don't poison anyone!

Momma C has been cute as a button, too. Even though she swore up and down that she wasn't going to lift a finger, she's been hanging around the kitchen like a hawk all day long. I see her tasting things and adding dashes of this and pinches of that along the way.

I pulled the gargantuan bird out of the oven a few minutes ago, and now I'm staring it down, wondering how the hell I'm going to get it inside in one piece. Forget carving it; I have no clue where to even start with that.

Maybe the guys have a chainsaw. That ought to work.

Just as I'm about to have a mini panic attack over it, Reid struts into the kitchen. He's been amazing all day, too. Every twenty minutes or so, he comes into the kitchen to help us out. He never intended for me to do all of the work, but after about five or six times of me insisting that I wanted to do it, he finally stopped trying to help.

But, boy is he a welcome sight now. "Need some help there, Maddy?" He's being a little devil, playing on my earlier insistence that he stay away.

"Why, yes, dear." I arch a playful eyebrow in his direction. "Can you carry this to the table and carve it for me?" I try for my best June Cleaver impression, which has him laughing in hysterics.

I shouldn't be getting turned on at the sight of him carrying a turkey into the dining room, but watching his biceps flex as he effortlessly lifts the heavy tray makes my blood flame. Watching his taut, perfect ass sway out of the room is also a fairly yummy treat.

I love that everyone decided to keep everything casual and low-key. I never understood why some people get so dressed up just to eat. Give me elastic waistbands, please.

When I enter the dining room, my breath catches in my throat behind thick emotion when I see the scene before me. Everyone is seated around the table, which is beautifully set; it kind of looks like something out of a Norman Rockwell painting. Reid is sitting at the head of the table, and he pats the seat next to him for me to sit.

Before he sits, he raises his glass and clears his throat to get everyone's attention.

"Before we eat, I'd just like to say a few things. First, I want to say thank you to all of you for making today possible. I know I kind of threw this in everyone's lap at the last minute, but you all pulled together, and I just hope you had fun in the process."

Jack chimes in, ribbing Reid. "Yeah, nothing says fun like hauling a freaking six-foot pine tree off the roof of my car and into the house."

Logan adds, "I can't complain. This house is cleaner than a freaking Pine-Sol commercial!"

Reid just shoots them a playful look and continues with his speech. "Mrs. Crane, I really can't thank you enough for coming out here. It wouldn't be the same for Maddy and Mel, and I know I speak for everyone else when I say that we love having you here."

Momma C winks at him. I think she's a little smitten, because I see her holding back the tears at how sweet and kind he is.

"And last, but certainly not least, Maddy, thank you so much for coming into my life. I have no clue what I did to deserve you. I'm not even sure that I do, but I will spend every minute of the rest of my life making sure that I do everything in my power to keep you by my side. I love you, baby, and I hope you have a perfect Thanksgiving."

At his last word, he bends down to kiss me sweetly on the cheek. Everyone erupts in "hear, hear"s, and they all clink their glasses together.

Momma C leads us in a blessing before we eat, and my heart swells with love for this woman who has been my surrogate mother for the last eight years.

When she finishes, Reid carves the turkey, and everyone begins passing dishes back and forth. My plate is full to the brim, and so is my heart. I've gotten everything I've ever wanted because of Reid.

I reach my hand out to grab his and squeeze gently. "Reid, I love you. Thank you. This has been the best surprise, the best weekend, in my whole life."

He winks at me and says, "Anything for you, Maddy. Anything at all."

"Oh, I'm so glad you said that, because if you think I'm cleaning all of this up after cooking all day long, well, then, you are sorely mistaken."

He laughs and offers me up a sexy lopsided grin. "I got the dishes, babe. You're off for the rest of the night. Well, at least until everyone goes home. Then you're all mine."

We're all sitting in the living room watching *The Wizard of Oz*, and while everyone is lost in conversation, I can't help but notice that Reid has been checking his phone nonstop all night. Come to think of it, he's never really on his phone, but the last few weeks it's been like a constant presence—always in his hand, always buzzing away on whatever surface he's left it on.

Who could be calling him, anyway? We're all here.

Something's not adding up here.

Unpleasant thoughts take root in my head. Is he cheating on me? God knows he's got plenty of women to choose from—all of them certainly hotter and more experienced than I am. Maybe he's been keeping some of them on the side all this time. I try not to let my mind go there. I remind myself of all of the sweet gestures that Reid's done for me since we've been together. A cheater doesn't text nearly every hour to see how you're doing. He wouldn't buy me flowers at every opportunity—at times just a single red rose—if he was sleeping with someone else.

When would he sleep with someone else, anyway? We've spent practically every night together.

But you only had sex with him once.

You don't have to spend the night to have sex.

At the thought of him sleeping with someone else, I can't help but think about how foolish I was to insist that we didn't need a condom. My heart and mind are battling fiercely over what to believe. One thing is for certain, I do not like this version of myself - this questioning, insecure, uncertain version of the Maddy that I've been trying to erase over the last few months.

It's stupid, really. I have no reason to think he would hold on to his old ways. I've let him in and he's let me in, and now all of a sudden I'm a scared little girl who is just making up excuses to make things seem imperfect. It's just like what I did with Jay before I left.

Shake yourself out of this. He's a good man, Maddy. He wouldn't do that to you.

He catches me looking at him, and his brows furrow into a quizzical stare. I smile quickly at him, letting him know that everything is okay. I fake a yawn to play it off that I'm just tired. He smiles back and resumes his conversation with Logan and Bryan. They're probably still analyzing every little detail of the football game from before.

When everyone finally does leave, it's almost ten o'clock, and I am bone tired. Between last night—and then again this morning in the shower—plus all of Reid's revelations, and this new crap with the phone calls, I'm surprised I even have the strength to walk up the stairs and crawl into bed.

He called it our bed—a bed he bought so we could have our own beautiful memories.

He wouldn't do all of that for me, tell me his darkest secrets, and throw it all away on some other woman.

I fucking hope not.

I'm just about to pass out when Reid says, "I'm going to grab a quick shower before bed." He adds a sultry smile, and his eyes go all hooded before he adds, "Want to join me?"

"Reid, I really would love to, but I'm so exhausted. I really just want to curl up in bed and pass out for about twelve hours. I'm sorry, babe, but can I take a rain check?"

"Of course, sweetheart. How about a back rub when I get done? It'll help you relax."

Oh, my God, he's so adorable when he's this sweet. I force down my earlier doubts and try to hold on to the idea that he really does love me.

I'm being stupid, really. I'll just talk to him about it in the morning, because just thinking about diving head first into an "are you cheating" conversation exhausts me even more.

"That sounds amazing." I stand to get one of his T-shirts out of his dresser.

"Great. Be out in a few minutes, then." He pulls his shirt over his head in that sexy-as-hell one-handed grab from behind move that guys do. I wonder if they realize how sexy that is. It's probably the same for them watching us unhook and take off our bras without having to take our shirts off. I laugh at my pointless, although still funny, musings.

My whimsy is erased completely when I hear Reid's phone buzzing away on the dresser. I don't want to look.

Yes, you do.

No, you don't.

Crap.

While I'm stuck debating, the phone stops vibrating. I guess that solves the dilemma, then—as if picking it up under the reasoning that it was ringing would make my snooping less offensive.

Then it rings again, and I can't help but go to it. I'm like Sleeping Beauty drawn to the spindle I know I shouldn't touch. Nothing good can come of this. That much I know, but I can't help it. I've spent so long guarding my heart that the smallest suggestion, no matter how ridiculous it sounds even in my own head, that Reid is doing something wrong has me questioning everything.

I pick up the phone and slide the icon at the bottom to answer it. I open my mouth to say something, but no words come out. What do I say? There's no name attached to the number, and for a moment I think that's a good thing. If it was someone he spoke with or saw regularly, surely he would have her name and contact information saved. And then there's the small voice in the back of my head that's suddenly growing louder in volume, that's telling me saving her information, who-ever she is, would be the last thing he would want to do.

What would he file it under anyway?

Cheater?

The other woman?

Not Maddy?

I'm thinking of all of this as I wait silently for some kind of answer to this fucked-up situation that I've got-ten myself into. I still can't say anything, but when a young woman's voice comes through on the line, I can't help feel that wall around my heart snap back into place. Even though I'm rendered completely speechless, I sit and eagerly listen to the woman on the other end.

"Hello? Reid? Is that you? Hello? Is anyone there?" and then the line goes dead.

Before putting the phone back on his dresser, I look into his missed calls log. I'm a horrible girlfriend for this, I know, but my self-preservation is all I'm thinking about here. I am beyond shocked when I see that he has forty-five calls from the same number. I hear him getting out of the shower, so I don't have much time to look for more information—how long the calls lasted, how many times he called her, exchanges of text mes-sages. Instead of all of that, I quickly save the number in my phone. I bury whatever conflicted emotions I'm having over all of this. I need to be alone and figure out what the hell to do about it all.

I just don't have the energy—physically or emo-tionally—to confront him about it tonight. Maybe it's because I don't want to hear his excuses. Maybe it's because I just don't want to learn the truth. But I choose to ignore it for the time being. Ignorance is bliss and all that crap.

When Reid comes back into the room, I pretend to be asleep. He spoons up behind me and nuzzles his lips up against my neck, kissing me in that sweet spot that sends shivers down my spine.

"Rain check on the massage, too, baby?"

My heart thaws a little at the tender tone of his words. "Is that okay? I think I'm even too tired to simply roll over." I know I'm being foolish, shutting him out like this, but feeling his hands all over my body while thinking about him possibly being with someone else has my insides churning. I know if he starts touching me, I'll break down.

"Shh. It's okay. Let's just sleep. I love you, Maddy. I love you so much. I don't know where I would be without you in my life. Thank you for giving me the chance to prove to you that I'm not a complete and total asshole."

I feel his smile against my neck. I want to believe him, and there's a very large part of me that does. Hell, four hours ago there wouldn't have been a doubt in my mind that he loves me and that he means every word he just said. But now—now everything is different. I don't want it to be, but it is. Even though I'm afraid he's going to crush me, that this girl, whoever she is, is going to come between us, I can't help but tell him that I love him, too.

Because I do. I love him so much. But love makes you weak, vulnerable.

It makes me everything I've been trying not to be.

It's the Sunday after Thanksgiving, and I still haven't found the courage to talk to Reid about the situation with the phone calls. I was able to avoid seeing him on Friday, since Momma, Mel, Cammie, Lia, and I hit up a bunch of Black Friday sales. Because Saturday was Momma's last day here, I was able to use spending time with her as an excuse to avoid him. I know I've been a coward, and I'm ashamed of myself that today I just pretended to be busy studying for finals, which start tomorrow.

I'm sitting on my bed back at my dorm stuck in a heated debate with myself over what to do about it all. I know that I can't talk to Mel about it. As much as she loves me, I know she and Reid are friends, too. Don't get me wrong—if Reid and I ever broke up, I'd like to think that Mel would be "Team Maddy," but I just don't want her to have to get involved until I know for certain what's going on.

I think I've figured out a way to get to the bottom of all of this. I nervously dial the digits of the number I've been dreading to call. I know that once I make this call, I'll have my answers. Whether they are the answers I

want or not, I don't know; only time will tell. I steel my
resolve and dial.

The other line picks up on the second ring, and a
deep male voice carries over the receiver.

"Hello?"

"Hi, Bryan. It's Maddy, Mel's roommate."

"Oh, hi, Maddy. I didn't recognize your number.
What's up?"

"Um, well, I kind of have a favor to ask you."

" Okay, sure. What can I do for you?" He's such a
good guy.

"Well, I figured since you're, like, a tech-god, that
you'd be able to help me figure out who a cell phone
number belongs to and help me do a little digging into
who they are." I really don't want to give him too much
more than that. It's unfair to expect him not to lie to
Mel. They're getting along so great, and I would hate
myself if I put anything between them.

"What's it for, Maddy? I don't usually do that kind
of stuff." He sounds unsure.

I know I'm going to have to give him something,
so I do what anyone in my situation would do: I lie.
"I've been getting a ton of calls from this number that
I don't know. I'm not sure who it is, and I'm worried
that it's that guy Mike who tried to drug me earlier in
the semester. I can't remember if I gave him my number, but I think I might have. I'm just worried that he's
stalking me or something. I don't want to get Melanie
all worried, and I sure as hell don't want Reid to flip out

over this. I just figured you were a good place to start."
I'm all but pouting at him, and then I realize he can't
see me.

Dork.

"Oh, wow. I didn't realize it was for something like
that. Yeah, of course I'll look into it. I'll see what I can
do. And I won't say anything to anyone until we know
some details."

"Thanks, Bryan. You're good peeps." As I give him
the number, I feel my guilt start to consume me.

"No problem. I'll call you when I figure anything
out."

I feel like a horrible person when I hang up with
Bryan. I'm glad I'm all alone so that I can wallow in
my own self-pity over this whole fucked-up mess. I
don't need anyone seeing me like this. I've never been
so thankful that all of the girls are out. Mel picked up
another shift at the lab, and Cammie and Lia are at the
library. They are incapable of studying here. Everything
distracts them.

I could use a distraction. But instead, I've got nothing but silence and my own thoughts. On the one hand,
Reid has been nothing short of amazing. And I love
him, I really do. He loves me, too. That much is clear.
But even if we do love each other, is that enough? I
don't think I can ever get past cheating. Then again, on
the other hand, he might not be cheating.

The more I think about it, the more I lean toward
him not being a cheater. It just goes against everything

I know about him. He's even said it himself, that no one knows him better than I do, and I just can't imagine him turning to someone else for any kind of physical contact when he really does seem to be happy with me.

And then there's the impossible-to-ignore fact that he makes me happier than I've ever been in my life. I could be lame and quote some cheesy-ass chick flick saying that he completes me, but that's a load of crap. He doesn't make me whole; he doesn't erase the pain I've felt for most of my life. Being with him isn't some cure-all to everything I've ever dealt with, but when I'm with him, I'm me. I'm the person I have always wanted to be—fun, lighthearted, playful, flirty, sexy, seductive, and loving. He's opened me up to the possibility of a completely different future than I ever envisioned for myself—a future that I just can't imagine him not being a part of.

If I'm being completely honest with myself, I know in my heart that he isn't cheating. I think I'm just using the idea of him being a cheater to protect my heart from the pain of whatever secret it is that he's hiding from me. I'm bracing myself for the unknown.

Before I drift off to sleep, my last visions are of Reid and me making love, and I remember the vows I made to myself back when the semester started, and ironically all three apply here.

I will choose to be happy and not let this—whatever it is—get in the way of here and now. There's no sense in getting all upset over something that could be nothing.

I will appreciate the beauty in everything that Reid and I are together—in everything that we bring out in each other.

I've already let love in. He's not only in my heart; he owns it. Now I just have to keep him there and never let him go.

Chapter 14

Reid

It's the Monday of finals week—my last finals week—and I'm anxiously waiting at a table in the student café, waiting for my weekly lunch date with Melanie. Hanging out with Mel makes me fall even more in love with Maddy, if that's possible. Melanie is like the little sister I never had, and I can't help but smile and laugh when I'm around her. Mel's happiness is that infectious.

Rather than getting straight to business—a.k.a. pulling one over on Maddy—I try for some normal conversation first.

"So how do you feel about your finals?"

She gives me the side-eye. She knows me too well at this point. "Oh, cut the crap, Reid. I see it in your eyes. What are you up to now?"

I fake a wounded look, but again she sees through it, so I just come clean. "Well, I'm graduating, and I thought what better way to celebrate that than with a vacation. It's too damn cold up here in the winter, so I was thinking of taking Maddy away somewhere. You know, to celebrate me being done with this place and all. Well, done until my internship starts, but in my head I'm done."

It has nothing to do with me wanting to see Maddy in a bikini for a week.

Or out of a bikini, for that matter.

Nope, not that at all.

"Eww! You are so thinking about her naked right now. You've got that far off-look in your eyes." She throws a French fry at me.

I don't admit that she's right. I can daydream about my girlfriend—my hot, naked girlfriend - all I want.

" Okay. Okay. I'll help. You know I always do. So what do you need from me?" she asks.

"Well, has she ever wanted to go anywhere specific? I'd like to do something tropical, far away from this frigid wasteland. We've both had a really rough semester, and I'd like to just have her all to myself for a week."

Melanie seems lost in thought. I can see her raking through her Maddy-files to try to dig up some useful tidbit for me. Then the light bulb goes off over her head.

"Well, it's not tropical, but it's still a beach, so I'm not sure if you'll be interested. When we were in high school, I remember her mentioning something about wanting to go to Montauk Point out on Long Island. After her parents died and she moved in with her Aunt Maggie, she never had the chance to go back home again. I never asked her why going to Montauk was special—if it was a family vacation spot or something like that. She didn't seem like she really wanted to talk about it, and she never mentioned it again. I remember her being very lost in thought while we were talking about it."

"That's perfect, Mel. Thanks." The wheels are definitely turning in my head.

"Sure, no problem. So much for seeing her in a bathing suit for the week, huh? I mean, it's not much warmer down there than it is up here." She thinks she's pulled one over on me. She thinks she's so funny.

I lean in across the table and almost whisper, "There's always the hot tub, Mel."

Maddy

It's Wednesday morning, and I'm walking across campus to meet Bryan at the computer lab. He said he's found out some information for me, and since Mel is busy at her economics final this morning, now is the perfect time for us to meet without anyone else finding out. I wonder if this is how Mel and Reid felt when they had lunch together that first time, like they were sneaking around, doing something they knew they weren't supposed to be doing. There's a big difference here, though; their intentions were always good. I have to admit that I feel like I'm sneaking around behind Reid's back.

Absolutely nothing is going on with Bryan and me, but it just feels wrong. Whoever is attached to this number is a part of Reid's life and not mine. And I went and just took it from him.

Bryan greets me warmly from behind his desk. It's funny; I've seen him hundreds of times since Mel started dating him, and even though I know he is one, he's never struck me as the geeky type. Yet seeing him here sitting high atop his desk like he's King of the Computerland or something like that that makes me chuckle.

"Hey, Maddy. How are you? How did your psych final go yesterday?"

I know he's genuinely interested because he helped me study the other night when he was over. "Ehh— I've been so distracted with everything that I'll just be happy if I pass." I'm really quite conscientious about my grades. Failing for me is getting anything less than an A, so for me to say that I'd be happy to get a D means some serious shit is going on upstairs.

Anxious to get this over with, I ask, "So what did you find, Bryan?"

He looks at me intently before saying, "Well, you'll be glad to know that it wasn't Mike who was calling you." He's searching my face for a relieved look, but it's not there. When he doesn't see it, he continues. "Which, by the look on your face, isn't a surprise. What is this really about, Maddy?" His tone has changed; he's all stern and serious now. He's got me figured out already, and we're only a few sentences into this conversation.

Shit.

Time to come clean, Maddy.

He stares me down for a few long moments, and I have no choice but to own up to the truth. If I don't, he'll just withhold the information I'm waiting on.

"You're right, Bryan. This was never about Mike." I take a deep breath, searching for the words. "It's Reid. He keeps getting calls from this number, and he's always on his phone. One night while he was in the shower, I looked through his call history and copied down the number. I figured you were my best bet at finding anything out. So did you find anything?"

He looks disappointed in me. Hell, I'm disappointed in me.

"What did you think I would find, Maddy? You know Reid loves you, right? Why didn't you just go to him with this?"

His questions make me feel so incredibly guilty. Right now I wish I had just gone to Reid. It would have saved me so much restlessness this week.

"I don't know. I mean, I have issues with letting people get too close. Reid has obviously worked past those issues, but when I saw the calls, my first thought was that he was cheating on me. I knew I just had to protect myself in case he actually was. It's foolish, really, because if I find out he's cheating, whether he tells me on his own or I find out through you, it will break my heart just the same."

Bryan sees that this conversation is getting a bit too deep for the main room of the computer lab, so he pulls me off to a smaller section that no one is using. He powers up a computer and sits down in front of the screen.

"The area code is from a small town not too far from here—Denning."

When I hear the name of the town, my face pales and my stomach drops. That's where Reid grew up. The feeling that I was betraying him before is nothing compared to what I'm feeling now. I know how much he hates his past; he's got more than enough reason to do so.

Bryan notices my reaction. "Are you okay, Maddy? You don't look so hot."

I try to keep my composure, knowing that it will falter more as he tells me what else he's learned. "Yeah, Bryan I'm fine. I'm just going to get some water."

I just need a minute to process all of this, so I walk across the room to the small water cooler by the door. I could stop this whole thing now. I don't *need* to hear what Bryan has to say. I could just leave it alone and let Reid deal with it. And then an idea takes root in my mind. What if it's Alex? There's no way I can let this go now that she's in my head. She's a horrible human being—the worst kind there is—and she's calling Reid after all these years. Suddenly, this deep-seated need to protect Reid is born, and I know I have to get to the bottom of this. Walking back to Bryan, I feel stronger— ready to face the truth.

"Okay, I'm ready now. Sorry about that," I apologize, but Bryan just looks at me with that "don't be ridiculous" face.

"All right, figuring out the person attached to the number was a bit difficult since it was a cell phone, but with the new online reverse look-up interfaces out there, it wasn't too difficult."

I'm lost. If it's more than checking my email or reading up on some of the gossip sites, I don't understand it.

Since he doesn't want to make me feel like an idiot, he just laughs a little at the glazed-over look that must be on my face and continues, "So anyway, I found out that the number belongs to Katelyn Donovan."

I hadn't realized it, but my heart stopped beating, waiting for him to say a name. When he didn't say Alex, or any kind of variation of the name, it started beating again. I let out a huge breath that I didn't realize I was holding.

I can only imagine the emotions that Bryan sees fleeting across my face, but, honestly, at this point, I just don't care. It's not her; it's not Alex. Thank God.

"After I found out *her* name," he pauses here to shoot me a wry look, "and that *she* wasn't Mike, I figured I might as well go ahead and find out a little bit more about her."

"You mean you knew this whole time that it wasn't about me and Mike, and you didn't say anything?"

He doesn't respond; he just smiles a small, cute smile. God, he's so much like Mel it's not even funny.

"Yes, I knew, Maddy. But I also knew that if you came to me and didn't want anyone else to know, then this must be pretty important to you. I didn't want you to have to worry about any of it, so I did what I promised I would, and I looked into her for you."

"Thank you, Bryan, so much. I can't tell you how much I appreciate it. So what did you find?"

He clicks away on the computer and pulls up some files, a few pictures, and her Facebook page.

"Even though the number is from Denning, it doesn't look like she lives there anymore. She's actually a college freshman at SUNY New Paltz. She was raised by her father, Joseph. Her parents divorced when she was in middle school, and her mom skipped out. From what I could find, it looks like her mom never came back into the picture."

I look at the screen where he's got her picture open, and she's beautiful. She kind of reminds me that blonde bitch who was hanging all over Reid back when we first met. But she's different somehow. There's a sweet innocence to her face; she looks like she has some class and self-respect. Hell, that'll make any girl look more beautiful than that tramp.

I can't help but think that while Bryan did find out a ton of information, the most important being that it's not Alex calling him and that he's not cheating—well, that can't be eliminated completely, but the fact that she lives three hours away from here makes it highly unlikely—I still feel lost. I mean, what do I have? All I've got is her name and what college she goes to. That's not much to work with.

Bryan starts shutting down the computer he was using. "I'm sorry I couldn't find out more, Maddy, but honestly it doesn't look like there's much to find. What are you going to do about it all?"

"I'm not sure, Bryan. I honestly haven't thought about that part. I can't exactly confront Reid. What would I say? 'I was snooping around your phone because I thought you were cheating on me, even though you've professed your love to me time and time again. Oh, and you've also told me things about you that you've never told anyone else'—wouldn't want to leave that out. I really got myself in a mess here, didn't I?"

I can see him mentally taking stock of the whole thing. "It doesn't look pretty, Maddy." He runs his hand through his ink-black hair and then strokes his thumb and forefinger along his jaw as he's trying to come up with some kind of solution. "Do you want my honest opinion, Maddy?"

I hate it when someone asks if you want to know their "honest" opinion. It means they're just going to tell you something that you already know but you just don't want to admit to yourself.

I nod at him, cuing him to go on with what he thinks I should do.

"Talk to Reid. You're in the wrong here, but if this girl is trying to call him, something must be going on. And you're not going to feel any better about all of this until you tell him. You can't build a relationship on lies. Don't get me wrong—I don't think what you did is a deal-breaker, but he deserves to know. More importantly, you need to deal with the fact that your mind and your heart immediately went to the assumption that Reid was cheating. You have to figure out a way to work all of this out, and you need to do that with Reid, not with me digging up information on some girl he might not even know."

So apparently Bryan is an expert in relationships in addition to being one in computers.

I hate to admit that he's right, but, well, he is. "I know you're right, but I'm scared. Scared of how he'll react, of who this girl is, of what will happen to us. But I know I have to talk to him—it's the only way to get to the bottom of it. Thanks again, Bry. I owe you one."

Walking back to my suite, I still feel like crap over everything. I'm not in any way closer to figuring out what the hell I'm going to. I just know that I want to crawl into bed and sleep. Finals are kicking my ass, and I still have this huge poetry paper that isn't going to write itself. I just don't want to do any of it. What I want is to bury my head in the sand and forget about the world around me. I want to go back to last weekend and not pick up Reid's phone.

How on earth can I bring up Reid's past to him and make him confront it even more than he already has? What right do I even have to do that to him? He trusted me, and I broke that trust. I know more than anyone what it meant for him to open up to me like that. Thinking about Reid and what I've done to him, all without him even knowing, makes me want to be with him. It makes me want to curl up in his arms and let the world fall away. I'm pretty sure he's got his last final tomorrow morning, but I take a chance of interrupting him and give him a call.

Of course he picks up on the first ring.

"Hey, baby." His voice instantly calms my aching soul, and I have a renewed sense that maybe everything will work out. "How's your paper going?" The man remembers everything. Okay, fine, not everything. What is it with guys and remembering to put the toilet seat down? I think it's in their DNA or something.

"Ugh, I haven't even started yet, but I know what I want to write. Once I sit down and actually focus on it, I'll be fine. How's studying going?" This kind of mundane conversation soothes me.

"Great, actually. I'm just about wrapping up. What are you up to?"

Of course he would drop everything to spend time with me. He's awesome like that.

"Nothing, really."

"Is everything all right, Maddy? You sound off." His voice is laced with concern, and it crushes my heart.

"Yeah, I'm fine, babe. I promise." All of a sudden my desire to see him, to just be in the same room with him, is overwhelming. "I guess I just miss you. It's so lame, I know, but I haven't seen you since Sunday and it's Wednesday night, and well, since we started dating, that's the longest we've gone without seeing each other. Texts only go so far. I miss you." My emotions are on the surface, and despite everything I've done wrong, I just want him to make it better.

I know I don't deserve his comfort, but right now I need it, and I'm going to take it while I still can.

"So can I come over, then? I don't want to keep you from your paper, so I won't stay long, but I'd love nothing more than to see you."

If he were any sweeter, he'd give me a cavity, for crying out loud.

"That would be perfect, Reid. The paper isn't due until tomorrow afternoon anyway, and my morning is completely free, so you're not keeping me from anything." I know that if I don't reassure him that he's not keeping me from my paper, he'll be worrying about it all night. He's beyond sweet, but he's also neurotic as hell.

"Perfect. I'll grab some takeout and a movie, and I'll be there in like an hour. Love you." He sounds so happy and I just can't help but feel lighter knowing that he'll be here soon.

"I love you, too, baby. See you in a bit."

As I end our call, I clear my brain of everything that's happened over the last few days. Right now, none of that exists. Right now, it's just me and Reid. Everything else can fade away, because no matter what happens, I will always love him, and I have to believe that he will always love me.

There's just too much pain involved in thinking otherwise.

Chapter 15

Reid

Sushi, a movie that's not a chick flick, and rose
in hand, I knock on Maddy's door. Don't get me wrong,
I don't hate her choice in movies; I just wanted something a little different tonight. Besides, I think I'm one
romantic comedy away from having to hand over my
guy card.

I'm in awe of the sight before me as Maddy opens
the door. She's wearing a really short pair of shorts.
I'm no expert in women's fashion, but they really just
look like glorified underwear. I love them instantly.
The thin tank top she's wearing isn't bad, either—not
bad at all.

"Hey, baby. I got sushi. I know you said you were
craving some the other day."

She smiles back at me. I think it knocks her out that I actually listen when she speaks, and then I go ahead and remember what she says.

I hand her the rose I brought for her, and she rolls her eyes.

"You don't have to get me flowers every time you come here." She holds it up to her nose and inhales the sweet scent. The deep red of the petals makes her eyes shine.

"Sweetheart, you said I was the first person to buy you flowers, and I want to be the last person. So, yes, I have to give you a flower every time I come here because I want you to be reminded that it will always only be me who loves you." I bend down and plant a soft kiss on her lips, grazing the knuckles of my free hand across her delicate cheek. Her eyes roll again, but this time out of pleasure instead of annoyance.

When the kiss breaks, I playfully slap her ass and direct her into the little kitchenette. We set up our plates, grab a few drinks, and make our way over to the couch.

"What are we watching tonight?" she asks as she walks over to the DVD player.

"*The Departed*."

She shoots me a disappointed look that I've brought over what she calls a "boy movie." She's so freaking cute, though.

"Just give it a chance. You might like it. It's actually good." I know it's pointless to try to convince her, but she relents and sits down next to me.

"Okay, fine—you win. So what's it about?"

"It's about the mob and the Boston Police Department. They're both trying to find a rat who is feeding the other side information. It won Best Picture a few years ago."

She seems to shift away from me a little at the description.

"Don't worry, babe. It's not too bloody. I'll hold you if you get grossed out."

I wink and smile at her. Flirting always seems to loosen her up, but she's still tense. I pull her close to me and wrap my arms around her as the movie starts. She doesn't say anything. She just rests her head against my shoulder and cuddles into me. Before long, her head is on my lap, and I hear her yawning. I start to play with her hair, knowing that it relaxes her. It relaxes me, too. About thirty minutes into the movie, she is out cold, lightly snoring away. I don't have the heart to move her. Plus, I like having her on my lap like this. I watch the rest of the movie by myself, trying not to disturb her every time I have to lean forward to get a bite of my dinner.

As the final credits roll on the movie, I start to move my legs to try to get some feeling back into them. The movement causes Maddy to wake, and she just looks up at me all dreamily.

"Hey, sleepy. I guess we can officially say that you're not a Scorsese fan." That comment earns an eye roll. This is why I love her. Within two minutes of waking up, she's cheeky.

"Come on, let's get you to bed. You've got a paper to write in the morning, and I've got some stuff to do, too."

"Stuff? What stuff? I thought you were done with your finals today." She's getting used to my antics, and she's gotten pretty good at grilling me, trying to figure out exactly what my next move is.

I arch an eyebrow in her direction. "Just stuff. Let's leave it at that." The grin I flash her is a surefire way to let her know that it's more than that.

She gets up from the couch and, after she rubs the sleep from her eyes, she holds her hands up in front of her in an "I give up" gesture. She stretches, arching her back. Her breasts stand out, nipples protruding through the thin fabric of her top. My groin twitches with desire for her. She sees it and leans into me seductively, and since I'm still sitting, she provides me with an excellent view down the front of her shirt.

"You know, you don't have to go. You could stay here. Unless you've got 'stuff' to do tonight." She moves to walk away.

Oh, no, you don't.

I grab her wrist and pull her back so she's standing in front of me. My face is in a direct line with the small sliver of her belly that is uncovered by her top. I lick along the waistband of her shorts, and I can feel her insides clench and shudder as I do. I wrap my hands around her tiny waist and hook my thumbs into her shorts and panties. Pulling them down slightly, I lick again, this time lower, in that danger zone between her belly and her sex. She shudders again.

I lower my hands down the back of her shorts and squeeze her ass while pulling her closer to my face at the same time. She shifts slightly, spreading her legs almost imperceptibly, but it's enough for me to notice. I take her up on the offer immediately.

Wrapping my hands around her hips, under her skimpy clothing, I pull the fabric away from her skin and slide it down her legs. Running my fingertips up the inside of her legs, I push her stance open wider. Her lips are glistening with her arousal. My mouth waters, and I can't hold back any longer.

Using my thumbs to pull back her folds, I expose her clit and kiss it lightly. Her knees buckle, and her breath catches in her throat. I blow on it lightly and kiss it again, this time with a little more force.

"Reid, your mouth is amazing. Oh, God…please."

How can I say no to that?

I roll my tongue around her hardened nub, and she's beside herself with pleasure. Moans and groans pass through her lips, but nothing that resembles real language. I pull back from her drenched core to look up at her. God, she's beautiful. Flushed cheeks, eyes aflame, breasts begging to be touch, licked.

Using my thumb, I trace small, fast circles over her clit and sink two fingers into her.

"Oh, fuck, Reid." Her legs are quaking, and I can feel her insides tighten and pulse around my fingers. She's close, and I want to make her come so badly. There's nothing more beautiful than watching her lose control, than bringing her pleasure, than showing her just how much I love her.

I reach my hands back up to encircle her waist again, and stand up in front of her. I switch positions with her and sit her down where I just was. Her legs can't hold her own weight, and I want her to enjoy this, not worry about holding herself up.

I push the coffee table back a little, giving myself some room to get down on my knees. I lean back on my haunches and situate myself between her legs. I pull them up over my shoulders so they dangle down my back.

Her eyes catch mine, and I see uncertainty there. I know this is all new to her, but she has to know how much I love her, how beautiful I think she is, how much she turns me on, especially like this, spread before me.

I run my tongue wetly up her inner thigh and try to reassure her. "God, Maddy. You are so beautiful. You taste amazing." Moving to the other thigh, I add, "I love you so much, and I can't wait to hear you scream my name."

Pulling her wet lips back once more, I dart my tongue into her core, and she gasps loudly. My fingers return to her depths and I massage her inner walls, rubbing my fingertips over that fleshy patch of skin that makes her thrash about in ecstasy.

I lick up to that tightened bundle of nerves and

pull it into my mouth, sucking gently, mimicking the motion of my fingers as they glide in and out of her effortlessly.

"Holy fuck! You're so wet, Maddy. I love it."

She whimpers and bucks her hips into my fingers. Running the pad of my thumb over her clit in furious circles has her coming hard. My name on her lips and her taste on my tongue is pure heaven.

"Reid! Reid—oh, my God, baby! I…I… ahhh…"

I love it when she can't speak.

I lower her legs from around my shoulders and stand, holding her in my arms. Carrying her to her room, I bend my face to hers and kiss her fiercely. When she pulls my tongue into her mouth and sucks hard, I nearly drop her.

"I love how I taste on your mouth, baby."

At that, I nearly sprint the rest of the way.

When we get to her room, we're all hands and mouths, lips and teeth. It's a fevered passion that's ignited between us. We're out of control with desire for one another, and in less than a minute we're both naked and on her bed.

She's spread out beneath me, hair fanned out beautifully on her pillow, and she reaches up to wrap her hands around my neck. Pulling me close to her, she kisses me. Our tongues stroke together as our bodies connect.

She's so tight and hot and wet. Sinking into her, the world fades away. There's just me and her and our love.

My hips pump a furious rhythm into her, and I grab her ankles up to my shoulders. I see her eyes roll back into her head as I bottom out in her.

"Reid…so…deep…I…gonna…come."

I feel her core tremble and clamp down on me. I'm lost.

A few more hard pumps into her, and I come, calling her name. She wraps her arms around my sweat-drenched shoulders and pulls me to her. I collapse into her as we both work to catch our breath.

I roll off her, knowing that I'm crushing her, but still needing to be close. I move behind her and spoon her, sweeping her hair from her neck. I place my lips softly on her nape and whisper, "I love you."

We drift off to a blissful sleep, wrapped in the safety of each other's arms.

A small smile curls up the corners of my lips, knowing that we're in for more of the same bliss this weekend.

Chapter 16

Maddy

I'm sitting at my desk, writing this stupid poetry paper, and all I can think about is last night. After Reid explained that the movie was about finding a rat, I just wanted to run away. Talk about irony. I wanted to tell him about everything, I really did. I just couldn't.

Maybe it was wrong of me to act as if nothing was going on, to act as if I wasn't hiding something. Even when we were making love, it was in the back of my head. "It" being that I'm going to hurt him. Because that's what it comes down to. No matter who Katelyn is, no matter how they're connected—it won't even matter that the whole situation might be connected to his past. What matters the most is that my initial reaction was that he was going behind my back, that I didn't trust him, and that I thought he was doing wrong by me.

All of these feelings of guilt brew while I'm stuck here writing about love and beautiful things like that. The paper doesn't come easily, but three hours later I'm done and on my way across campus to hand it in. It's not my best work, but it's on time and complete. Right now, I'm not capable of much more than that.

It's hard to believe that three short months ago, my life was so vastly different from what it is today. I guess with the semester ending, I'm in a bit of a reflective mood. So much has happened in such a short time that it really is quite overwhelming.

I can't say that I'm completely over my parents and the feeling of emptiness that I'll always associate with them being gone, but the family I have here in Cammie, Lia, and Mel has strengthened me in ways I never thought possible.

My relationship with Reid has shown me so much that I never knew about myself. He taught me how to love again, despite the pain. I really have found my best friend in him and now I'm so afraid that I'm going to lose him. Losing him would be like losing a part of my soul. With that thought in the center of my consciousness, I make the decision to tell him everything that's going on. The longer I keep it hidden from him, the longer the betrayal will go on; he'll be hurt one way or the other, but if I don't tell him now, if I wait weeks, even months, to tell him, he'll be even more hurt. I'm not exactly sure how I'm going to go about it all, but I have at least tonight to figure it out.

The girls and I are having a "girls' night in" tonight. With the semester coming to an end and finals being ridiculously crazy, we haven't had much time to spend together, so when Lia suggested that we have a *Friends* marathon, eat junk food, and drink cheap wine all night, everyone jumped at the idea.

Lia nearly tramples over me to get to the chips when I get back to the suite.

"Please tell me you got salt and vinegar chips! I am so craving those." She looks like a rabid beast sorting through the bags I've brought home from the supermarket. I don't know how she eats the way she does and still maintains her figure.

"Yes, Lia. I got you your chips. You only texted me ten times today to remind me to get them for you." I roll my eyes at her, and she just sticks her tongue out at me in return.

Cammie is already elbow deep into the carton of ice cream, and Mel is slicing open the roll of chocolate chip cookie dough. I can feel the bellyache settling in already, but I know it'll be worth it.

When what must be the tenth episode of *Friends* comes on, I hear Mel squeal with delight.

"Omigod! This is my all-time favorite."

Mel is a complete and total *Friends* junkie. We spent many late nights watching reruns. I'm pretty certain that we've seen every single episode—twice.

I must admit that this is my favorite one, too. It's the one where Ross is trying to get Rachel back after making a list of reasons not be with her. Phoebe's line of reasoning that he's her lobster—that lobsters mate for life and walk around holding claws—is not working. In the end, Rachel realizes that Ross went to great lengths to save her from being stood up at prom. She is overcome with emotion and puts aside her feelings of hurt. Again, the irony is not lost on me that this episode is rather fitting for my current situation with Reid. In the end, I hope he can see that he's my lobster.

Lost in my musings about Reid, I'm completely unaware that someone is knocking on the door. Before I can even realize it, Reid is standing before us, smiling slyly at our little pajama-party scene.

"Oh, please tell me I didn't miss the naked pillow fight." He's trying to stifle a laugh, but he's failing miserably.

Feigning irritation, Cammie asks, "What are you doing here? This is a girls' night, so unless you grew a pair of breasts overnight, you have to leave. No boys allowed!" She's in full little girl mode, hands on her hips, sternly tapping a toe. I can't help but laugh out loud at her little act.

"Oh, Cam, believe me—if I grew a pair of my own tits, I'd be at home playing with them right now, but since I didn't, I figured I would come over and borrow Maddy's for a while."

"Reid!" I yell at him. "I can't believe you just said that!" My face is bright red with sheer embarrassment.

"What, babe? I can't compliment my girl on her great rack?" His eyes are dancing with mirth, and his lips quirk up at the corners. He's gorgeous, but I still can't help but roll my eyes at him.

I walk over to where he's standing and wrap my arms around his waist. Looking up into his deep blue eyes, I know there will always be just him. I will never love anyone as much as I love this man. He's everything I never knew I wanted and never thought I deserved.

"Seriously, Reid, what are you doing here? It's girls' night. I thought you were going out with the guys?"

At my questions, I see him sneak a peek at Melanie, and I know something is up. Before I can say anything else, Mel is walking out of my room, wheeling a small suitcase behind her.

I can't help the exasperated sigh I let out at being duped yet again, but I will admit that there is a very large part of me that likes him surprising me like this all the time. "What did you guys do this time?" My tone is more anxious than angry.

"I didn't do anything. Well, nothing except plan a little vacation for us. And, as usual, I had a little help from a friend." He smiles over at Mel while explaining all this to me.

I'm struck completely speechless. "We're going on vacation? Where? When do we leave?" Okay, not completely speechless, but I'm definitely in shock.

"Calm down, babe. Have I ever been unprepared? I've got everything covered. All you've got to do is get changed for the car ride, and then we're off. Everything else is taken care of, as usual."

And it's just that simple. He takes care of every last detail. He takes care of me, and I love him so much for it.

"Road trip? How far away are we going? Why don't we just wait until the morning? It's almost midnight." When he said "vacation," I immediately thought we were taking a flight somewhere. I can't think of many places within driving distance that make for the ideal vacation spot, but I have a fairly strong feeling that Reid has this all thought out.

"Just get changed and get your sweet ass in my car. I got this." He leans back against the counter and crosses his legs in front of him. Tapping the face of his watch, he says, "Let's get a move on."

Five minutes and a completely pointless conversation with Mel about where Reid is taking me later, I'm walking out of my dorm and into the dark of the night to drive to some unknown location that my incredibly sweet boyfriend has determined to be an excellent vacation spot.

I can't help but think that maybe this little vacation will give me the perfect opportunity to get everything off my chest. Smiling a little, I laugh at the idea that I'll have the whole week to make everything up to him.

About an hour into our road trip, Reid stops at a gas station, and I am feeling sick to my stomach. I've never been good on long car rides. But this time is much worse because of all of the crap I ate earlier.

As Reid walks past my door to go inside to pay the attendant, he leans in the window and asks if I want anything.

"Dramamine, please. I'm not feeling so hot." I know my insides are also churning for reasons other than the car sickness and bellyache, but I won't share that with him just yet.

"Sure thing, babe. Be right out." He kisses me briefly before walking away.

When he comes back to the car, he hands me my pills and a bottle of water. Reaching into the back seat, he pulls out a small travel pillow and a blanket.

"Why don't you close your eyes and sleep a little?"

He kisses my forehead as he drapes the blanket around me. I recline the seat a little to try to get comfortable, and before I know it I'm drifting off to a peaceful slumber where little old lobsters walk around with their one true love.

When I wake up a few hours later, it's still dark. I don't recognize where we are, not that there's much around that would really help distinguish our location. The highway is small, two lanes in each direction, and it's lined with tall pine trees. There aren't any shopping centers or gas stations to note. There aren't many other people on the road, either.

I pull the seat up and stretch a little before I lean my head over to rest on Reid's shoulder.

"Where are we?" My voice is soft, sleepy.

"Somewhere."

Okay, I see how it is. He's not going to tell me anything until we're there. "Is it even worth it for me to ask any more questions?"

"You can ask whatever you'd like, sweetie, but I'm not answering anything." He looks down at his watch and then glances out to the horizon. "Besides, we should be there soon."

I relent and just nuzzle up close to him. It's quiet and peaceful anyway, so I enjoy the silence. The only thing I hear is the rumble of the Mustang, and the only thing I feel is the beating of Reid's heart beneath my hand.

After a few minutes, the sun begins peeking its head up over the horizon. It's absolutely beautiful. Shades of red and orange dance with one another. They mingle and intertwine, creating colors that have never been seen before, that will never be seen again. As the sun gains height in the sky, the colors transform into a soft fuchsia and violet combination that is more beautiful than any picture of the sunrise I've ever seen before.

Reid catches me gazing out at the scene before me, and he smiles. This must have been part of his plan. He's so incredible.

"It's beautiful, Reid. Did you time it this way? I mean, is that why we left when we did?"

"Maybe. And yes, it's beautiful, but not as beautiful as you." He kisses the tip of my nose before returning his attention to the road.

We drive a little farther, and I'm so lost in the stunning sunrise before us that I'm not paying attention to much else. Before long, I see a lighthouse come into view. The pines have disappeared, and a smooth, flat landscape rises up to greet us. I look up and see a sign that tells me we're five miles away from Montauk Point.

I can't speak. I can't think. Time stands still, and, while I'm sure that the rest of the world is still going about its business, for me everything has stopped.

A few minutes later, Reid pulls into a small parking lot that leads down to the beach. Before he turns off the ignition, I somehow register that Imagine Dragons' "It's Time" is playing over the radio. There's no other song that's more fitting for what I'm about to do.

Reid gets out of the car and walks around the hood to come open my door. He grabs my hand and pulls me out of my seat. I hold on to him for balance—for strength, really.

"Still in a daze from sleeping, huh? Come on—let's take a walk down by the water. The sea air will wake you up."

I can't respond; my voice is stuck behind the huge lump of emotion forming in my throat, so I just take his hand and walk.

We reach the water's edge, and the loud crash of the foamy white waves is both frenetic and soothing at the same time. The sand beneath my feet is soft and it gives under my weight, allowing my feet to sink in a little deeper. The water is lapping over my sneakers and is beginning to soak my feet. At the feel of the salt water on my skin, I collapse under the weight of my memories.

I don't brace myself for the fall. My bottom crashes down into the wet sand, and my palms are scratched by the abrasive surface beneath me. I try to keep my emotions at bay, but, like the water moving before me, they're too powerful, too huge to reel in. No longer having the energy to keep it all inside, I begin cry-ing—full body-wracking sobs. Reid is beside me in an instant, holding me tight to his side, running calming fingers through my hair as he tries desperately to calm me down.

"Maddy...I...I don't know what to say. What's wrong, baby? Please talk to me. I hate seeing you like this. Please tell me what I did wrong."

His voice is barely above a whisper, or maybe it's a normal volume, but I just can't hear it above the sound of my sobbing cries.

Rubbing circles on my back, he says, "Shh. Shh. It's okay. I'm here for you. I'm so sorry, baby. I just wanted to take you away to somewhere relaxing. Melanie said you always wanted to come here, and I just thought...oh, God, I don't know what I thought. I'm so sorry I upset you. Please talk to me. I want to make it better. Please."

I can hear his voice a bit more clearly now that my tears are lessening, and there's a rising panic in it.

He shifts slightly so that we can look at each other. He cups his palms around my face and swipes his thumbs under my eyes to wipe away the tears. It's pointless, really, because more follow in their wake. His deep blue eyes search mine for some kind of answer, for some semblance of the Maddy he knows, but I just can't find her right now.

All I can muster up is the ten-year-old version of me, who stood in a place not unlike this one. The words of the priest echo in the background noise of my brain. I can feel Aunt Maggie's hand squeezing mine lightly, the wind caressing the skin on my face, the sun forcing me to squint my eyes a little. I feel the gut-wrenching pain—the kind of pain that is so much worse than any actual physical wound. The physical kind of hurt can be bandaged; it will heal in time. But the emotional wounds never heal fully, and they are so easily reopened, even when you think they've scabbed over. The scars remain, and mine have been brought right back to the surface.

In the scene that's replaying in my mind, the priest is saying something about them "eternally resting in peace." Aunt Maggie urges me forward, closer to the water. A small wave laps up over my shiny new black dress shoes. It's cold, so cold, but I actually welcome the numbing feeling it brings. At the same time, we both drop two red roses into the deep blue water before us— one for each of my parents.

The priest begins saying the words of the Lord's Prayer as he opens the urn that holds their ashes. Blessing what remains of my parents, he scatters their ashes into the wind, and then they're gone. They're off in their heaven, dancing to no music for no reason, riding the endless waves of the sea to the farthest corners of the world, leaping across the stars in the night sky, forming the clouds into whimsical shapes.

I'm brought back to the here and now by Reid's voice, which, like mine, is laced with thick emotion. He's on the edge of tears, and I realize that I still haven't said anything.

Reid squeezes my hand and looks into my eyes, begging me to say something.

"You didn't do anything wrong, Reid. Please believe me. You couldn't have known what this place means to me. No one knows. I don't think I even shared it with Melanie in all the years I've known her."

"Will you share it with me? It's obviously important, and I want to be here for you."

I see a tear trickling down his cheek at the thought that he's brought me pain somehow. I wipe it away with the pad of my thumb and lean into his side. He wraps a strong arm around my shoulders and kisses the top of my head with soft, loving lips.

"We scattered my parents' ashes here. Well, not this exact spot, but it was a beach in Montauk. It was the last time I saw them, the last time I spoke to them and told them that I loved them. I watched them float away on a sea breeze, fall into the water, and wash out to sea. That was when I knew they were gone. Aunt Maggie didn't have the money for a burial, definitely not for two, so she had them cremated. With me moving upstate to live with Aunt Maggie, there was no point in a gravesite and headstone anyway. There was no one to visit them. A few days after the ceremony, my house was sold, and my things were packed away. I moved in with Aunt Maggie right away and was never able to come back to see them, to see my parents again—to sit quietly on the beach and talk to them, to feel the comfort that their final resting place would give me."

At my admission, his eyes are wide and apologetic. "Maddy, I am so, so sorry. I never would have brought you here if I'd known it would make you so sad."

I dig deep into my soul and realize that I can look at this as either a sad moment or a happy one.

I choose happy.

"No, Reid. I mean, yes, I'm sad. I love my parents so much and miss them more than anything. After they died, there were mornings when I would wake up and almost forget that they were gone. Those few minutes when they still existed, if only in my mind, were the best minutes of my day. And then reality crashed down on me and the darkness set in."

He shakes his head, acknowledging my feelings; he's had the same ones, I'm sure.

"After a while, I stopped waking up in that blissfully unaware state. They were dead, and that wasn't something I was going to forget. I always liked to think that they were wherever I was—their ashes following me everywhere. Still, I missed them."

"I know what you mean about waking up unaware. Some days, you know when something big happened, my first thought would be 'I can't wait to tell Shane,' but of course I couldn't. I remember this one time. I hit a homerun during my last varsity baseball game of my high school career. As I was rounding the bases, I scanned the crowd for Shane's face. Of course my parents weren't there—we'd stopped caring about each other long before that game. It was at that point that I realized I was completely on my own."

Even in the midst of my own pain, I want to take his away his. I want to wash it all away and heal us both.

"I know my reaction isn't very convincing, but please believe me that I'm not sad."

He's not buying it; I probably wouldn't, either.

I try to explain it to him. "Don't you see? You've brought me back to them."

"You never cease to amaze me, Maddy. You are so strong, and I am constantly in awe of how you always look at good side of things. I love you."

We spend a few long moments huddled together in the sand, just holding on to each other through the pain, both lost in raw memories of the families we no longer have.

But we have each other.

When some of the heaviness lifts, I remember the Friends episode from last night. Thinking that the beach scene before us is fairly fitting, I laugh a little.

"What's so funny, baby?"

He's going to think I'm a dork, but whatever. "Nothing's wrong. I was just thinking that you're my lobster."

His face is contorted in all sorts of confusion, and he asks, "Is that a good thing or a bad thing?"

"It's good, Reid. Really good. I love you."

I stand and pull him up with me. We spend the rest of the morning walking up and down the shore of this beautiful beach, hands clasped together, reminiscing about the people we've loved and lost. It's healing and cathartic for both of us, and when we get back to the car, I feel lighter and happier than I've ever felt before.

Chapter 17

Reid

SPENDING THE MORNING WALKING along the shore of the beach is far better than any tropical vacation ever would have been. I've always felt close to Maddy, even when I was pushing her away, but after everything we shared this morning, both good and bad memories, I know that she is a part of me—heart and soul.

We pull up to the hotel and check in. It's mid-morning, and the sun is shining brightly The place is beautiful—a nautical theme without being lame.

I slide the key card in the door, and when Maddy sees the suite she nearly squeals with joy, clapping her hands together, jumping in the air a little.

"Reid, this place is gorgeous. I love it."

"And I love putting that smile on your face. I would move mountains to see that smile." I squeeze her tightly, lifting her into the air, and spin her around. I let her slide down the length of my body. She arches an eyebrow when she feels my groin harden beneath her.

She laces her hand around my neck, and her fingers tangle through my hair. Pulling my face to hers, she kisses me passionately. It's not fevered and fast, but slow and seductive. She's tasting, licking, and nipping at me with such sensuality that I've grown painfully hard behind the zipper of my jeans.

Grabbing my hand, she pulls me into the bedroom. She removes my clothes, slowly; her eyes never stray from mine. When I'm naked before her, she runs her hands over every inch of my chest and back as she leans in for yet another earth-shattering kiss. She pushes me all the way to the bed until the backs of my knees hit the mattress. Pushing me down to the mattress, she begins removing her clothes in the sexiest striptease I have ever seen in my life. She's not calling on her inner stripper. No, what makes this as sexy as fuck is the innocence and trust in her eyes. Every item of clothing is removed slowly, deliberately. She's pulling the fabric along every inch of her body, and it makes my fingers itch with need to touch her.

When she's disposed of all of her clothing, she crawls on top of me, straddling my throbbing length. There are no words; even if there were, there's no need for them now. I can see her love for me brewing at the surface. I know I'm conveying the same look.

Reaching down between us, I nudge into her dripping wet core, and she sinks down onto me so slowly that I can feel every pulse and beat of her sex.

"Fuck, Maddy! You're driving me crazy. Ahhh…I love you." I'm barely holding it together.

When she leans down to kiss me, I wrap my hands around her waist, and pull her up and down along my aching cock.

She doesn't say anything; I don't think she can, but every time I bottom out in her, I feel her insides quiver in pleasure. I move her so we are sitting upright together. She's now straddled on my lap, and I push into her hard and deep. Reaching around with one hand, I grab her ass and move her in rhythm with me. Using the other hand, I rub slow, sensual circles around her pulsing clit.

"Ohhh…Reid…yes, faster, please…yes…oh, baby, I'm coming."

Her back arches, forcing her perfect breasts close to my mouth. I lick and suck furiously, feeling her inner muscles clamp down on my swelling erection.

When she comes a second time, from only my mouth suckling her sweet nipples, I lose it. Two more hard pumps into her drenched channel, and I come with more force than I ever thought possible. I entangle my arms around her slim body and pull us both down onto the mattress.

She places her head on my chest and runs her fingers through the light spattering of hair on it. I love it when she does that. I pull the blanket that's folded at the bottom of the bed over us and kiss the top of her head.

"I love you, Maddy. How about we take a nap, and then I'll take you out to a fancy dinner to celebrate the end of your first semester?"

"That sounds perfect, except one thing."

"What's that, babe?"

"We'll go out to celebrate you graduating and starting your internship. I'm so proud of you, baby."

My face nearly splits in two at her praise. It's been so long since someone was genuinely proud of anything I've done.

"We'll celebrate both, then. Let's get some sleep now. I'm sure we'll need our energy for later."

I feel her smile against my chest, and in a few short minutes her breathing has evened out and her hand has stopped tracing patterns lightly in my chest hair.

I fall asleep knowing that when I wake up, my pain won't be gone, but it will be bearable; it will be less. Life can't be painful when the most beautiful thing in the world is curled into your side, keeping you warm and safe and protected from the ghosts of your past.

Maddy

When I wake up from my nap, Reid isn't at my side, but there's a note.

Hey, baby,

I had to run a few errands, and yes, they involve a surprise for you. I got you some lunch from the deli down the road. It's in the mini-fridge. I'll be back at five to pick you up for our date. See you soon.

I love you xx

I eat lunch out on the balcony and enjoy the fresh air and the scenery. I get lost in my book, one that I haven't been able to read lately because I was so preoccupied with finals, and before I realize it, I need to get in the shower and get ready for our date.

After my shower, I dry my hair so that it curls in soft waves around my face. Keeping my makeup clean and simple, I feel sexy and beautiful.

As I walk toward the bedroom to get dressed, I realize that I have no clue what is in the suitcase. I'm sure that Reid told Mel what to pack, but Mel's fashion sense tends to lean more toward the "less is sexy" mantra.

When I open the closet and find a gorgeous black dress hanging before me, my breath catches in my throat. There's a note pinned to the hanger.

I can't wait to see you in this—and out of this.

I love you xx

I slide the silky fabric over my head, and of course it fits like a glove. It's not so short that it's slutty; it hits me just a few inches above the knee. The asymmetrical top shows off my cleavage nicely, but in a classy, sophisticated way—not a "hey, come look at my boobs" way. The most interesting feature is that it's one-sleeved.

One arm is completely bare, while the other is covered to the wrist in a light, billowing organza fabric. There are shoes, too, of course. My amazing boyfriend thinks of everything. I'm a little afraid to open the box of Jimmy Choos, but my inner shoe goddess is jumping up and down with glee. I've always wanted to a pair of these but could never afford them. They're silver, sparkly, strappy stiletto peep-toes. I am in love with them.

I check myself in the mirror once more before applying a final touch of nude lip gloss. Grabbing the silver clutch that Reid also left for me, I head to the door, feeling much like Cinderella waiting to meet her Prince Charming.

When the elevator door opens, Reid is right there waiting for me, single red rose in hand. He scans me from head to toe, and he looks pleased. He should; he did pick everything out, after all.

"Hey, beautiful." He pulls me to his side and kisses me softly.

"Hey, yourself. Look at you! You clean up real nice." I'm not used to seeing him in more than jeans and a T-shirt or his workout clothes, but tonight he looks like he could be on the cover of *GQ*. The light blue button-down shirt makes his eyes glow almost unnaturally. The shirt stretches tight across his broad, strong chest and back. I can see the bulges of his biceps when he moves, and it makes my mouth water. His strong, thick legs and fantastic ass are covered in freshly pressed black dress pants. I didn't think he owned anything other than sneakers, so I'm pretty sure that the shiny black dress shoes are new. I can't help but smile at how utterly beautiful he is.

"Ready to go?" I am anxious to leave, to be occupied with us, to not be focused on what I have to tell him over dinner.

"Sure. I just need to do one more thing." He pulls a long, sleek black velvet box from his back pocket, and I'm speechless.

I'm choking back tears, mostly happy tears—some of guilt. "Reid, you didn't have to do this. You've already done so much for me, spent so much on me. And now this? I can't accept this."

"You're the only woman I know who doesn't like getting presents. Please let me give this to you. I love you, and I want you to have it." He cracks open the box and what rests inside is absolutely breathtaking. It's unlike any necklace I've ever seen—not a regular chain and pendant. There are two separate chains intertwined, except they each look like small ropes encrusted in hundreds of small diamonds. One rope is covered with black diamonds, and the other is white. They are braided together, mingling with one another in a simple yet stunning pattern that sparkles and reflects every spot of light in the room.

"Reid, this is too much. I…"

He doesn't let me finish my sentence. Taking the necklace from the box, he steps behind me and sweeps my hair to one side. When the chain is clasped at my nape, he kisses me softly right below me ear and whispers, "I love you."

He moves in front of me and adjusts the necklace. "When I saw this, I had to get it. It is the perfect symbol for us. I saw the black and white, and immediately thought of our past and all the crap we've both had to deal with, and the white made me think of all of the good things we've shared together. How they link together and rest on one another made me think of how, without you," he kisses the tip of my nose before finishing his speech, "I wouldn't have the strength to move on from everything. You've made me realize that life can be good again and that not everything has to be sad. So believe me when I say that when I saw this, I just knew you had to have it, because it was us."

"That is the sweetest, most romantic thing I have ever heard in my life. Thank you so much, and not just for the necklace—which, by the way, is the most beautiful thing I've ever owned. But for bringing out the happiness in me, when all I felt was pain. I love you so much."

"Not that you didn't look beautiful before, but that necklace makes your eyes sparkle." He kisses the tip of my nose and says, "Come on. I've got much more planned for the night." Lacing our fingers together, he leads me toward the doors where the valet is waiting with his car.

Dinner is simply amazing. He's brought me to a small, intimate seafood restaurant. The candlelight

flickers and dances across his face as he talks anima-
tedly about his internship, which starts in a week. I love
hearing him talk about helping kids. Shane's suicide
and how his parents treated him afterward really dam-
aged Reid, and I know that being there to help others
will help him deal with his demons. It might not chase
them away completely, but I know that it will give him
a purpose in his life; it will bring him peace, knowing
that he's comforting others . I think that's why he treats
me the ways he does. I can't be mad that he spoils me,
especially when it makes him this happy. But it makes
me feel so guilty, because I know I don't deserve it.

We share a piece of chocolate molten lava cake for
dessert, and I am stuffed. "Ugh. I can't fit in another
bite. That was delicious."

He slides a small gift bag across the table, and I roll
my eyes.

"No! I will not accept another gift from you. The
dress, shoes, and necklace are more than enough." I'm
practically yelling at him over giving me a gift.

He just shakes his head and laughs at me. "Maddy,
just shut up and open the bag, which, by the way, is
the only thing I paid for, so don't get all in a tizzy over
spending money on you."

I roll my eyes at him, but I'm confused. I reach
into the gift bag and pull out a small glass jar filled
with sand. My brows knit in confusion, and I just stare
blankly at him.

He responds to my silent question. "You said you wanted to be able to have a place where you can visit with your parents. We can't be here all the time, so I thought I would give you a piece of the beach to bring home. Now you'll always have them with you."

I'm shocked into silence at his thoughtfulness. "Reid...I don't know what to say."

"No need to say anything. Come on. Do you want to take a walk on the boardwalk and let everything digest? You know, before the heavy activity?" He winks his baby blues at me seductively, hinting at the other part of his plan for the night.

"A starlit walk on the beach sounds amazing. A walk anywhere sounds amazing, as long as it's with you."

He finishes up signing the credit card slip, and he walks behind me to pull out my chair—always the gentleman.

When we get outside, it has gotten noticeably colder than it was before. The breeze that was cool and calm and warmed by the abundant sunlight earlier on an unseasonably warm fall day is now harsh and bone-chilling. We don't last more than five minutes before we're racing back to the car to get the heat on.

"I'm sorry, babe. I guess I'll just have to bring you back here in the summer." He reaches into his pocket to check his phone, which has just buzzed.

I've heard it a few times tonight, but since we were in the restaurant surrounded by other people, I didn't say anything. It was just an excuse, really, but now that it's just us here in his car, I know I have to tell him. I can't let this go on any longer, because the guilt is eating me alive, especially after everything he's done for me.

"Who is that, Reid?"

He simply dismisses me, saying, "No one." He moves to shift the car into drive but stops when I keep talking.

"But I've seen you check your phone a few times tonight. Actually, I've seen you on your phone a lot recently."

His face hardens, and there's a palpable tension building in the car. Maybe starting off by accusing him wasn't the best idea.

He's trying to force back his anger, but I see it boiling just below the surface. I have to navigate this conversation carefully. He finally says, "I said it was no one—no one important, anyway. I don't even know the number."

I reach across the console, and grab his hand and squeeze to try to reassure him. He calms a little, but I know his outburst is inevitable.

"Reid, I have to tell you something. Please don't be mad." I register the look of shock on his beautiful face as he careful considers his next words.

" Okay, I promise that I'll try not to, but when you're suspicious of me all of a sudden, it might not happen."

I see glimpses of the Reid I knew when I first met him—cold, hard, mercurial. I inhale deeply and brace myself for the fallout.

"Back around Thanksgiving, I noticed that you were always checking your phone. One time while you were in the shower—well, it rang, and I picked it up."

"You did what?" His eyes widen in shock, and I can hear the hurt in his voice. "Why would you do that? What did you expect to find out?" He's baiting me and I know he knows the answer; he just wants to hear me say it.

"I…I don't know why, but I just thought it was some girl you had on the side. I knew that you slept around a lot before me. I knew that you had needs, needs I hadn't met until the night before, and I just figured you were keeping up with your old ways while you were waiting for me to come around."

He recoils from my words as if I've physically slapped him. He roars back at me, "I can't fucking believe that, Maddy! You're really going to throw my past in my face like this? Haven't I done everything in my power to make you realize how much I fucking love you? And one stupid little insignificant thing like a few calls - from a number that I don't even know - and you automatically assume the worst of me? How could you fucking think that I'm cheating on you?" His voice is venomous and booming; it's angry, and it's laced with hurt. He's clenching his fists at his side and I can see veins bulging in his neck as he's trying to rein in his rightful anger.

"Baby, I'm…"

"Don't fucking call me baby!" He's yelling at me, and I can feel tears sting the backs of my eyes. His shoulders slump and he rests his head on the steering wheel. He looks defeated and pained. "I love you and I trusted you with everything, and you go and snoop on me. Tell me, Maddy, who was it? When you picked up the phone, who was it?"

I know that if I start talking, I'll cry, and I have no right to be upset, to want his sympathy, but I just want him to pull me into his arms and tell me that everything will be okay. When I don't answer immediately, he slams his fists against the steering wheel, making me jump.

"Who the fuck was it, Maddy?"

"It was a girl. She didn't say anything more than hello. I didn't say anything to her. I didn't know what to say, but when I heard a woman's voice on the line, I…I'm sorry I jumped to conclusions. It's just that…I was scared. I thought you were going behind my back, and I love you so much that the thought of losing you took over in my mind. I'm so sorry. I never meant to hurt you."

It's menacingly quiet. I know I have to tell him the rest. It's now or never. I made my bed, and now I have to sleep in it.

"There's more." My voice is small, barely a whisper.

"What do you mean, 'there's more'? What more can there be? You don't trust me."

His quiet and hurt tone makes my gut clench. I messed up so bad. I just wish I could take his pain away.

Now seething, he says, "Fucking tell me, Maddy. Tell me everything."

Here goes nothing.

"After the call ended, I saw that you had a ton of calls from the same number, so I wrote it down and brought it to Bryan. I figured he could help me find out who it was."

His sarcasm is getting the best of him—eyes rolling, face contorting in various shapes of disbelief. "And did he? Did you find out what you needed? Why the fuck couldn't you just come to me? God, Maddy, I don't know what to fucking do with all of this!"

I can hear the anxiety and panic rising in his voice. In the small confines of his car, he looks like a caged animal.

"I don't know why I didn't go to you. I'm so sorry. It's been killing me."

"You? This is killing you? Oh, that's rich!" He laughs sarcastically. "Tell me what he found." His tone is deadly flat and the calm that's at the surface belies the fury that I know is simmering below.

"When Bryan told me that it was a cell phone from Denning, I, well, I just didn't know what to think. I was concerned for you, honestly. I thought it was Alex. I don't know why she would be calling you after all this time, but I didn't want her to hurt you again. You had just told me about Shane and your family, and, baby, please believe me. I was really worried."

His anger recedes marginally, and it seems as if he's softening to me slightly as I voice my genuine concern.

"Once he told me that the number was from Denning, I immediately dismissed the idea of you cheating. Please, you have to believe that. I can't apologize enough for going there first. It's just that I kept my heart guarded for so long that it was a knee-jerk reaction."

He pinches the bridge of his nose and then rubs his eyes as if that will erase the tension. Regaining his sense of the Reid I know and love, he turns in his seat and looks me in the eyes. "That's why I never picked it up. It's not a number I know, but I recognized the area code immediately. There's no one from there I want to talk to." He's trying to explain everything calmly, but he's far beyond that.

I try to reach for his hand, but he pulls away. He's right to still be angry with me, but it hurts that he doesn't want me to touch him.

He sees my hurt, and I can tell he's debating what to do. The sense of relief I feel when his fingers lace with mine is huge. Maybe there's a chance we can recover from this.

"Please, Reid, you have to believe me. I'm so sorry. I love you so much, and I will do everything I can to prove that to you. I'm so, so sorry, baby."

He doesn't say anything in response. He just holds

my hand, running his thumb across my knuckles. I pull our entwined hands up to my lips and kiss his hand tenderly, lovingly. Tears are streaming down my cheeks, not because I want him to feel bad for me, but because of the overwhelming emotion I feel in this moment.

A weight has been lifted that I've told him all of this and that he hasn't gone running from me. I love him so much, and I know I will do everything that I can to make this right. We've survived so much worse than this; we have to make it through to the other side.

With his other hand, he reaches up to wipe away my tears. The feel of his hand on my skin makes my heart swell. We'll be okay. We have to be.

He speaks first, breaking the long, emotion-filled silence. "I'm not going to lie, Maddy. I'm mad—really fucking mad. But," he pauses and takes a deep breath, "I love you. As much as I don't want to understand why you thought I would cheat, I do. I was a complete dick before I met you, and I treated you like shit at first. Just promise me that from now on you'll come to me."

Just as I'm about to make that promise to him, his phone buzzes again. It's the elephant in the room at this point, and he just chooses to ignore it. He says nothing; he just hits the "ignore" button and returns it to the compartment in the console. As soon as the phone returns to its cradle, it buzzes again. The sound of it vibrating against the hard plastic of the gearshift reflects the return of the tension that I thought was gone.

"Reid? Why don't you answer it?"

He gives me a look that suggests I've sprouted another head, then sighs in disbelief at my suggestion. "Why? Because there's no one from that hellhole of a place that I used to call home who I want to talk to."

As much as he wants to make it seem like he's done with that place, I can hear the hurt in his voice; I can see the pain in his eyes. He's a long way from healed.

When it buzzes for the third time, I surprise even myself at the suggestion that I answer it for him. It's simple, really: if he's not strong enough to do something, then I'll do it for him—with him. I will be the rope of light when he is in the darkness.

"Why would I let you answer it? I don't even know who it is. Nothing good is going to come of it, so let's just leave it at that."

Maybe if he knows who it is, he'll talk to her. Maybe he'll recall something about the name? It's a small town, after all; maybe they knew each other. I have to take a chance and share my last piece of information.

"Her name is Katelyn Donovan. She's a freshman at New Paltz. She grew up in Denning and was raised by her father. Her mom left when she was a kid and hasn't been back since."

He looks shocked and terrified at the same time, but he doesn't say anything.

"Reid, please let me do this with you. She obviously has something to share with you if she's been calling this much. Let's just see what she has to say, and we'll deal with it. I'll be by your side the whole time—I promise. I love you."

Once again the phone buzzes, but this time he picks it up out of the cradle. He just stares blankly at the screen, obviously contemplating whether or not to answer. Sliding his thumb across the bottom, he takes the plunge and answers.

Chapter 18

Reid

I'm scared out of my fucking mind, but Maddy's
right. The calls aren't going to stop until I answer.
"Donovan" sounds familiar, but then again, it's not an
uncommon name. Bracing myself for the unknown, I
pick up the call.

"Hello?" The word trembles in my throat, and I
hate that I sound weak.

"Hello. Is this Reid Connely?" Her soft, sweet voice
wobbles with disbelief.

"Yeah, it is. Who's this?" My weakness is gone. I've
steeled myself for whatever it is she has to tell me.

"My name is Katelyn." She pauses briefly before
adding her last name.

"What do you want? Why have you been calling?"

I'm being harsh—being an asshole, I know it, but honestly, I just want to get this over with and get on with my life.

"Um, well…it's about your mom, Reid."

My world spins. The phone almost slips out of my hand, but I catch it and pull it back up to my ear.

Slowly, and in as controlled a voice as I can muster, I say, "I don't have a mother. She's dead to me."

I hang up and turn the power off. Shifting the car into drive, I pull out into traffic to head back to the hotel. I don't look over at Maddy; I can't. She'll make me talk about it, and I just can't right now. It's easier to just bury it deep down and leave it there.

The fifteen-minute drive back to the hotel passes in complete silence. There's nothing to say, really.

Walking into our room, Maddy wraps her small arms around me from behind and rests her cheek against my back.

"Do you want to talk about it, Reid?"

I chuckle a little at the ridiculousness of her question. "No, I most definitely do not want to talk about it. My parents are dead to me. They disowned Shane and stopped acknowledging my existence simply because I had recognized his. There's nothing she has to say that I want to hear. I'm going to shower and go to bed. I just want this day to be over." I stalk out of the room without a backward glance. I just want to be alone.

I take longer in the shower than I would normally, but I want the scalding water to burn away the memories and the pain. It doesn't work.

I come out into the bedroom and am pulling on a pair of sweats and a T-shirt when I hear a voice out on the balcony. What the fuck?

I creep out into the living room area of the suite and stay out of view. I can hear Maddy's end of the conversation in bits and pieces. I take a few steps closer but still remain hidden from her view.

"I understand, Katelyn…"

I don't hear the rest of the sentence. My stomach flips, and my fists clench involuntarily. The blood is rushing in my ears with the fury I feel at her betrayal. How could she?

She's talking again, and I refocus my efforts to hear what she's saying.

"I will. I'll try to talk to him. I can't promise anything. He's hurting, but I will try to talk to him about it. Okay, I'll call you tomorrow. 'Bye." She hangs up and slides her phone into her back pocket. As she turns to come in through the double glass doors, she sees me and gasps in shock.

Imagine how I feel.

"Oh…hi…I was just checking in with Mel."

She's stumbling over her words. She's a terrible liar, but this time I've caught her red-handed, and I'm not going to let her get away with it. She tries to walk around me, but she can't. A "deer in the headlights" look flashes across her face, and she looks up into my cold, hard eyes.

"Who were you on the phone with, Maddy?"

"I told you…"

"Don't fucking tell me it was Mel!" The growl of my voice makes her jump back. "I heard you, so tell me the fucking truth. Who was on the phone?"

She's shaking in panic. Her voice trembles as she begins her confession.

"It was Katelyn."

I hold my stare. I knew this much already, but at least she's telling me the truth now.

"And can you tell me why the fuck you called her?"

"I'm sorry, Reid." Tears start to stream from her eyes; she's beside herself with sobs. I don't have the energy for her apologies, for her emotion. I'm engulfed in a sea of anger.

"Quit the fucking tears, Maddy, and tell me why the fuck you called her."

I'm standing over her, crowding her space, and I realize she's still shaking. I grab her arm and walk into the living room. Spinning her around so that she's facing me, I ask her once more to tell me what the hell is going on.

"When I heard you say that it was about your mom, I had to call and find out what was going on. She's your mom, Reid. Doesn't that matter to you?"

"It's not your fucking business! Doesn't it matter to you that she disowned both of her sons—that she hasn't contacted me in the last three years! Doesn't *that* fucking matter?"

"She's sick. She's dying. She needs your help, Reid. You're her last chance." Maddy's practically yelling at this point, but I don't want to hear what she has to say.

I yell at the top of my lungs, "I don't care what she needs! She wasn't there for me when I needed her, for Shane when he needed her. She was our mother, and she just turned her back on us! What kind of mother does that? I never want to hear from her again."

Maddy's spine straightens, and she pokes me hard in the chest.

"You're a fucking selfish bastard! Do you know what I would give to have my parents back in my life? But I can't, because they're dead - really and truly dead. Yeah, your mom was a shit for doing what she did, but she's alive—maybe not for long - and she needs your help, and you're being an asshole for ignoring her. If there's even the smallest possibility that you can help her, then you need to do that. What if she dies?"

"She's already dead as far as I'm concerned!"

"No, she's not, Reid. She's alive. My mom is dead. I'll never have her back again, but you can help yours. I know that if she dies, and you don't help her, you'll regret it for the rest of your life."

Her anger is receding slightly, and I almost want to cave, but I don't.

"There is no way in fucking hell that I am going to her. Do you understand me? Losing your parents doesn't give you a license to do whatever the hell you want in my life. It sucks that your parents are dead, but they never hurt you like mine did to me. Making me talk to my mother isn't going to bring yours back, so cut this fucking Mother Teresa shit and get over yourself. The world doesn't revolve around you and your pain, Maddy. Just because my life isn't the same as yours doesn't mean that you're better than me. How dare you fucking judge me!"

"You know what? No, I'll never understand how anyone could turn their back on their mother, because that's something I would never do. And is it so horrible of me that I want you to do the right thing, to be the man I know you are? You're wrong, Reid, and no matter how much I love you, I can't stand beside you while you let your mother die."

We're saying ugly, evil, mean things to each other. My throat hurts from yelling and screaming, and Maddy looks exhausted at the energy she's spending trying to convince me to talk to my mom.

She practically runs to the door and grabs my keys off the side table. "I can't stay here with you. I'll be back later when you calm the fuck down and hopefully come to your senses." With that, she storms out.

I pull the bottle of champagne that I bought earlier out of the fridge.

Don't have much to celebrate now.

I walk out to the balcony and gaze up at the stars. Popping the cork out into the night sky, I slink back into the chair on the balcony and stretch my legs out onto the railing. I finish the bottle in minutes and move on to the mini-bar. When that's empty, I head down to the bar and try to drown my anger.

It doesn't work, and when I stumble back into the hotel room sometime around 3 a.m., I pass out without even registering that Maddy is not beside me.

Chapter 19

Reid

Somewhere off in the distance, I hear pounding, banging. My head is foggy from the alcohol. The piercing light coming in from the windows is painful. I never drink, and this hangover is massive.

I look next to me, but Maddy isn't there. Maybe she's on the couch? I don't remember hearing her come in last night, but then again, after my fifth shot of whiskey, I didn't remember much of anything. Looking over at the bedside clock, I realize it's already past eleven. She's been gone for nearly twelve hours! I try to get out of bed, but my legs are unsteady as the room spins. When I get to the living room and see that the couch is empty, I sober and my stomach tightens.

She never came back.

When I hear the banging again, worry sets it. Trying to calm down, I tell myself that it's probably Maddy. I don't think she had a room key on her. I walk my wobbly legs to the door and look through the peephole, and the world fades away. I unlock the door and nearly crumple to the floor when the police officer flashes his badge as he introduces himself and his partner.

"I'm Officer Rivera, and this is my partner Officer Murphy. Can we come in?"

I don't say anything. I just move to the side and let them enter.

"Is your name Reid Connely?" Officer Rivera asks, but it seems like he already knows the answer, so I just nod in return. "And do you own a 2008 black Ford Mustang?" he continues.

"Yes, I do, officer, but I haven't driven it since last night." They take stock of my appearance. I'm sure I look like a hot mess, and I can guarantee that I smell like the pint of whiskey I drank last night.

"Was that before or after you were intoxicated, young man?" Officer Murphy nods his chin over at the small coffee table, which is littered with tiny bottles of mini-bar liquor.

"It was before—I swear. My girlfriend and I got into a fight, and she took my car to get some fresh air. She... oh, God...please tell me that she's okay. Where is she?" Tears are burning in my eyes, and a huge lump is forming in my throat.

She has to be safe. I can't lose her—please tell me that they're here because they thought she stole my car or something. Please let her be okay.

"I'm sorry, son, but she was in an accident last night…"

The rest of his words fade off in the background as I collapse to my knees. I hold my head in my hands and sob wildly. No! No! No! This can't be happening. I feel my heart break in my chest as I think about her being hurt.

I feel a hand at my back and see another reach around to help me up. Officer Rivera says, "She's alive but in critical condition. She's at St. Francis Hospital. We've been trying get in contact with you all morning. When we reached her next of kin, Melanie Crane, she gave us your number and told us that you were staying here. We've been trying to call the room and your cell, but there was no answer. If you'd like, we can take you there to see her. Ms. Crane is on her way as we speak."

I numbly drag some clothes on and get myself together to leave with the officers. I can't do this; I can't face the possibility of her not surviving. I was such an asshole to her last night, too. I need to see her, to apologize to her, to tell her I love her. She can't leave me. This can't be happening.

I enter the hospital, and I'm immediately assaulted with the harsh, biting smell of antiseptic. It burns my nostrils and eyes, but I'd be lying if I said that it was the only thing causing my tears. If I thought I'd felt pain before, I was kidding myself. Maddy is the strong one; Maddy is the light to my darkness. I need her like I need my next breath, and even the mere thought of losing her stills my heart.

Mindlessly, I hit the call button on the elevator and go up to the third-floor ICU waiting room. A nurse comes up to me, but I can barely acknowledge her presence.

"Sir? Can I help you?" Her voice drifts in through the fog of pain and worry that's engulfing me.

"Madeleine Becker. My Maddy's here. I need to see her."

"Are you family?" No, but she's mine—she's my everything.

I just shake my head as the tears stream from my eyes. "No, I'm not. She's my girlfriend. We're supposed to be on vacation…" My words drift off, and the nurse escorts me over to some chairs.

"Wait here, and I'll see what I can do for you."

She moves over to the nurse's station and flips through a few files. In a few short minutes she's walking back to me, her face unreadable, her demeanor calm and even.

"She's in critical but stable condition. The severe concussion caused some brain swelling, so she's unconscious right now, but she might be able to hear you. Would you like to see her for a few minutes?"

I don't know why I'm allowed to see her since I'm not family, but I assume that Melanie must have had something to do with it. I just follow the nurse to a small, dimly lit room.

I hear the constant beep of some machine in the background as my eyes land on Maddy's battered and broken body lying on the bed. There are tubes and needles coming out of and going into each arm. Her head is bandaged and bloody. Her left arm is in a cast up to her elbow. Her beautiful face is bruised and swollen. A fresh stream of tears pours from my already bloodshot eyes at the sight of her in this condition.

I walk to the side of the bed, and horror sets in. What if she doesn't wake up? What if she dies?

I hear the nurse start to explain some things. "Her face looks worse than it is. The bruising is mainly from the air bag, but her nose and right orbital bone are broken from the impact. Right now, we just have to wait for her to wake up."

I wipe the tears away from my eyes, not at all ashamed of my inability to control my sadness. "When will that be?"

"We'll just have to wait and see. Hopefully, it will be soon. Sit and talk to her. It might help."

The nurse exits, leaving just Maddy and me in the room. I pull the chair up next to her bed and sit beside her. I take her frail hand in mine and pull it up to my lips. I taste the salt of my tears, and I break down.

"Maddy, baby, please wake up. I'm so sorry, baby. I take back all those horrible things I said before you left. Baby, I'm so, so sorry. Please, please come back to me.

Maddy..." My voice is lanced in pain and spiked with emotion. It sounds foreign even to my own ears.

After a few minutes, the nurse returns to tell me that someone else is here to see her. Melanie.

When I walk back out into the waiting room, Melanie races into my arms. Tears are streaming down her freckled face.

"What happened, Reid? Please tell me she's going to be all right! I was so scared when they called. Where were you when this happened? How come they couldn't get in touch with you?" She's in a frenzied panic, and I'm so afraid to tell her that it was all my fault.

I'm lost to my pain and guilt. I collapse to floor in front of her, sliding down the length of the wall behind me. Melanie sits down with me and pulls my hands into hers. She prompts me to start talking, and I put together what I can.

"We got into a fight. I said some really shitty things. She left because she was mad at me. I went and got drunk because I was so angry. I didn't even realize she was gone until the cops showed up at the hotel this morning."

There's no need to elaborate any more. The bottom line is that it's my fault she's here, just like it's my fault that Shane is dead. Why do I cause people so much suffering? Why am I such a screw-up? If I just would have listened to her, agreed to have her help me face my past, to help my mom, then she'd be safe. We'd probably be making love, basking in the afterglow. But instead we're here, waiting for her to wake up and return to us.

I'm crying again, or still, and Mel slides over next to me and leans her head on my shoulder. "It'll all be okay, Reid. She's stronger than anyone I know. She has to be okay." Mel is then lost to her own tears, and we're holding on to each other through the painful thoughts of losing the person who is most important to both of us.

When Mel calms down slightly, she stands and pulls me up with her. Vaguely, I realize that Cammie is sitting in the chairs in front of us. She offers up a small smile of sympathy.

"I'm going to see if I can visit her now." Mel walks off to the nurse's station, and I slink down into the chair beside Cammie.

I lose the battle with my emotions yet again, and I break down. Cammie holds me and tries to calm me down, but it's pointless, really. The only person who has ever been able to help me with my emotions is unconscious in the next room—all because of me.

"I fucked up so bad, Cam. I said such horrible things to her. Oh, God, what if she doesn't wake up? What if I lose her? I can't…" I begin hyperventilating at the thought of losing Maddy. She's my world, and without her I know I'll return to the shadow of a man I once was.

"Shh. Shh. It's okay, Reid. She'll be okay." She holds my shoulders and pulls away from me; she looks me in the eyes and says, "Reid, sometimes we say horrible things to the people we love the most. You can really only hurt the ones you love. I'm not saying Maddy is just going to up and forgive you, but you love her, so you'll do everything in your power to make it up to her. And because she loves you, she'll let you." She smiles a small playful smile, trying to lighten the mood, but nothing will lighten my darkness, nothing but Maddy.

A few hours later, Mrs. Crane shows up, disheveled and tear-stained. Mel fills her in on all the details, and they cry with one another at the thought of Maddy suffering, of her not waking up. We're all huddled together in the waiting room. Jack is here, too. He drove Cammie and Mel. It's not all that shocking that neither one of the girls would have been able to make the drive by herself. Lia and Logan were already on their way home for the first part of winter break, so they couldn't make the drive with everyone else. Cammie has been on her phone pretty much the entire time she's been here, filling everyone in on Maddy's progress.

Watching Mel and Mrs. Crane holding on tightly to one another makes me think of Maddy. Everything makes me think of Maddy, but this scene makes me think of everything she said to me about my mother before she left. Sparks of realization and feelings of deep-seated remorse start to consume me as I think back over her words.

No, she's not, Reid. She's alive. My mom is dead. I'll never have her back again, but you can help yours. I know if she dies, and you don't help her, that you'll regret it for the rest of your life.

The harsh reality is that if Maddy doesn't wake up, if I lose her, I will never be able to hold her again, to tell her I love her. I'll never get to wake up in her arms and feel her trace imaginary patterns on my chest.

Out of my peripheral vision, I register that a doctor is approaching us. "Are you Madeleine Becker's family?"

We all stand to hear what he has to say.

Mrs. Crane speaks for the group. "Is she okay? When will she wake up, doctor?"

"The swelling is starting to decrease. Her vitals have been strong since we got her stabilized when she came in. The accident wasn't a direct impact, so she looks worse than she is. If the swelling continues to diminish, there's a chance she might wake up tomorrow or the day after."

My heart begins beating again, and my lungs drag in an unsteady and shaking breath. "So she'll be okay? She's not going to die?" I feel like the weight of the world has been lifted from my chest. All of a sudden the light has returned to my life, and I can breathe again.

"No, son. It looks like she's going to be just fine. She just needs to wake up. Why don't you all go in and spend a few minutes with her before you head home for the night? We'll call you if anything changes."

Cammie and Jack go first, and they're done quickly. When she comes back out to the waiting room, her eyes are puffy and red from crying. She's shaking, so Jack tries to calm her. They walk outside, telling us they'll be in the car.

Melanie goes next. She takes a little longer than Cammie, but her reaction is the same—puffy, red eyes, chest heaving through the sobs. Mrs. Crane holds her daughter through the pain, rubbing slow, calming circles on her back. She passes Mel off to me so she can say goodnight to the next closest thing she has in this world to the girl she just placed in my arms.

Mrs. Crane comes out a few minutes later and pulls Mel back into her arms. There are tears in her eyes, too, and her breathing is heavy. She's trying to stifle her emotions, to be strong for Melanie, and I feel a pang of guilt that there's no one there to comfort her.

"You guys go ahead. I gave Jack the information for the hotel. You can stay there tonight. I'm just going to sleep out here in the waiting room. I'm sure you could all use a hot shower and a meal after having to drive down here. I promise I'll call if anything changes."

Momma embraces me warmly and cups my cheek as she goes to leave. "She'll be okay, Reid. She has to be."

I hug her back and kiss the top of her head before releasing her.

They don't argue; there's no point, really. An army couldn't drag me away from her. They walk through the ICU doors to a waiting elevator, and I'm alone.

I walk slowly to Maddy's room, silently praying to a God that I don't believe in for Maddy to wake up. And maybe if I'm lucky, she'll forgive me when she does.

Chapter 20

Reid

I SIT IN THE CHAIR I SAT IN EARLIER and pull her hand into mine once more. I know I should say something, anything, but no words come. I just hold her hand and cry. I cry for the pain I've caused her, for the pain I'm causing her now, for the pain I'm feeling deep in my soul that I've been carrying around for far too long. Drawing on her inner strength, I think over everything she told me.

The thought of Maddy dying without me being able to tell her how sorry I am runs through my brain. For the first time since Shane died, I permit the idea of allowing my parents into my life again. What if my mom is having similar thoughts? What if she just wants to tell me one last time that she loves me? I know I would never forgive myself if couldn't tell Maddy that I loved her one last time, hold her in my arms once more.

I'm not ready to come around completely, but for the first time since my parents turned their backs on me, I'm not completely closed off to the idea.

I spend the rest of the night wandering aimlessly between the coffee machine and the waiting room. Around two in the morning, the nurse gently shakes my shoulder to wake me. My neck and back are killing me from sleeping in the waiting room chair, but I'd sleep in a chair forever if it meant that Maddy would be okay. I suddenly panic, thinking that something must have gone wrong.

"What is it? Is she okay?" I'm immediately awake; my discomfort is forgotten.

"Yes, Reid. She's just fine." We've been on a first-name basis since her shift started and she saw that I wasn't going to leave.

"I just thought you might be more comfortable in the recliner in her room." She smiles and starts walking toward Maddy's room. When we're standing in front of the chair, she says, "I got you an extra pillow and a blanket. Now, I might have to kick you out when my shift is over, but I couldn't watch you sleep out there."

"Thank you, Carolyn. It's really nice of you." I pull the blanket up and try to settle in, but the relentless beeping from the machines is keeping me awake.

I slide the chair closer to Maddy and try talking to her.

"Maddy, baby. It's me, Reid. I just wanted you to know that I'm here. I'm waiting for you to wake up, and I'm so sorry, baby. Please just wake up. I love you." Pulling her hand up to my face, I kiss it lightly and rub her knuckles across my cheek.

And then it happens.

It's slight, but I feel it; I feel her hand move in mine, so I start talking again.

"That's right, sweetie—I'm here, and so is Momma Crane and Mel and Cammie and Jack, too. We're all here for you, and we all love you so much. I love you, baby, I love you so much. Please wake up for us."

She squeezes my hand again, and she begins to stir in the bed. I can't hold back the tears of joy and relief that spring from my eyes.

"Can you hear me, baby? Please open your eyes. Please, Maddy, wake up please."

She stops what little movement she was just making, and my heart sinks. I plant my face on the bed next to her hand and sob like a baby.

When her hand reaches out and her fingers trace over my cheek, I stop breathing completely.

"Hey, why all the tears?" Even though her voice is cracked and raw, it's still the most beautiful thing I have ever heard in my life.

She coughs at the effort she exerted over those simple words.

"Shh. It's okay. They're happy tears now. God, I'm so happy you're okay. I love you so much, Maddy." I'm kissing her fingers and whatever part of her hand and arm that isn't covered in the cold, hard cast. "Let me go get the nurse for you, sweetheart."

"No, don't go. Please. Just stay with me. Tell me what happened."

For a moment, I selfishly hope that maybe she won't remember our fight. Maybe she won't remember all of the hateful things I said to her.

"You were in an accident, baby. You were at an inter-section about to make a left turn when someone blew the red light on the other side. They swerved to miss you and almost did. It wasn't a direct impact, but it was still bad. You've been out cold for almost an entire day."

Maddy tries to adjust her position in the bed, but I hear her gasp in pain.

"Please, Maddy, let me get you the nurse. She'll get you something for the pain. I'll be right back in."

Carolyn returns with me and checks Maddy's vitals. When the doctor comes in to examine her, I leave the room with Carolyn, feeling lighter and more hopeful than I ever have in my whole life.

As the doctor exits, he lets me know that he's given her something for the pain and that she'll probably be drifting in and out of sleep for a little while. Before returning to her, I call Melanie and let her know that Maddy is awake, that she'll be okay. Mel tells me they'll be there as soon as they can.

After I hang up with Mel, I'm back at Maddy's side in less than a minute, holding her hand once again. I'll hold her hand forever if she'll let me.

She goes to speak, but I quiet her immediately. She needs her rest.

"It's okay, Maddy. I'm right here. I'm not going anywhere. Sleep, baby. I'll be here when you wake up. I love you." I want to smooth my knuckles across her cheek tenderly. I want to kiss her soft sweet lips, but I don't want her to hurt. I never want her to hurt again. Instead, I just lay my head next to her hand and let the beep of the machines lull me to sleep beside my love.

Chapter 21

Maddy

The knock on my door wakes me from my light sleep. I straighten myself up in bed and tell whoever it is to come in.

"How are you feeling this morning, Ms. Becker?" Dr. McNamara is hopeful that I can go home today, and so I am. I've been recovering quickly, but since I had a few broken bones in my face and nose, I had to have some minor surgery after I regained consciousness to reset them. My face is still swollen and sore, but I've been reassured that the scars will barely be noticeable.

"I'm still a little sore, but I'm definitely ready to get out of here. A week in the hospital is not exactly what I had in mind." I muster up an insincere laugh. It's the best I can do at this point. I really just want to go home.

Out of all the doctors I've seen here, I like Dr. McNamara the most. She's young—can't be more than her mid-thirties. Her kind brown eyes crinkle in the corners when she talks to me, and I can hear her genuine concern in every word she says.

When she sits down in the chair next to my bed to review my discharge papers, I see a look of worry work its way across her face. She reaches out to hold my hand, the part that's not in a cast, anyway.

"Your final blood work came back from the lab this morning." She pauses a beat as she reads over the paperwork in my chart, as if she's verifying something.

"Great. Does that mean I actually get to go home today?" I feel like a little kid at Christmas or on the last day of school.

"It looks that way. You're all cleared to go." She goes over all the medications I need to take when I leave here—antibiotics to stave off possible infection, anti-inflammatories for the swelling, scar prevention cream for my stitches.

"Thanks, I'll get these filled as soon as I get home." Despite my lingering aches and pains, I'm practically leaping from the bed to pack up my things.

"You'll also want to fill this prescription and call your gynecologist when you get settled in at home."

In all the chaos of the accident and then the surgery afterward, I had completely forgotten about my birth control pills. I glance down at the slip of paper in my hand, expecting to see one thing, and the world falls away from beneath me when I see something completely different.

"I think you gave me the wrong prescription, Dr. McNamara. This says pre-natal vitamins. I need one for birth control pills." My hand is shaking as I reach my arm out to give it back to her.

She looks back over her paperwork and then shuffles her chair closer to the bed.

"I'm afraid not, Ms. Becker. As part of the normal blood work-up, we do a pregnancy test, and yours came back positive. Since your numbers are still relatively low, I would assume that you aren't very far along at all—a few weeks at the most. And considering your reaction, I'll also assume that you didn't already know."

"But I can't be. I'm on the pill. I was on the pill. I got it from the campus clinic, and I was religious about taking it every day. How? I don't understand?" I'm freaking out. Pregnant! How the hell did this happen?

"How long have you been taking them?"

"About a month or so—I think. I was supposed to start a new pack the morning after the accident."

"And when was your last period?" She pulls her smart phone out of her lab coat pocket and opens up what I assume is the calendar function.

"Um, I think it was in the beginning of finals week, but it was really light. The doctor at the campus clinic said that it's possible for my periods to be light or to not come at all, so I didn't think much of it when it only lasted a day or so."

"Did they also tell you to use another method of birth control for the first month as an extra precaution?"

"No, they never mentioned that." The world stops spinning. How could they forget to tell me something so important?

She clicks away at a few more things on her phone and glances back over my chart one last time before sliding her phone back in her pocket and placing my chart across her lap. She leans forward and holds my hand in both of hers. She is in full-on doctor mode as she begins explaining how this all happened.

"For some women, the pill doesn't always work right away. It's very rare, but as a precaution most doctors will tell their patients to use another method of birth control during the first month while their bodies adjust to the new hormones."

Fuckity fuck fuck!!! This is real.

"I suspect that what you thought was your period was the spotting most women experience early in their pregnancy. All things considered, you're very lucky, Ms. Becker."

I can't help the scoff that comes out of my mouth. I'm sorry, but did she just say I was lucky? What the hell is there about this situation that's lucky? "Yup, that's me. Your regular old four-leaf clover."

Dr. McNamara gives me a glaring side-eye at my flippant attitude.

"For starters, you're alive. And more importantly, so is your baby," she chides me, but softens at the last part.

My baby.

And then it's all-of-a-sudden more real. There is a tiny person growing inside me. A person made up of me and Reid.

So many thoughts scramble my brain, but the most prominent one is of Reid. How will he react? We've barely been together a few months, and now a baby! He never signed up for this—hell, neither did I.

Then I think of our fight over his mother and all those horrible things he said about her. I'm trying to look at this from every possible angle. She is definitely less than worthy of Reid's attention after how she treated Shane and then Reid after Shane's death, but the bottom line is that she's his mom. Reid is here because of her, and I just cannot wrap my head around how he could be so cold and callous to the person who brought him into this world.

If he can so easily erase her from his life—whatever justifiable reason he may think he has—what is going to stop him from wiping me out one day? What's going to happen when he stops loving me? I've been trying to keep them subdued, but my old insecurities are beginning to consume me, and suddenly my walls are snapping back into place.

How would it be possible for me to look into the eyes of my child and hand him off to Reid, knowing that he let his mother die without fighting for her? It wouldn't. There's enough pain and suffering out there in the world. I can't imagine having to deal with the guilt of his mom's death hanging over me, over us, over our child, when there's something he can do about it to make it right.

If he's capable of cutting his mother out of his life when she needs him, could he be capable of doing the same to me and our child?

That last thought hits me like a ton of bricks—our child. While the idea of having a kid when I'm eighteen years old scares the freaking crap out of me, I can't deny that I would be beside myself with joy that I would finally have the family I've wanted for so long. This little tiny person would be a part of me—nothing can come between that.

Unless you're Reid.

I'm pretty sure my face is a contorted mess as I try to process it all. This is just too much to take in, and I'm so thankful when Dr. McNamara stands up to leave.

"I should have your final paperwork done shortly. You should be out of here by lunchtime. Don't forget to get those vitamins filled along with everything else."

Standing at the door, she pauses, her hand hovering over the handle. She turns back around to me and walks back to the bed.

"Maddy, can I just say one thing?" Her tone is cautious, as if she's treading in unfamiliar waters here.

"Sure. Anything."

"Don't worry about it—about being pregnant, I mean. You can worry all you want, but it's not going to change things. Do you want your first thoughts of your child to be ones of regret or remorse? Worrying does not change your situation, so just let it all play out and embrace the path that's laid before you—you might find that initially your road is dark and lonely, but eventually the sun will rise and light your way."

I can see her trying to visibly rein in her emotions, trying to take back her words.

"I'm sorry. I've overstepped my bounds. It's none of my business how you deal with this and how you feel about it. I just...well, I just didn't want you to feel alone. That's all."

Guilt rests heavily in my throat, making me choke on my words a little. "No, believe me, it's all right. You didn't overstep any bounds. That was actually really helpful advice."

"Good. Then I guess I'll see you later."

When she gets to the door this time, she offers a small smile and a quiet nod in my direction. And then she's gone.

I'm left in the room all alone with thoughts about Reid and our baby, about his dying mother and our dying relationship.

I really wish I could ask for some pain medication. I could use something to numb some of the all-encompassing grief that is sucking me down into an abyss of darkness. Tears threaten to drown me, and my chest heaves as I try to draw oxygen into my lungs when the sobs set in.

And of course this is when Reid chooses to enter the room. He practically sprints to my side when he sees that I'm crying. Tenderly brushing away the hair that's fallen in my eyes, careful not to touch my bruises, he lightly presses his lips to my forehead. He doesn't say anything; he doesn't have to. It's like an unwritten language of love and support. When one of us is hurting, the other just holds on tighter, letting the strength seep into our bones, deep into our soul. It's never draining or exhausting because we're always there to give our strength back in return.

While he's brushing his fingers lightly through my hair, I think about how amazing he's been while I've been recovering. He's brought me flowers almost every day, and the morning after I woke up, the first thing I saw, besides his shining blue eyes, was the jar of sand from my parents' beach. He told me that he knew I would want them with me as I healed.

Now more than ever, though, I just wish he would listen to his own words and let his mother back in his life while he still can. Suddenly, a gnawing unsettled feeling begins to swallow me whole.

The timbre of Reid's calming voice breaks through my thoughts.

He tips my face up to his and grazes his lips over mine. Physically, I react right away. I've missed him, and right now all of this inner turmoil is making me desire his comfort and affection that much more.

"Talk to me, babe. What's wrong?" He pulls me into his side, and I nuzzle in the crook of his arm.

"Dr. McNamara gave me my discharge papers and said I'd be good to leave here shortly." Okay, so I'm beating around the bush a little, but I'm just trying to delay the inevitable.

He crinkles his brow in confusion. "That's good, though, right?"

"Yeah, of course it's good. It's just that she told me something else, too."

He doesn't say anything. He just looks at me, his eyes willing me to continue saying whatever it is that I have to tell him. I just can't spit the words out.

"And that would be? What did she tell you, Maddy?"

I know that when I say these next two words, my world will change irrevocably.

"I'm…I'm pregnant." The last word comes out on a sob. I hear him gasp in shock, as I figured he would. The bed shifts as he leaps from it, as if he can't get away from me fast enough.

He's wildly pacing the floor next to me. "How? I mean, I thought you said you were on the pill." He's trying to hide it, but I hear the accusation in his voice.

"Of course I was on the pill. You saw me take them every morning, Reid. The doctor mentioned something about needing a backup form of birth control for the first month."

"Why didn't we, then? Why didn't you tell me about that? Shit!" He runs both hands through his hair and pulls on the ends in frustration.

"Don't you think I would have told you, if I would have known? The doctor at the clinic forgot to mention that little gem, so now here we are."

I'm hurt, and I won't hide it. Does he think I lied to him? He doesn't want this; I knew he wouldn't. I know it's stupid, but all of the crap with his mother and my current feelings of anger aside, there's a huge part of me that was hoping he would smile and kiss me and be elated.

Being happy after hearing that your girlfriend of less than three months is pregnant is not an equation that adds up for a twenty-one-year-old college graduate. He slumps down into the chair, and he looks utterly defeated—shoulders sagging, head held in his hands.

Shaking his head as it's cradled in his hands, he says, "What the fuck are we going to do? I fucking start my internship in a few weeks, and it already took an act of God to get them to postpone it because of the accident."

He might as well have slapped me.

Actually, I might have enjoyed a smack about the face more than I did his words.

"So this is my fault, then? I got knocked up because I didn't follow instructions that I was never given, and then I went ahead and got myself into a car accident with the sole purpose of screwing up your plans." I roll my eyes skyward, and seething anger takes over. "And you had absolutely nothing to do with any of this? Did it ever occur to you that I wouldn't even be in this freaking hospital if it wasn't for you? You want to blame someone—blame yourself and your stubborn ass."

I no longer care about the pain radiating through my body as I storm out of the bed and start packing my things up. Shoving things into my little suitcase with one hand is difficult, but I refuse to let him help. I refuse to soften to him.

Reid steps between me and my suitcase. He's towering over me, glaring me in the eyes. "And tell me how on earth this is all my fault?"

I've never been afraid of his physical size, and, even though he's threateningly crowding my space, I won't start now. He may be pissed, but I know he's not going to hurt me—physically, anyway. His words, however, are certainly going to rip my heart to shreds.

"I said, tell me how this is my fucking fault." His voice snarls in anger, and I flinch.

I look up into his eyes, which are no longer a peaceful and calming blue. There is a storm raging there, and I am about to unleash its fury.

"How? Well, it's simple, really." My tone is like that of an adult trying to calmly and patiently explain a simple task to a child; that is what I'm doing, after all.

"I did not have sex with myself. If you recall, I've only ever had sex with you. So while I'm not completely free of blame, I did not do this," I point to my flat stomach for emphasis, "all by myself."

He may have half a foot of height and nearly one hundred pounds of weight more than me, but I refuse to back down, so I move in to his physical space for this next part.

"And I'm in this place and screwing up your precious internship because you refuse to do the right thing and call your fucking dying mother!" I don't scream; I don't yell. My quiet, calm, even tone conveys my fury well enough.

I turn away from him and go into the small bathroom to collect a few things. When I come back out into the room, he is practically vibrating in anger.

"So we're going to come back to this again? When are you going to stop throwing my fucking past in my face? She hasn't meant anything to me for the last five years. That's it—it's over. So get off your fucking high horse and deal with it. Why is it such a big deal to you, anyway?"

"Why is it important to me? Are you really that thick-skulled that you don't see it?"

"Maybe I am just that dumb, Maddy. So please do me the favor and enlighten me, please." His voice is dripping in sarcasm, and in this moment I recall every reason I ever had to stay away from Reid in the first place.

"Because my mom is dead, and I'll never get to tell her I love her again. I never had a chance to make my peace with her, to say goodbye. You do, and you're being an asshole for not taking advantage of it." I choke down my tears but somehow find the strength to continue. "And because I'm going to be a mom. There's a person growing inside me who, yeah, okay, I definitely didn't plan, but I can't change that. I can't change the fact that I will love this child with everything that I am, and I don't think I can be with someone who doesn't share those same feelings. What happens when you have enough of me and our baby? Will you just walk away like you're doing to your mom?"

"That's low, Maddy. You know what she did to me, to Shane. You know everything about me, and you're going to throw it in my face like this. You know I love you and that I could never turn my back on you."

While I can see the truth in what he's just said, he left out the most important piece of information.

Our baby.

He's walking toward me with his arms outstretched. I put my arms up in front of me, to protect, to defend, because I know that if he wraps his strong arms around me I'll give in; I'll surrender to his love for me, but I can't act with only my needs in mind.

"No, Reid. Do not touch me. Please just get out. I want to finish getting packed up so I can leave."

His face sinks, and he looks as if I've physically attacked him.

"Are you leaving me? Is this it? Are you saying that we're over?" There's disbelief and pain in his words. Anguish settles in over his beautiful face, and I want to make it go away. I want to curl up in his arms and let the world fade away so that it's just the two of us in our own little bubble, but I can't. It's not just the two of us any longer. I can't be with him and trust him to be with me until I know he is fully capable of loving me and our child the way we deserve to be loved.

Tears are burning in my eyes, but I refuse to let them fall. I will be strong for me and for our baby. This baby deserves a family that loves him unconditionally, and I can now see that Reid is not capable of unconditional love. He needs time to work out his past, because no matter how much he thinks he's over it, he's not.

The thought of going on without Reid is just unbearable, but I have to. I have to do this for me, for my baby—to protect us.

With walls firmly in place, I ready myself for the inevitable broken heart.

"Yes, Reid. I…I can't stay with you. This baby deserves love—" he opens his mouth to say something, to tell me he does love the baby and that he loves me, but I know he'll say anything at this point to keep me from saying the rest, "—I deserve love, and until you realize that you deserve love, that you are not to blame for Shane dying, and that your mother deserves love, too, I know I can't be with you."

Eyes wide and sincere, his heart bleeds open in front of me. He looks like a lost little boy—and that's essentially what he is.

"But I can't be without you. You can push me away all you want, but I will fight for us. I will fight until my last breath to show you just how much I love you, how much I will always love you."

Our eyes are locked, and he's furiously searching mine for some clue that I'm balking here, that I don't mean what I'm saying. He's pleading with me to take back my words, but the Reid I know is fully aware of their truth.

The knock on the door startles us from our hell. Momma peeks around the corner.

"Guess who's all cleared to go home?" Her cheery sing-song voice is a stark contrast to the icy atmosphere. Lost in the happiness that's consuming her with me being well enough to finally leave, she doesn't even notice what's going on.

She stands next to me and pulls me to her side. I rest my head on her shoulder and try to refrain from crying and sobbing in pain at my broken heart.

"I just saw Dr. McNamara in the hall, and she gave me these." She waves a few papers in front of me, indicating that I'm all set to leave.

I turn away from Reid because I just can't bear to see what I imagine is my pain reflected in his eyes. I reach down for the handle on my suitcase and, with my good hand, click the button to extend the handle.

Momma wraps her arm around my shoulder and starts walking toward the door. She's starting to figure out that something's not right. "Smile, Maddy. You're going home. You've got me, Mel, and Reid to take care of you. Everything is going to be just fine. Well, just fine as soon as we make this five-hour car trip."

I only wish that last part were true. I would give anything at this point to know in my heart that Reid will be there to take care of me and our baby.

As Momma and I walk toward the door, Reid lingers behind us in the room. Momma stares at him blankly. "Aren't you coming home with us, Reid?"

He regains his composure and swallows his pain. "Yeah, of course, Momma. I just need to head back to the hotel and get Cammie and Jack. I've got his car. Actually, why don't I drive back with them, and that'll give Maddy enough room to stretch out in the back seat for the long drive. I'll meet up with you guys later."

He walks toward me slowly, and I'm savoring every last second I have with him. I want to memorize the rough stubble that's grown on his hard, chiseled jaw, his deep ocean-blue eyes that are swirling in anguish at the moment, his soft, full lips, his rich brown hair that feels like silk between my fingertips.

He stops directly in front of me and cradles my cheeks in his large palms. He gently strokes the pads of his thumbs under my eyes, where tears are streaming down. Leaning into my ear, he whispers, "Goodbye for now, sweet Maddy. I love you. I'll always love you, no matter what, and I will prove it to you." His lips softly graze my cheek, and then he's gone. He's walking past me - out of the door and out of my life.

As Momma and I enter the hallway, I can see Reid all the way at the end. His dark silhouette is illuminated

by the bright sun shining through the sliding glass
doors.

I can't help but think how fitting an image it is.

Reid, the love of my life, has always been the darkness in search of the light.

I hope for his sake, for my sake, and for the sake of
our baby that he can finally find it.

The End

Acknowledgments

WHEN I STARTED WRITING *Let Love In*, I did so mainly because I had a story to tell. I realized somewhat quickly that it was a story worth sharing. So I sent it out to a few of my friends and family who enjoy reading. Encouraged by their overwhelming response, I knew I had to self-publish the novel and get it out there for more people to read. It has been a crazy journey to get to this point, but I have really loved every minute of it.

I have to say thank you to all of those people who read my work before it was released. Your encouragement, suggestions, and support were all a huge help in keeping me motivated. Lori L., Lisa L., Mollie M., Nicole L., and Kristy B., thank you so much for being there for me in the early release stages. You are all awesome, and

I can't possibly begin to express how your reviews kept me going.

Being an independent author/self-publisher is very lonely at times. There's so much information to wade through, so I owe a great deal of gratitude to my editor, Joy at Indie Author Services; my cover designer and fellow indie author, H.B. Heizner; and all of the amazing bloggers out there who helped me along the way.

For months, the house went uncleaned, rugs unvacuumed, dishes unwashed. Needless to say, my family never complained. Boys, I love you more than the sky, and I hope that one day you can find your true passion and embrace it. I know I might have been in front of the computer more than you would have liked, and that it will be years before you can ever read this, but I just want to say thank you for being the best kids I could ever ask for.

To my husband—I don't even know where to begin. You've always been my biggest cheerleader, oftentimes having more faith in my abilities than I had in myself. There's no way for me to sum up in a few lines how I feel about you. Just know that I love you and that you will always be "my lobster."

Last, but certainly not least, I owe so much to you— the reader. Thank you for reading Maddy and Reid's story, and for your continued support. I hope you enjoyed Let Love In and that you're looking forward to Let Love Stay, the second book in the Love Series.

Follow me:

Facebook: https://www.facebook.com/MelissaCollins.
Author?ref=hl

Twitter: @mcollinsauthor

Web: www.melissacollinsauthor.com

–Melissa Collins

Made in United States
North Haven, CT
04 January 2024

47058895R00193